D0536632

# getting rid of Mister Kitchen

*Also by Charles Higson*

King of the Ants
Happy Now
Full Whack

# getting
# rid of Mister
# Kitchen

## Charles
## HIGSON

LITTLE, BROWN AND COMPANY

A *Little, Brown* Book

First published in Great Britain in 1996
by Little, Brown and Company
Reprinted 1996

Copyright © Charles Higson 1996

The moral right of the author has been asserted.

A CIP catalogue record for this book
is available from the British Library.

ISBN 0 316 88106 6

Typeset in Palatino by
Palimpsest Book Production Limited,
Polmont, Stirlingshire
Printed and bound in Great Britain by
Clays Ltd, St Ives plc.

UK companies, institutions and other organisations wishing
to make bulk purchases of this or any other book
published by Little, Brown should contact their local
bookshop or the special sales department at the address below.
Tel 0171 911 8000. Fax 0171 911 8100.

Little, Brown and Company (UK)
Brettenham House
Lancaster Place
London WC2E 7EN

# For Paul

# ONE

All weather forecasters are liars. What is the point? I mean, what is the point of a forecast which is only at best fifty per cent accurate? That's not a forecast, it's a guess. It's a lie. They stand there and they waffle on and on about high pressure fronts and isobars and wind chill factors, and whether it's raining in Spain, as if I care whether it's raining in bloody Spain, and they show you little pictures of clouds – which actually rain – and satellite pictures, and radar pictures, and it's all lies. Have you noticed now how they've taken up telling you what the weather was like today? 'And today was another sunny day.' I bloody know what the weather was like today. Christ on a bike, they even get that wrong sometimes.

Weather forecasters are false prophets. Their position is the reverse of Cassandra's. Cassandra, you may remember, was the ancient Greek prophetess who was cursed always to prophesy the truth, but never to be believed. Weather forecasters are cursed never to prophesy the truth, but always to be believed. Although, obviously, the curse is on us rather than them.

They should be banned, they should be shot, they should be stabbed by lightning and drowned in rain tubs.

I say this because last night they'd all announced that it was going to rain today. 'Thunder clouds, storms, heavy rain, wear a mac, stay indoors . . .' And so, this morning, expecting dark skies, I hopped out of bed and gaily rolled back the big roof blinds only to be poleaxed by an intense explosion of light which seared into my

1

brain. It was gorgeous, a gorgeous bloody day. The sky a clear, dark blue, streaked here and there with high, pale wisps of white cloud. A Mediterranean sky. I must confess I gave a little cry as I was temporarily blinded by this foreign sun, burning down, shining, glancing off glass and metal, thick and liquid and heavy.

They'd lied to me again, the fuckers, those mendacious crooks at the Met Office, and there I was, sightless, swearing, fried, with needles inside my head, dry to the core and bad-tempered.

I waited for the hurting to cease and my retinas to settle down and I looked at the clock; it was quarter to eleven, which was a pain in the arse, as I'd wanted a lie-in. But the bloody sun had woken me. If I'd been warned I could have worn my blackout mask, my blindfold.

So, you see, I blame the whole thing on the weather forecast. I started the day on the wrong foot, pissed off and out of joint. If they hadn't got it so wrong, none of this would have happened.

Let me tell you about it – this thing that happened to me. I don't know if there's a moral to this story, or even a point, but it happened, so there you are.

I stretched, my backbone popping all the way down, and dressed in baggy shorts and green vest. Ready to face the world. Ah, well, at least it wasn't so bad getting up at the crack of dawn when the weather was like this.

I clambered down the steps from my sleeping gallery and sorted out some coffee. While I waited for the cafetiere to do its thing I checked my Psion to see what the day held in store. My short-term memory is not what it could be (my long-term memory is no better) and I constantly have to update my various organisers, charts, diaries, filofaxes, scraps of paper; the alternative memory storage facilities for the burnt-out hard disk in my head.

It being the weekend, I could have done with getting out of town, sitting on a beach somewhere with a cold chicken and a bottle of tequila, but I saw I had a full

2

day ahead. There were a couple of guys coming to look at the car and some bint from the *Observer* was due in the afternoon to do me for 'A Room of My Own'. Which would mean tidying the place up a bit. But that wasn't till later so it could wait. There was also the message, 'BIRTHDAY DINNER'. I'm sure the bloody gadget had the details of exactly whose birthday and where the dinner was to be held, but I couldn't for the life of me remember how to access this extra information. So I chose to forget it. If it was important someone would give me a ring.

I poured a small measure of Jameson's into my coffee and put the TV on to catch the end of the Saturday morning kids' programmes, hoping *Taz-Mania* might be on. For about half a second I contemplated going round to the baker's for some croissants, but decided I could not be arsed. Instead I rummaged in the kitchen cabinets for something suitable. I found a bag of microwave popcorn, put it in the machine and left it exploding away as I went down to pick up the papers. There was a pile of them spilled on the floor, *Sun, Mirror, Guardian* and *Telegraph*. I read the broadsheets for the gossip, the cultural stuff, the arts and whatever, and I read the tabloids for the news. There's far too much of it in the big papers, the tabloids manage to sum it all up in some pithy headline like 'Fuck off Krauts' or something. I mean, let's face it, there's basically just too much news in the world. You can't take it all in, you can't react to any of it. One decent news programme a week on the BBC would be about right. Sift out what's news and what's just noise. Who ever reads last week's papers? Last year's? Even yesterday's papers have a sort of sad, unimportant feel about them. No, none of it really matters.

I looked at the front of the *Telegraph*; more Africans were dying. They'd started by killing each other and then nature had got in on the act and now they had another full-scale disaster on their hands. Cholera it was this time. Jesus, change the name of the country and it could be a paper from any time in the last twenty-five years. Every year millions more of them seem to snuff it in some new apocalypse, and it never seems to make any difference. Next year there will be millions more around to die of something else, starvation or AIDS or war or something. And their population just keeps on growing and growing. It's not just Africa, I've got nothing in particular against that lot, what I'm saying is that none of it matters. The Berlin Wall's come down, apartheid's been given its marching orders, the Arabs and the Israelis are still at each other's throats, the Irish have bombed some people, the Muslims have bombed some other people, right-wing-survivalist-God-fearing-Christian-Cadbury's-fruit-and-nut-case militiamen have bombed some more, the USSR and Yugoslavia have split into a load of countries that nobody can remember, let alone give a shit about, the Russians are shooting and bombing the crap out of their neighbours, the Iraqis are doing the same to the Kurds . . . we've had boom-bust-boom-bust, the Japs are all set to rule the world, the Japs are going bust, the Krauts are all set to rule the world, the Chinese are all set to rule the world, the Koreans are all set to blow up the world, America has a crack problem, England hasn't won anything in any major sporting event anywhere in the world for as long as anyone can remember, and it's all just blah blah blah . . .

What difference does any of it make? There's too much news, too much blather, and the more you watch, the more you read, the more you listen, the less you know, and in the end you come to the conclusion that nobody knows nothing and nothing changes.

Anyway, I was just reading some choice bollocks in the *Sun* about a pop star being caught with the wrong woman when the buzzer went. I pressed the button on the intercom and asked who it was.

'Hi, it's Mister Kitchen,' said a male voice, made

4

thin and reedy by the speaker. 'I've come about the car.'

'You're early.'

'Took me less time to walk round from the tube than I thought.'

I considered telling him to sod off but thought I might as well get it over with. It would be one less thing to do later.

I went downstairs again and opened the front door.

He was a skinny chap, about my height and age, with little, round blue sunglasses, some sort of sixties mod-style haircut and an unhealthy complexion. On his feet were ridiculously large black boots, far too rugged for wearing around London, and over his arm was a neatly folded grey mac.

'Hi,' he said. 'I've already had a look at the motor. I assume it's that one.' He pointed to my Saab parked outside.

'Yes.'

'Looks fine to me.' He came in without being asked. 'I'll write you a cheque.'

'Don't you want to talk about it at all?'

'What's to say?' he said and I watched him clump up the stairs in his great boots. I closed the door and followed.

I couldn't place the man. His accent was flat. He was either a prole who'd come up in the world or a pitiful middle-class guilt-tripper trying to sound more of a man of the people than he really was. Estuary English, I think the current jargon is. That no-man's-land of speech and style that allows the 'cor-blimey-love-a-duck-apples-and-pears' cockney wide-boy to appear not quite so plebeian and the 'I-say-chaps-what-ho-you-horrible-little-man' middle-class twit with a chip on his shoulder to sound not quite so privileged. Class Esperanto.

I suppose it's the accent I'm expected to adopt. To fit in. Being a youngish, London, man-about-town, nouveau entrepreneur kind of a bloke. But a man's got to have

5

some kind of pride. You can't crawl in the darkness all your life and still look forward to a decent obituary.

You see what I was saying about being in a bad mood. Just this twerp's accent had put my back up.

When I got to the top of the stairs he was draping his mac over the back of one of my chairs. He smiled at me.

'Rain later,' he said with authority. 'They said so on the weather. It's coming over from the North Sea, apparently. Wind's turned. We're going to be getting it from Siberia.'

'Siberia?' I said. 'That *is* interesting.'

'Yeah, apparently,' he replied and looked around the flat, nodding his head. 'All one room, is it?' he said fatuously.

I'd had it done before I moved in, had most of the top floor removed, so that all that was left of it now was a platform for my bed opposite the huge skylights which I'd knocked into the roof. The rest I'd opened out so that kitchen, dining room, sitting room, office, whatever you wanted to call any of the parts, was one big space, broken by low walls and movable screens. The only other rooms were a tiny bathroom and spare bedroom.

'I'd be worried the place would fall down,' said Mister Kitchen, gawping up at the light streaming in through the roof.

'A team of very expensive builders and architects ensured that there is not the remotest possibility of that happening,' I said.

'Doesn't it get cold in the winter?'

'I hit upon the novel idea of having heating installed.'

'Expensive, though.'

'Not particularly. It's all insulated, double-glazed. Probably more energy-efficient than any of the other buildings in this road.'

'Yeah, but still . . .' He turned to me and grinned. 'You can obviously afford it, though, can't you?'

6

'Mister Kitchen,' I said grinning back at him, 'much as I'd love to stand here all day fielding your witty insights, I am rather busy. Now, I believe you were going to write me a cheque.'

'How come you're selling the Saab so cheap, then?' he said, raising his eyebrows in a failed attempt to look canny and raffish. 'There something wrong with it?'

'I wasn't aware that I was selling it cheap.'

'Very popular car, the old model nine hundred. Hippest car around at the moment. Your Saab enthusiast don't like the new model, reckon it don't look like a Saab ... more like a BMW. Thought it might be snapped up before I got here. Tell you the truth, that's why I'm early,' he said, tapping the side of his nose and winking chummily. 'The early bird catches the worm. As they say.'

'Yes, they do say that, don't they, Mister Kitchen?'

'Maybe I ought to take a little peek beneath the bonnet. Just in case you're trying to sell me a pup.'

'Listen,' I said, trying to disguise my impatience, 'I'm picking up a new car on Monday. I meant to get round to selling this one ages ago. I've left it rather late so I need a quick sale. Okay? There's nothing sinister about it. If you're not interested, fine. I've got plenty of other people coming to have a look . . .'

'Woah, woah, woah. Hang on to your horses. I didn't say I wasn't interested. Calm down, my friend. I just need to be sure.'

'Mister Kitchen,' I said, 'Perhaps you're not aware of the philosophical statement "Don't look a gift horse in the mouth".'

'I am aware of that saying. I am also aware of "Beware strangers bearing gifts".'

'How about "Write me a cheque, or fuck off and stop wasting my time"?' I countered.

'You're quite a rude man, aren't you?' said Mister Kitchen.

7

'That's neither here nor there,' I said, and offered him a biro.

Am I rude? I don't know. Sometimes life just seems too short. There's certainly something about me that winds people up. I'm good-looking, slim, confident, well spoken, well educated, well off and I have a full head of hair, all qualities that the average Englishman despises. Plus I have a difficult streak, a compulsion to state the opposite view to whoever I happen to be talking to at the time. Waking up out of sorts wasn't helping, either. I was feeling particularly uncharitable this morning.

'You're all the same,' said Kitchen, picking up one of my steel lamps and scrutinising it. 'You public school types. You've got no shame, have you? No concept of how you come across to other people.'

'Here we go,' I said.

'You talk loudly on buses, and in restaurants, and you don't care that everyone can hear you. You have no idea of how you sound. You're rude to waiters and shop assistants, you're arrogant and . . .'

'This is all absolutely fascinating, Mister Kitchen.'

'Don't get me wrong,' he said. 'I'm not having a go. I'm just stating a fact.'

'Well, that's a relief,' I said.

'Where'd you get this lamp?' he said, frowning. 'All this gear . . . This expensive crap that all you lot seem to have. Where do you get it? Is there some special shop in Knightsbridge, or somewhere, that sells this stuff to people with more money than sense?'

'There is, in fact,' I said. 'And another in Chelsea, and a third in Covent Garden. Not to mention Glasgow, New York, Milan . . .'

'I bet it cost you a fortune.'

'It cost me nothing, Mister Kitchen. I made it.'

He picked up an iron piece about four foot high, with three spikes, like some medieval torture instrument. I'd made it during my gothic phase, about two or three

8

years ago, when I'd been experimenting with downers and heroin.

'What's this supposed to be, then?' he said.

'It's a candlestick,' I told him. 'Based on a sixteenth-century Catalonian design. Represents Christ crucified between the two thieves.'

'How much you sell one of these for?'

'That particular item, the Leveller, though no longer available, used to sell for somewhere in the region of six hundred pounds.'

'Fuck me. Money for old rope, innit?' he said and winked at me again, this time conspiratorially. I honestly believe that he thought he was being friendly.

'I couldn't live somewhere like this,' he said, putting down the candlestick.

'I doubt if you'll ever get the chance, Mister Kitchen.'

He attempted to give me a withering look. 'You sleep up there, do you?' He was looking up to my gallery. 'Don't you worry about falling out?'

'Mister Kitchen?' I asked. 'Are you completely mad?'

'There you go again,' he said, gesticulating with one hand like a man knocking on a door. 'There you go again, thinking you can say these things to people. Thinking you have some God-given right to abuse people. You think you're so superior, don't you? Well, let me tell you something, my friend, underneath that stuck-up, overprivileged exterior you're vulnerable, you're soft, and one of these days somebody's going to turn round to you and say, "No! No, my friend, you cannot act like that. No."'

'Mister Kitchen, I seem to be missing something here. Correct me if I'm wrong. But this is my home, my flat. You came in here uninvited, acting for all the world like one of the less civilised contestants on *Through the Keyhole*, insulting me, insulting my work . . . and somehow this means that *I* am rude. Is there something I'm not getting?'

'You see, you don't understand.'

9

'What is it you object to, exactly, Mister Kitchen? My voice? You resent the fact that I speak in a certain way?'

'I told you I don't mean anything by it,' he said, smiling. 'It's nothing personal. It's just that you have to be told. It's for your own good. I'm just stating the facts.'

'Let me state a fact, Mister Kitchen. Let me state several facts. Nothing personal, all for your own good. Your hairstyle is ludicrous, your clothes ridiculous, your accent preposterous. Your general manner is revolting. You are a self-righteous, boring prig. A phoney. And it's not "Strangers bearing gifts", it's . . .'

I didn't get any further than this, because Mister Kitchen hit me. Punched me on the nose, to be precise. It didn't particularly hurt, too many corrosive drugs had been squirted up there for that. There's nothing much breakable left and most of the nerve ends have been fried. But it can still bleed – in fact bleeding is about what it does best – and bleed it did. I tasted blood down the back of my throat and felt it dripping down my stiff upper lip.

'You people,' said Mister Kitchen, angrily. 'You think you rule the fucking world, don't you? Well, let me tell you, my friend, there is no more British Empire, the aristocracy is dying on its feet. Everything's gonna change. Your days are numbered.'

I hit him back. It seemed the only way to shut up his tedious wittering. It surprised him considerably. I've got a fair punch and I got him in the eye, knocking off his sunglasses. He yelped something like 'Blimey' and staggered a bit.

'I am not an aristocrat, you stupid cunt,' I said. 'I am an ordinary middle-class man who can't be bothered to pretend that he's something else. Now, do you want to buy my fucking Saab or not?'

He rushed at me and put his hands round my throat, knocking me backwards on to my long sofa. His right eye was weeping and blinking where I'd hit him.

10

'I'm a better man than you'll ever be,' he cried.

'That was never in question,' I replied, gouging him in his good eye, which caused him to let go of me.

'I'm not a good person,' I said. 'But I'm a happy person. Unlike you. You seem so bitter. Calm down. Enjoy yourself.'

'Don't patronise me,' he said, his voice shaking. 'People like you have patronised me all my life.'

'I'm not surprised,' I said.

With that he picked up a wine bottle which had been broken in the scuffle and brandished the jagged end. I looked around for something to defend myself with and saw the Leveller.

By this stage I'd really had enough. I was thoroughly bored by the whole sorry scene and just wanted it over, but there was no stopping the man. If I let things carry on it could easily escalate into a major hassle. I pictured endless dreary hours spent with him in police stations and solicitors' offices, explaining myself. So, as he came at me with the bottle, I picked up the candlestick and stuck it in him. The leading point went in just beneath his ribs. His eyes and mouth went very wide; it was something of a Frankie Howerd look.

'It's Greeks,' I said, and he frowned at me.

'Huh?'

'"Beware of Greeks bearing gifts". An obvious reference to the Trojan horse . . .'

But he wasn't listening. He dropped the bottle, tottered back a couple of paces and fell to the ground. He kicked his feet very fast like someone riding a tiny invisible bicycle, and then became still.

I sat on the sofa and wondered what to do. I needed to think straight, because it was dawning on me that perhaps killing him hadn't been such a great idea. I mean, you do understand that at the time I had no choice? It's just that there were consequences I should have considered more carefully, and, perhaps if I hadn't been woken prematurely and dicked about by the weather forecasters, I might have chosen to act differently.

Right now I needed to be calm and rational and clear-headed, so the first thing to do was to drink another large measure of whisky, and have a thick line of coke, which meant somehow forcing the stuff up my raw and pulpy nose, which was still bleeding from Mister Kitchen's punch. In fact a couple of spots had dropped on the sofa. I pulled off my vest and held it to my face, then hurried into the bathroom, picking up the whisky on the way.

I filled the basin with cold water and plunged my face into it. I held it there as it slowly became numb, then sucked in through my nose. A wash of cold water, mucus and blood gushed down my throat. It was fairly painful, but it seemed to do the trick. I sat on the edge of the bathtub drinking whisky and waited for everything to dry and seal up. After a while I felt suitably unplugged and went up to the gallery to chop some coke. It was like snorting into a hollow face; the powder seemed to shoot straight up into my brain. So I smoked a large joint to bring me level again.

Feeling relaxed, level-headed and lucid, I lay on the bed and mulled over my options.

Contacting the police was the obvious first choice.

I'd had a couple of brushes with the law in my time . . . a speeding thing, a drugs thing and a nightclub brawl type thing, and I'd managed to keep them quiet. A bloody expensive lawyer and the best PR man in London had seen to that. But killing someone was quite a different matter. I have to tell you, without wanting to show off in any way, that I was on the verge of becoming relatively famous and bloody rich. My right-hand man, Crispin Butler, was even now out in Japan negotiating a deal that would put me into the major league, and something like this could scupper the whole shebang.

I could do with Crispin right now. He did all my

paperwork, all the fiddly stuff, all the delicate negotiations. I would swan in every now and then and show off a bit, impress the client, but he did all the contracts, all the diplomacy, all the real nitty-gritty. He had a cool head and would have known what to do in a situation like this.

Me, I was all over the bloody shop.

So, the police were not an option. The alternative was to dump the body somewhere. This seemed an infinitely more sensible plan. How on earth could they ever trace the killing to me when, and if, they found the body? I mean, the man was a git, he was bound to have scores of enemies with legitimate reasons for topping him. All I needed was a bit of time to cover my tracks.

Yes, the obvious solution was simply to ditch the body and destroy the murder weapon. I could melt the candlestick down in the small forge at the studio. And the body? Well, I knew just the spot, in Lincolnshire.

I smiled. What could be simpler?

It was now quarter past eleven. The woman from the *Observer* was due at five, that gave me nearly six hours. Two to get out of town, two to hide the body, two to get back, then do the piece. That was a good alibi, in case I ever needed one, to be seen calm and relaxed at home having my photo taken.

Yes. Good.

I pulled on a fresh vest, then went down and got a clean sheet from the airing cupboard. I lined the sheet with newspapers and black bin liners and pushed Mister Kitchen on to it, using the candlestick as a handle. Once he was in place I set to pulling the spike out. This proved to be an unexpectedly tough job, and it was some minutes of huffing and puffing and bad language before it finally popped out, releasing a gloopy flow of blood. Luckily the plastic bags and the newspaper contained it all, and I managed to wrap him up in a nice neat bundle which I tied with string. It was all too obviously corpse-shaped, however.

13

Now, I live in a fairly quiet part of St John's Wood and have no nosy neighbours that I'm aware of, but if someone were to see me carrying what was clearly a dead body out to my car, eyebrows might be raised. So I rolled him up in one of my rugs, a worn and faded Persian thing that may well have been valuable but at that moment I really didn't care.

I went outside to the Saab and opened the boot, then ran back upstairs and hoiked Mister Kitchen on to my shoulder. It was a bit of a struggle getting him down the stairs. I slipped once, crashing into the banisters, but at last I managed to get him in the boot with only some grazed fingers to show for it.

I work with large pieces of wood and heavy metals all the time, so I'm fairly strong, I suppose, but the effort of getting Kitchen into the Saab had severely knackered me. I shut the boot and sat on the pavement for a couple of minutes, panting and sweating. Then, once I'd got my breath back, I locked the flat, got into the car and set off.

As I say, I knew the ideal spot in Lincolnshire to lose a body, about a two-hour drive if I put my foot down, but I hadn't even got out of Kilburn when the car began to lurch and stall. It was only when I glanced at the fuel gauge that I saw what the problem was.

Empty.

I pulled over to the side of the road, and cursing myself for a bloody fool, got out. I'd passed a garage not too far back, so I grabbed my small petrol can from the boot and set off in that direction.

14

# TWO

There were a couple of dirty homeless types hanging around the petrol station forecourt. One of them came over to me, a tall, skinny chap with a big nose and a haircut that was an unpleasant cross between a mohican, a white rasta and, let's face it, a girl. He was wearing vast boots, army fatigues and a long baggy shirt with a very tight moth-eaten jumper over the top of it.

'Can you spare us some change, mate,' he said pathetically, with a hopeless display of humility, his voice theatrically woebegone and estuary to a painful degree.

'No,' I said and smiled pleasantly enough. I carried on walking towards the cashier.

'Come on,' he said. 'You can afford it.'

'No,' I said.

'Why not?'

'Fuck off,' I explained.

'Rich cunt,' said the beggar. I smiled again, and went in to tell the uninterested cashier about my car, then I went back out to fill my can at one of the pumps.

The air was heavy and hot under the canopy, thick with fumes, smoggy and polluted. Traffic clattering by on Kilburn High Road sent up dust which hung in the damp stillness. Any other day I'd have enjoyed the alien sensations, like being in LA, or Athens, or somewhere, but today it was just one more irritation.

I paid for the petrol, and as I left the forecourt, the second homeless type tried to hit me for some change as well. He was shorter than the other one, squat

15

and poxy, with a haircut that couldn't be described as anything except a bloody mess. He had a Scottish accent and was wearing blackened, shiny jeans and a checked lumberjack shirt.

I naturally refused to give him any money, either.

'Why not?' he said.

'Why?' I replied.

'You've got money and I haven't.'

'And if I gave money to every vagrant that asked, I'd very soon end up like you, with no money at all.'

'Then we'd be equal, eh? Isn't that the point of democracy?' He was following me out of the station and up the road.

'No,' I said. 'That is not the point of democracy, or even socialism. It is not that we all end up as peasants, but that we all end up as kings. No second class, only first. You come up to my level, I don't come down to yours. You see?'

'Well, give me some of your money, then, and I'll be on my way up,' he said, with the look of a man who thought he was being clever.

'And I'll be on my way down,' I said.

'We'll meet in the middle, eh?'

'No,' I said. 'I don't think so.'

'Why not, huh?'

'Because, to tell you the truth, I'm not a great believer in equality.'

'But you just said . . .'

'That was just a little lesson on socialism for you. Me, I'm a follower of Darwinism. Survival of the fittest, all that malarkey.'

'Oh, go on, give us some pennies.'

'Is that the best you can do?'

He shrugged.

'You are the worst beggar I have ever encountered,' I said. 'Don't give up the day job.'

'Look, you can afford it.'

'Let me tell you about begging,' I said. 'Begging is

only begging if there's a choice. My choice. I have to be allowed to choose whether or not to give you any money. It's not an obligation, it's not automatic. As soon as it becomes obligatory then it's no longer begging, it's simply a form of taxation, a form of social handout for you. You cease to be a beggar and become just someone else signing on. Now you either live by these rules, or give up.'

'You're a bloody fascist, pal.'

'I suppose, when it comes down to it, I probably am. And as such I really don't have to worry about being nice to you at all.'

He gave up at this point and spotted some people at a bus queue he could pester.

A few minutes later I reached the Saab and emptied the can into the petrol tank. Then I got in, did a U-turn and went back to the petrol station. By the time I got there, beggar number two was back with his chum. When they saw who it was in the car, they started to yell abuse, and as I got out they came scurrying over.

'You going to give us some money, then, or what?' said the tall one.

'Bugger off,' I said. 'I explained to your friend here.'

'Don't you tell me to bugger off.'

He pushed me back against the car and jabbed a finger in my face.

'I don't like your type,' he said.

'Neither do I,' said the Jock, and he crowded me out as well.

'It seems nobody does,' I said.

'You going to give us some pennies, now, then, eh?' said the Jock.

The two of them jostled me along the car, taking it in turns to give me a shove. The cashier was watching but wasn't about to come to my rescue, nor was a middle-aged guy calmly filling his car at another pump.

'Times are changing,' said the tall one.

'I know,' I said. 'Come the bloody revolution, I'll be

first up against the wall. But let me tell you, Geronimo, a couple of anti-motorway protests and sleeping in a cardboard box does not a revolution make.'

With this I kneed him in the bollocks. Him being so tall, I didn't do much damage. I couldn't quite get my leg up high enough to cripple him, but it was enough to make him let go of me.

As he stumbled backwards, the Jock grabbed hold of him and dragged him away.

'Come on, Rhubarb,' he said. 'Leave the wanker alone.'

I watched them walking away. Lumberjock said something and the tall one laughed. They looked back at me, then the Jock stuck out his arm and waved my wallet triumphantly in the air. They then bolted in different directions. I tried to chase them, but the Jock ran through the traffic and I got stuck. By the time I got across the road I'd lost sight of him. I swore and went back to the petrol station.

This was not a good development.

I sat in my car. With the amount of petrol I'd put in from the can I'd get about thirty miles, maybe forty if I took it easy. Which meant I had a range of only twenty miles at most. Plus, I needed to report all my cards stolen. And time was ticking away.

This really was a major headache.

Perhaps I could scrape together some cash out of my drawers and pockets and jars at home, otherwise I'd have to think of someone I could borrow some off . . . I was mulling over the problem when a car hooted at me from behind and I had to move off.

Home, then, and take it from there.

When I got back it was ten to twelve. I was losing too much time.

I made the relevant calls to cancel the plastic in my wallet, then set about finding some money. If you're anything like me you have the general notion that your home is probably stuffed with cash, that if you only looked you'd find a forgotten fortune hidden away. But

18

I ripped through the place and managed to find just sixty-six pence. Twenty pence from a jacket, thirty-six pence in one- and two-pence pieces from a tin in the kitchen, and ten pee from the bottom of a desk drawer.

So I'd have to go on the scrounge. Beg like those sorry fools at the petrol station.

I took another line of coke and sat there and thought. Who lived nearby? And no matter how hard I tried, no matter which angle I came at it from, the one same answer kept coming up.

Carrie.

There were no two ways about it. If I didn't want to waste hours farting about all over town, I'd have to try Carrie.

I suppose I'd better tell you, we almost got married once. Two years ago, or maybe more. You know what my memory's like. It was all set, a big white wedding with a vicar and champagne and hats and then she announced that she was pregnant. Well, I mean, what could I do? You can't just spring a thing like that on a man. It put a whole different complexion on things. Marriage is one thing, but babies . . . It was all becoming a bit too real.

So I walked. What choice did I have? Now, I'm not boasting, you understand, it still makes me sweat a little, thinking about it. I don't suppose it's the done thing, is it? To walk. But, you know, it would have been meaner of me to stay, wouldn't it? To stay and offer her some hope, to offer the poor kid some kind of future, to do all that and *then* walk.

I tried to explain all this to her, but she was a little hysterical at the time and couldn't really take it in. I think she probably understood, deep down, but that's not the same as accepting, is it? Isn't there some country song that goes 'I've forgiven but I can't forget'?

Hell, there are probably a million.

She was all right. Had the baby, no problem. Soon got herself a new boyfriend, a fashion photographer. At least, that's what he had been, I think he'd given up the

19

fashion side because he was away so much, and was trying to find other work nearer to home. So she was happy now.

I'd seen her since Jack's birth, of course. I gave her money towards his upbringing. She was always fairly civil towards me, but every time we met I could see something in her face, something unsaid. It was like there was a big neon sign, flashing on and off behind her eyes, with some important message that I just couldn't read. So I tried to see her as little as possible, in case the message was something unpleasant.

So, you see, of all the people I knew in London, she was the one I least wanted to borrow money off, but desperate situations demand desperate remedies.

Carrie, here I come.

I realised that my hands were bleeding, from when I'd hit Mister Kitchen and from the various knocks I'd taken manoeuvring him down the stairs. I washed them and fixed them up as best I could with some Band Aids. Just a few more nicks, cuts and scars to add to the collection. Working manually, as I do a lot of the time, you're always injuring your hands, so that after a while you don't notice any more.

I looked at the clock. Quarter past twelve. Was I being stupid? Should I just wait until tonight? Till it got dark? Get everything out of the way? Get properly prepared?

No. If I stopped for a moment I knew I'd fall apart. The only thing I could think of was Mister Kitchen in my boot, slowly cooking in the heat. It was as if I could already smell him, and until I got rid of him, I wouldn't be able to relax.

I went downstairs, out into the street, and the sweat turned to ice on my body.

There was someone poking around the car, peering in through the windows.

Keep calm, I told myself. Don't give anything away.

'Can I help you?' I said, my voice holding reassuringly firm and forceful.

20

'Oh, sorry. Yes. Hello,' said the man, straightening up. He was a round, middle-aged guy with thinning hair and a blue business suit. 'Is this yours?'

'Yes,' I said. Nonchalant. Casual. Desperate.

'Doug Fish,' he said and shook my hand.

I must have looked vacant.

'Doug Fish,' he repeated. 'I rang yesterday about the motor. The old brum-brum. Your Saab.' A worried look came over him. 'You've not sold it already, have you?'

'No,' I said automatically, too relieved to think straight, and instantly I could have kicked myself. If I'd only lied and said yes, I could have got rid of him.

Bollocks.

'Hot enough, isn't it?' Doug said, pretending to wipe sweat from his brow. 'But it's going to get cold later. Bit of rain, they reckon.'

'It's coming from Siberia,' I said.

Doug nodded and ran his hand admiringly down the Saab's paintwork. 'It's in good nick, isn't it?' He had a Midlands accent and an irritatingly cheery manner.

He squatted down and inspected the tyres.

'Any chance of a test drive?'

I had to be civil to the man. I'd already killed the last guy who came to buy the car; I didn't want to get aggress-ive with this one or the police might spot a trend.

'It's a little inconvenient, actually, Doug. I've got other people coming to have a look. I don't want to be out . . . If you'd like to come back tomorrow?'

He tutted and sucked his lower lip. 'Could be sold by then,' he said. 'No matter.' He clapped his hands together. 'But a little look at the engine, eh?'

'Of course.' I opened the bonnet for him and he peered in. I could tell he didn't know much about cars by the way he adopted a thoughtful expression and pointlessly tweaked a couple of wires and tapped the odd piece of metal with a pen.

'All looks in order,' he said, then had a poke around inside.

21

'Roomy, isn't it?' he said, sitting in the driver's seat and running his hands round the steering wheel. 'What's it like for boot space?'

'Not bad.'

'Mind if I take a look? With my line of work it's a necessity, generous luggage capacity.'

'It's locked.'

'You got the keys, ain't ya?' He laughed.

'What I mean is, it's stuck.'

'Stuck?' He went to the boot and tried to prise it open with his fingertips. 'That's not very good, is it?'

'There's a guy coming over this afternoon to fix it. As I say, if you want to come back tomorrow . . .'

'You're not hiding something?'

'I beg your pardon?'

'In the boot?'

'Like what?'

'Like rust, or dents . . .'

I laughed. 'No, no, no . . . It's just . . . The lock sometimes sticks, but I'm having it fixed. It's not a major job.'

Doug thought about all this.

'I'll tell you what I'll do,' he said. 'I'm seeing another couple of motors today, so, you know, I might see something I like. If not, I'll maybe pop back tonight. And if you sell it in the meantime, well, that's the luck of the draw, isn't it?'

'Fine. Okay, Doug. Nice to have met you.' I shook his hand then waited as he got into his car. He waved and pulled away. I watched him to the end of the road, then jumped in the Saab and drove off in the opposite direction. Towards Chalk Farm, and Carrie.

Carrie lived on a cul-de-sac, in a nice little two-storey semi with ivy growing up the walls. I parked out front, which was a first, and which I took to be a good omen.

I almost didn't recognise the woman who answered the door. She was fat, puffed up. Shiny-faced and sweating buckets in the heat. It was easy to see why. She was

22

hugely pregnant. I'd had no idea. Christ, how long was it since I'd seen her?

'Carrie,' I said. 'How's it going?'

'What are you doing here?' she said flatly.

'I won't lie,' I lied. 'I thought I'd come round and . . .' I looked at her belly and raised my eyebrows . . . 'see how you were getting on . . . It must be due quite soon now. When's it due?'

'Six days ago.'

'Right . . . Six days ago . . .'

'What do you really want?' she said.

'I need to borrow some money.'

'Forget it,' she said.

'No, no, no,' I said, putting a foot in the door and gently easing it back. 'Not much, just a tenner to see me through the day. I've had my wallet stolen.'

Carrie began to cry.

'What is it?' I said. 'What have I done? What's the matter?'

'Nothing . . . It's just this.' She held her guts. 'I get so weepy all the time. Tony's away on a shoot in Azerbaijan and I'm going bananas here without him. I thought, when I saw you, I thought . . . You didn't even know I was pregnant, did you?'

'No.'

She looked like she was going to crumple to the floor, so I took her head and pulled it against my chest, where it felt hot and damp.

'There, now. Come on now, Carrie.' I carefully edged her back inside and closed the door.

'There, now . . . Bad timing. I'm sorry. I'll go.'

She suddenly gripped hold of my forearm. 'No. No. Stay, now you're here. Stay.'

We went through to the sitting room, the nouveau-traditional knocked-through affair, but it still felt small and cramped after my place. Carrie was an interior designer, or at least she had been before children, so the place was immaculately done, with distressed walls

23

and Shaker furniture, only the bright plastic kids' toys spoiled the effect. There was one piece of mine here, a low iron table which I had given her soon after we met. There was a half-finished puzzle laid out on a tray on top of it. Carrie'd always loved doing puzzles.

'Where's Jack?' I asked.

'Mum's taken him out for a walk. He was driving me crazy . . . She was driving me crazy. She's been here for two weeks . . . It's so overdue. I thought at first I'd be all right by myself. I thought I was strong. Hell, I am strong, but my hormones are in chaos . . . I'm just . . .' At this, she burst out crying again.

'How is Jack?' I asked. 'Is he walking yet? He must be how old now? One and a half? Two?'

'He's four.'

'Four? Really? You know I've always had a rotten memory.'

'No you haven't,' said Carrie bitterly.

'What?'

'You can remember the things you want to remember,' she said. 'You can remember short cuts round London and cricket scores and every member of the magnificent fucking seven . . . It's just the important things you forget, like the names of your friends and the birthdays of your own family.'

'Horst Bucholz and Brad Dexter,' I said.

'What?'

'They're the two no one ever gets. I mean, everyone knows Steve McQueen and Yul Brynner and James Coburn and . . .'

'SHUT UP!' Carrie was weeping like a maniac now. I held her and rocked her gently, looking over the top of her head to see if there were any pieces of the puzzle I could fit.

'So . . . Azerbaijan,' I said. 'Is that for a news magazine? A newspaper . . . ?'

'A fashion shoot for *Elle*. Winter coats. He was supposed to be back, but they've had rotten weather. Not

24

cold enough. The forecasters all said that at this time of year . . .'

'I thought Tony was giving up the glamour stuff,' I said.

'He tried, but we got so short of money. I couldn't get any work. He's had to go back to it. Oh, God, it's a bloody nightmare. We're so broke.'

'You should have asked me.'

'Tony doesn't want that. I don't want it. I mean, money for Jack is one thing . . .'

I sneaked a peak at my watch. It was twenty to one. Hour and a half there, hour and a half back. Oh, bollocks, at this rate I'd be trying to bury him at Watford Gap services. The last thing I needed right now was to get dragged back into Carrie's domestic politics.

'What's the puzzle?' I asked. 'What's the picture?'

'It's a Sherlock Holmes thing,' said Carrie, letting go of me. 'There's a book that goes with it.' She sat up and wiped her nose. 'You have to finish the picture, then solve the mystery from the clues in it.'

'Sounds complicated.'

'Mm.'

Silence descended.

'Listen,' I said after a couple of weeks. 'I'd really better go.'

'I'm so fucking scared,' said Carrie quietly.

'What? I mean, why?'

'Last time it was easy, well, not easy, it was the hardest bloody thing I'd ever done in my life, but at least I didn't know what I was letting myself in for.'

'What d'you mean?' I asked, looking at my watch again, the second hand relentlessly ticking round and round.

'It rips you apart,' said Carrie. 'It tears your guts out. The whole thing takes for ever. It's the worst possible thing you could imagine.'

'What about the miracle of childbirth?' I said.

25

'The miracle is that anyone survives . . .' She laughed again.

'Listen,' I said, patting her knee. 'I'll borrow some money somewhere else.'

She looked at me and there was the sign flashing on and off.

'I really am in a bit of hurry,' I said. 'I know you don't believe me . . .'

I had to keep calm, in case anyone ever asked her . . . 'No, he wasn't acting suspiciously, he was the same old shit he always was . . .' Yes, fuck it, she wouldn't trust me if I was nice to her. Be brisk. Be brutal.

'Well, good luck, honey,' I said and prised my arm free from her grip. As I stood up, she lunged at me and fell to the floor. I helped her back up on to the sofa and she was gasping and groaning like somebody being murdered in a radio play.

I looked down and there was liquid trickling down her legs.

'Oh, God,' she wailed. 'It's started . . .'

# THREE

Yes, as one life is snuffed out, another comes into the world.

Oh, bollocks.

'I'll ring for an ambulance,' I said.

'An ambulance?' Carrie was crouched on the floor clutching her great lump and panting like a dog.

'Isn't that what you do?' I said. 'Call an ambulance?'

'Not if you've got a bloody car.'

'Oh, no, Carrie. Carrie, honestly, I can't . . .'

'Do you want me to have it on the bloody floor?' she yelled, then whimpered and went back to her panting.

'Are you sure it's coming,' I said. 'It's not just a false alarm?'

Carrie sort of screamed.

I looked at my watch. This was not turning out to be my day. 'All right. All right . . .' I said. 'I'll take you up to the Royal Free, but that's it.'

Carrie looked at me and nodded, unable to speak.

I took her by the elbow and coaxed her upright.

'House keys,' I said, and she pointed to the table.

'And bring my bag,' she said, indicating an overnight bag by the door.

It took an age to get to the car. Carrie could only take one small step at a time, doubled over, holding herself, as if she was terrified that the kid would burst out of her like the Alien. She moaned with each movement, breathing all the while like someone who'd just come up for air after swimming the Channel underwater. I had an arm round her, dragging her forwards, mumbling inane

27

encouragements, when all I wanted was to say in a loud, firm voice, 'Get a fucking move on, will you?'

At last we made it and I belted her into the passenger seat, the straps going above and below the monstrous bulge.

I drove like a maniac up Haverstock Hill, almost wanting the police to stop me so I could do the old 'She's having a baby' routine and get them to escort us, sirens wailing and lights flashing. But isn't it always the way? Whenever you want to be stopped for speeding it never happens.

It released a fair amount of tension, though, driving like I was in a car chase, squealing in and out of the traffic, jumping the lights, going way too fast, but no matter how fast I went, it wasn't fast enough.

I parked in a fairly random manner and got Carrie out of the car and through the doors into the hospital. I yelled at a porter to get a stretcher or a wheelchair or something. He just nodded and ambled off.

'She's about to fucking drop,' I yelled after him, but he paid me no heed. Indeed, none of the staff seemed to have any great sense of emergency. They probably dealt with this sort of thing all the time; hysterical couples who thought the thing was about to pop out at any moment. And was it? Well, I didn't know. This whole process was something of a mystery to me. In films all that seemed to be required was some hot water for the woman and a ready supply of cigarettes for the man.

In a while the porter returned with a chair. We peeled Carrie off the pillar she'd been clinging on to, and the porter wheeled her into the depths of the hospital.

I trotted alongside. I didn't have much choice; Carrie was holding on to my arm with a grip of steel.

Eventually we arrived in a little cramped and windowless room with a single bed in it. Various pieces of equipment stood around, waiting ominously. The porter and I manhandled Carrie on to the bed, a complicated affair with joints and metal levers and pistons. I couldn't

28

help studying it from a professional point of view. I wondered if I should consider bringing out a range of furniture based on surgical designs; the maternity bed, the wheelchair, the operating table . . .

The porter muttered something and shuffled out. We were left alone.

'Okay, honey,' I said. 'You're okay now. You're in safe hands. I'll leave you to it, eh . . . ?'

She sank her fingers deeper into my flesh and gave me a fierce look. I didn't try to pull away. I don't think I could have broken her unnaturally superhuman grip if I'd tried.

'Carrie, really, I . . .'

She replied with a low animal growl which very definitely wasn't human and latched on to me with both hands. She stared at me with a wild, wide-eyed expression that was quite terrifying.

'Carrie . . .' I pleaded, but it was no good, she was too far gone. Like someone on hallucinogenic drugs, she was on another planet.

After a while a middle-aged black midwife with Michael Caine glasses and a no-nonsense, 'What's all the fuss?' type manner came in with a young nurse.

'Let's have a look at you,' said the midwife, and she removed Carrie's knickers. She rummaged around for a few seconds, then her manner changed abruptly.

'Crikey, love,' she said. 'It's all systems go.'

'Is it on the way?' I asked.

'Baby's head's half out,' she said, and the whole atmosphere changed. The nurse bustled around switching things on, and the midwife hurried out, only to return moments later with about a hundred other people; doctors, nurses, anaesthetists, trainee midwives, student doctors, observers; all we seemed to be lacking was a tea lady.

In the twinkling of an eye, Carrie had been greased and tied up with a bondage freak's orgy of straps, belts, tubes and monitors. All the while, someone from

29

administration was patiently trying to take down her particulars.

Carrie kept repeating the word 'epidural' between clenched teeth, until the midwife explained that it was too late for that. Carrie burst into tears.

'What do you mean it's too fucking late?' she screamed. 'Give me an epidural.'

'There, there,' said the midwife and patted her on the head.

'Well, give me something. Anything.'

The midwife passed her a sinister black gas mask thing and Carrie put it to her face and sucked. As she did so, she momentarily loosened her grip. I pulled away, but quick as a tiger, she got me again, pulling me off my feet. I toppled on to the bed and she sank her teeth into my forearm.

I yelled, but was ignored by all except the midwife, who smiled at me in a motherly way. It was beginning to dawn on me that Carrie's ferocious behaviour was nothing out of the ordinary.

Luckily her bite hadn't drawn blood, but there was a perfect set of deep teeth marks in my skin. I looked up at the clock . . . Twenty past two. Just over two and a half hours till the *Observer* bunch were due.

Ah, fuck it, Mister Kitchen would have to wait. After all, what better alibi was there?

'Where were you on the day of the murder?'

'I was in the Royal Free Hospital, Hampstead, delivering a baby, m'lud.'

'I'll stay, Carrie,' I said, trying to sound manly and caring at the same time, like one of those TV doctors. She smiled weakly up at me, then half sat upright in a sudden spasm of pain and punched me in the face.

At least it meant she let go of me. I sprawled back across the room and tripped over her overnight bag.

This gave me an idea. I rummaged through the bag, looking for her purse. It was no good, in our hurry to leave she hadn't brought it. I cursed myself for not thinking of it earlier and stealing some money while we were at the house and Carrie was distracted.

During all this, the team around the foot of the bed had been in conference. There was evidently something up. Two of them were dispatched on some errand. The others swapped jargon in hushed and urgent tones.

Carrie was rigid on the bed, sweating and growling.

'We've got a little problem, dearie,' said the midwife.

'Oh, Jesus. Oh, Christ . . .' said Carrie. 'Oh, shit.'

'You'll be all right, darling.' The midwife beamed at her then rejoined the pack staring up between her legs.

Another doctor came in, a young Asian guy who had the permanently tired, somewhat crumpled look that all hospital doctors seem to have. I gathered he was the registrar. He smiled distantly at Carrie and asked a few questions whilst fiddling about beneath her nightie.

'Baby doesn't want to come out,' he said.

'I thought it was half out already,' I said.

'He is,' he said. 'But he seems reluctant to come any further. He's got a very big head. Unfortunately, it's too far progressed for a Caesarean, so we'll just have to give him a hand, eh?'

Carrie yelled something unintelligible and grabbed hold of me by the bollocks.

I looked at her. She was a different person and seemed to have no idea what she was doing. Tears sprang to my eyes. I tried to prise her fingers loose as they steadily tightened.

'YOU BASTARD!' she suddenly yelled at me. Then a stream of words tumbled out of her. 'Oh dear God you bastard I never told you before bottled it all up terribly English aren't I oh you bastard I never told you what a prick you are you spineless selfish prick my life's been a fucking mess because of you you never could put anything else before your comforts could you I nearly died having Jack and it was two weeks before you came to visit us and then you were drunk and out of your head on bloody coke you just kept saying wow and giggling

31

you've got no idea have you no bloody idea at all God I hate you you screwed up my life for four years and now Tony's away the bastard why do I always get left alone?'

I couldn't reply. I couldn't breathe. But at least I knew now what those words were behind her eyes, the ones spelled out in bright and poisonous neon colours. They were flashing on and off now, so that I could clearly read them . . . 'YOU' and 'BASTARD', on and off, on and off, on and off . . . Like the name of a gaudy club in the worst part of town. A club with only one member: me. And I was bouncer, manager, barman and toilet cleaner too.

Carrie was still ranting on, her voice hoarse, almost a whisper.

'After you left I lay in bed plotting ways to kill you – ow – Christ I went through this alone before and this time you're here and it's not even your fucking child if there was a way if there was any way I'd give you all this pain all my pain mother mercy Jesus fuck damn I'm the King of the Swingers oh jungle VIP three threes are six three fours are seven deep breaths now but at least you're gone out of my life and I've got Jack and Tony and this one if it ever fucking comes out COME OUT YOU LITTLE BASTARD!'

With this she let go of me and hit the young nurse who was adjusting a monitor across her belly. In the confusion I got hold of the mask and sucked in a great lungful of gas and air until my head was detached from the agonising pain in my lower half. Then I sank to my knees and was sick into a bucket.

Still I was completely ignored by all and sundry.

Meanwhile, the anaesthetist had been busy injecting Carrie's nether regions with a gigantic, pantomime syringe, and the registrar now got hold of a pair of large scissors. I hauled myself upright and watched as he once again took up his position between Carrie's legs and set to work.

I realised he was cutting her open, snip, snip, snip, with the scissors. Somehow I'd never imagined childbirth was anything like this; an unholy and haphazard mixture of high and low tech. A ghastly cross between an abattoir and a science lab. All these fancy monitors and gadgets, all this expensive equipment, and the doctor was cutting her open with a pair of fucking scissors. My dispatching of Mister Kitchen had been a considerably quicker, cleaner and more efficient process. It struck me that it was a great deal easier to snuff somebody out of this world than it was to bring them into it.

I thought of all those times I'd read about childbirth, or seen it in films or on the TV, I thought of all the mentions in history books, the statistics, all those references to 'died in childbirth' which I'd never really thought about before, just imagined sickly young girls who weren't ready for it, but it was clear now, the human body just isn't designed to have children.

The next time some God-botherer tried to convince me of the Big One's existence and cited the wonders of nature . . . you know the sort of thing, 'How could all these perfect things exist if there wasn't a God?' I could counter with, 'If you think this is a perfect world you've obviously never seen a woman give birth, pal! A two-year-old could design a better method, like a fucking stork, or a gooseberry bush or something. There's got to be a better way than this gory circus of hacksaws and naked brutality . . .'

The registrar had now finished snipping, and he put the bloody scissors in a metal dish. A nurse then handed him what looked like a sink plunger attached to a long tube.

'We'll try the Ventouse,' he said and stuck the plunger between Carrie's legs. My God, he was going to try to suck it out! With some difficulty he attached the plunger to the top of the baby's head, then he turned on the suction and began to pull.

Nothing happened.

Nothing happened for several minutes. Then there were more urgent conferences. Carrie had subsided into a slobbery heap, burbling incoherent nonsense and crying continuously while the nurse mopped her brow.

Next, the doctor got a big spoon-shaped device, about two foot long, like an elongated ice cream scoop, or at least the steel outline of one. He greased it and slid it up inside Carrie. He then got hold of another one and slid it up the other side, before clipping the two halves together and creating a huge pair of tongs inside her – around the baby's head.

He said something quietly to one of the bystanders and took hold of the handle with a white-knuckle grip. He began to pull, gently at first, then harder and harder, his face straining with the effort, growing dark and sweaty. He put a knee up against the end of the bed to brace himself, and pulled even harder, his arms shaking, the muscles standing out in relief.

'Jesus Christ, man,' I said. 'You'll pull its fucking head off.'

The midwife gave me one of her little smiles, and moved me back from the proceedings. Everyone stood around watching the ghastly display as the doctor now pulled with all his might. Nobody seemed alarmed by his efforts, so I had to assume he knew what he was doing, but if the baby had a neck like a giraffe, I wouldn't be at all surprised. The doctor paused for a breather and the nurse now mopped his brow.

'It's all right,' he said. 'Nearly there.'

This whole thing, from arriving at the hospital onwards, had a disconcerting, nightmare quality about it. One of those nightmares where people do strange and terrible things with polite smiles, and you feel excluded from some secret ceremony.

As the doctor renewed his efforts I sneaked over for a closer look. Gripped in the forceps was a red lump, soft and squashy, bulging between the tongs like a moist dumpling.

34

'What the fuck is that?' I said, and as I said it I realised it was the baby's head. As I watched, it slipped fully out, followed by a white, slimy sac-like thing which I supposed had to be the baby's body. All manner of goo and gloop slopped out after it.

In a moment the cord was cut and pegged, and the baby was snatched up and whisked away by the midwife, who stuck a tube down its throat and turned it on. I heard it, deep down inside the child's lungs, sucking like a straw in a milk shake.

It was all peace and calm now. The doctor was sitting between Carrie's legs calmly stitching with a big needle and thread. The nurse was tidying up the filthy mess.

This really was the most bizarre scene I had ever witnessed.

They weighed the kid and wrapped it in a blanket and gave it to Carrie, who was lying in a stupor on the bed, shining, wet, drained and delirious. She looked at the ugly little thing like she had no idea what it was and made no effort to take it. In the end I picked it up and peered at it. Its head had been pulled into a cone shape by the Ventouse and dented by the forceps on either side. It didn't look at all human.

Even having watched it come out, I couldn't really believe that this creature had been living inside Carrie.

'There,' said the doctor, putting aside his needle and thread. 'A pretty good job, though I say so myself. Invisible mending.'

The nurse and the midwife inspected his handiwork, nodding appreciatively. 'She'll hardly be able to see the stitches.' The doctor shook my hand. 'I expect you saw that it was a boy. Congratulations,' he said and was gone.

Soon we were left alone. Me holding the baby, and Carrie quietly sobbing.

I looked at its mouth, opening and closing, its minute fingers wriggling and clutching at the blanket, and for an instant it opened the bluest eyes I had ever seen.

35

Then the midwife came back in and gently gave the baby to Carrie.

This time she took it.

I left her there and returned to my chores.

# FOUR

It was gone four when I left the hospital, and I was starting to feel weird; hot and dry and strung out. I got in the Saab and set off back through Belsize Park. I was all out of phase. I guess the strange interlude in the delivery suite had knocked me sideways. I was jangled, raw and itchy, like someone had tipped grit into my brain.

The worst part of it was, five hours after spiking him, I was still no closer to getting rid of Mister Kitchen. He was still festering in my boot, and I was still broke. I had no way of getting out of London. This pissed me off. It would piss anyone off. I mean, was it fair? All this shit falling down on me in one day? A man shouldn't have to put up with these problems. Sometimes you just felt it would be nice to be left alone by fate, or the stars, or God, or whatever it was, and allowed to get on with things. I'm a modest man. I really don't need a lot. All I really required of the world was a comfortable house, a plentiful supply of hot food, hard drugs and soft women, a nice car, all the latest electronics, a couple of decent suits, two or three holidays a year to someplace hot and ... Well, you know the sort of thing.

Was that too much to ask?

No. It was not.

But was I allowed to pursue my humble existence unimpeded?

No. I was not.

Instead of being left in peace I was fucked around, I

was knocked from pillar to post, I was tossed about like a dirty sock in a washing machine.

What had I done to deserve this?

Somebody cut me up and I blared my horn and yelled at him, swore in seven shades of shit.

What I needed was a drink. A cold beer and a whisky.

Carrie had never appreciated my drinking. I like to maintain a nice steady balance, a low-level fuzz, that just needs topping up every now and then, but with Carrie I was slipping into deep water. Towards the end I'd been drinking more and more. I guess I might have been getting close to becoming a drunk. And it wasn't helping, all that beer, all that wine, all those spirits. I was just getting more and more depressed. But, tell me, was I drinking more because I was depressed, or was I depressed because I was drinking more?

It all changed when I walked, of course. I no longer felt the need to oblivionise myself. I cleaned up my act. Dried out. I had it under control now, no problems, a nice easy half-bottle of whisky a day and maybe seven or eight bottles of Beck's. Shit, I was almost teetotal.

I stopped at some lights and a gold Mini with black windows and plenty of fancy trim pulled up alongside. There was a jungle track playing inside it so loud that the car had become one giant beat box. The vibrations shook the Saab and rattled my teeth in my skull. I closed my eyes and let the music fill me up. Ah, bliss. This was the buzz and the heat, this was a warm bath for my frazzled nodes. The sound was physical, magical. It shook me hard and things settled back to where they were supposed to be.

When the lights turned the Mini pulled away so fast I had no hope of keeping up. I heard the huge bass thump disappearing down the road, melting into all the other street sounds.

Music. That was the answer. Sad music, miserable music, sentimental, wallowing, self-pitying music. I needed the

38

blues, country and western, torch songs, Edith Piaf. I needed crying saxophones and whispering strings. When a man's down there's nothing better than some desperate music to cheer him up.

I snapped the front on my tape player and jammed in a cassette. An electric slide guitar gave a slam and a swoop and Elmore James yelled out, 'The sun is shining . . .' He paused. The guitar gave a great gulp and then plunged down like crashing steel . . . 'Although it's raining in my heart . . .' His voice hard and high and husky, soaring like his guitar.

'The sun is shining . . . Although it's raining in my heart . . .'

The music breezed through me until I was suffused by a white light of clarity and – PING – I got a little bit of my tattered memory back.

I remembered a hip flask in the glove box.

I took it out and unscrewed the cap while I drove.

I poured a nice golden burn down my gullet and smiled.

'You know I love you, baybeeyaaaaargh!' It was spine-chilling the way the word became a cry of pain . . . 'And I don't . . . Don't know the reason why.'

With the whisky fumes flowing out of my nose and the white light blowing through my brain I cheered up and sang along.

Things weren't so bad. I was remembering more and more now. Like how I didn't believe in fate, or the stars, or God. Didn't believe in any of that caveman mumbo-jumbo, not Zeus, Isis, Shiva or Beelzebub. None of it, not even luck. Good luck or bad. You could put it all in a sack and drown it, wouldn't make no difference to me.

Every night I pray to God. I ask him to grant me the strength not to believe in him.

I didn't believe in conspiracy theories, crystals, rabbits' feet or St Christophers. The Bible, the Koran, the Tibetan Book of the Dead, the Necronomicon, the weather forecast, it was all just double glazing. Vain attempts to keep out the cold. You want to know what I think? I think things just happen. And, as such, it was damned foolish of me to bathe in self-pity and rail against bad luck in a cruel and unjust world.

These things had happened and I could deal with them.

Lee Harvey Oswald shot JFK, I topped Mister Kitchen, and it was up to me to sort it all out.

Yup. And I could sort it all out. I could cope.

All I needed was another drink.

I drained the flask and it left a kind of hollow feeling inside. Not a spiritual hollow, you understand, not a hungry ache of the soul, more a hungry ache of the belly. Because, of course, I hadn't had anything to eat since my popcorn breakfast.

I'm not a big eater at the best of times. Somebody once told me you can eat or you can drink, but if you try both you're fucked. You bloat, you swell like an inflatable Elvis. So I generally get my sustenance from the bottle, but with the trials and tribulations that had been heaped upon me today I was in need of some extra fortification. I needed the comfort of food . . .

What the fuck is a tribulation, anyway? It's funny, all these old words that only survive in corny sayings. I told myself to look it up when I got home.

'I had a dream, I had a dream one rainy night . . . I was walking with my baby, and the sun was shining bright.'

I saw an Italian deli-cum-sandwich-shop by the side of the road and pulled over.

It was cool and dark inside, and the smells of the food made me feel weak and delirious. Big salamis hung from the ceiling, there were shelves of jars and tins, racks of bottles and bread, those bulky orange and yellow plastic bags full of dry biscuits and a huge glass-fronted display cabinet packed and oily with cheeses and olives and cold meats and salad and . . . Well, you know what an Italian deli looks like.

40

I waited while a couple of people were served in front of me, then finally the Italian guy got to me. He was about forty, with thick black hair and a mournful expression.

'Tomato and brie, please,' I said. 'On ciabatta . . .'

'We are out of brie. I'm sorry.'

'Make it salami and cream cheese, then.'

'Salami and cream cheese?'

'Please.'

He started to do his thing under the counter, with the practised smooth efficiency of someone who does nothing but make sandwiches all day.

'You want tomato and cucumber?' he said.

'What? You're out of salami as well?'

'No . . . You want it with? Is very heavy.'

'Sure, okay, some tomato, but no cucumber. Can't stand the stuff.'

'You need to make it more light. It help the digestion, you know?'

'Really?'

'I know a little bit about food, how it work. Is science, you know? How are the minerals work? The combination. What food is go with what. Now, for me, if I was going to a meeting, I wouldn't eat this sandwich, is too heavy. I would have some mineral water, a banana, some salads, lettuce, you know? Something light.'

'Listen,' I said. 'I don't want a fucking lecture, I want a fucking sandwich. I'm starving to death here.'

He shrugged and carried on with the preparations, cutting the bread in half, then wrapping it in paper before finally putting it into a little bag.

'Is your problem,' he said and handed it to me.

'Yes,' I said.

'Two pound eighty,' he said.

'Oh, bollocks,' I said, handing him back the bag. 'I haven't got any money.'

He looked at me. I felt very hot and tired.

'No one else is gonna eat this sandwich,' he said. 'Not today. Now I have to throw it away.'

41

'I'm sorry,' I said, and he just carried on looking at me.

'Get outta my fuckin' shop, okay?' he said after a while, and I did.

Outside, the light hit me like a blow, and I squinted as I got into the car. Flashes on my retina, shooting pains in my head.

What is it with people these days? Why has everyone got so worked up about food? It used to be you ate and that was it. Breakfast, lunch, dinner. Food. You eat to live. It's like breathing, it's a natural process. But these days food isn't just food any more. It's minerals and vitamins and calories and saturated fats and unsaturated fats and polyunsaturated fats. It's carbohydrates and E numbers and roughage and fibre. It's Yin and fucking Yang.

Food these days, it's medicine. It's not a simple process of chewing, swallowing and shitting. Going to the grocer's, it's like going to the bloody chemist. How long is it before we have to have our food prescribed to us? Restaurants will be like hospitals, with doctors for chefs and nurses for waitresses. 'Operating table for four, sir?'

Christ, you're hungry, you eat. It's not enough that mankind has existed for millions of years eating meat, fruit, fish, vegetables, milk, butter, cheese, eggs . . . Food. That's all it is. Just bloody food. But the scientists get hold of it and the health freaks and the pundits and the cookery writers and the scaremongerers and the fucking greens and we all think we understand it all so much better, but we don't, the more you know, the less you know, and in the end, you know what the problem with this country is? Everybody thinks they know what they're doing . . .

In the absence of any food, these thoughts sustained me till I got home.

I looked at the clock on the dashboard as I was parking: 4:35. That gave me twenty-five minutes to get everything

42

ready for the *Observer* people. I tidied up as best I could, hiding any evidence of drink and drugs.

Storage space has always been a bit of a problem. I designed the flat to look like a film set. It looks great, but there's no fucking cupboards. It was all very elegant and minimalist and Japanese; everything just so, everything in its place, but once I tried living in it I realised I'd made a couple of basic errors. Only an ascetic monk could have really appreciated the lack of storage facilities. You only had to live like a normal human being for a day and the place looked like a disaster. In the end I used the spare bedroom as a dump. So, whereas the rest of the flat looked immaculate and ordered, like something out of the pages of an interior design magazine, the spare room was like the very bottom-most pit of hell. It was a festering, terrifying snake-hole of junk, piled precariously high, thrown in, kicked and shoved into place, threatening at any moment to collapse and consume whoever happened to have strayed in there. It was the dark, secret heart of the place. And now I was adding to the chaos, lobbing in everything I didn't want to be seen.

I'd nearly finished when the buzzer went. I prayed it wasn't them, as I hadn't changed or washed yet.

It wasn't. It was Doug Fish.

'Doug,' I said. 'What do you want?'

'It's about the car.'

'I sold it,' I said, thinking on my feet for a change.

'No,' he said. 'There's someone tried to break into it.'

I raced downstairs, three steps at a time, and was back out in the sunlight in about half a second.

Doug was there with a uniformed guy from the AA who was inspecting the lock on the Saab's boot.

'I just came round with Alan,' said Doug, and the AA guy held out his hand. I shook it.

Doug shook my hand as well. 'We've been looking at another car, actually,' he said. 'Alan and I, and I said to Alan, "Why not pop round and see if the Saab hasn't been sold." Then we're just turning the corner and we

43

see there's two kids with a screwdriver trying to break into it. Lucky we came along, eh?'

'What happened to them?' I asked, looking off down the street.

'Oh, they scarpered when they saw us.'

'Not much damage done,' said Alan. 'Scraped the paintwork a bit. You left your radio cassette player in there. They were probably after that.'

'I forgot it,' I said, unlocking the driver's door. 'I've been a bit rushed.'

'How's the boot?' said Doug.

'Still stuck, I'm afraid.' I popped off the front of the radio and put it in my pocket. 'The guy's not been round to fix it yet.'

'And you still sold it, eh?' Doug shook his head. 'With a sticky boot . . . and now these scratches.' He tutted. 'You might have to knock a bit off, eh?'

'Yeah, maybe.'

'How much did you sell it for? I might be able to give you a better offer.'

'Signed, sealed and delivered, I'm afraid,' I said.

'That's life, in't it, eh? You sure you don't want Alan here to get your boot open? He's a whiz with motors.'

'No, honestly, Doug. It's okay. The guy I sold it to didn't seem unduly worried.'

'I'm intrigued now. What's in that boot?'

'Just a set of golf clubs.'

'Ah, well. Listen, if your other sale falls through, give us a tinkle, eh?'

'Sure thing, Doug.'

At last Doug and Alan fucked off and I was left with a dilemma.

Could I risk leaving Mister Kitchen in the car?

What if the thieves came back? What if Doug came back with Alan and got the boot open? What if . . . I know I was getting paranoid, but wouldn't you? With a stiff in your car? Specially the type of day I was having.

I checked there was no one around, then opened the

boot and hauled Mister Kitchen out, still wrapped in the rug.

If it was a struggle getting him down the stairs, it was even more of a struggle getting him up again. By the time I'd got him into the flat I was shattered, and filthy dirty from the dust which had fallen from the rug and stuck to my sweat.

And now I had to hide him somewhere. I couldn't have squeezed him into the dump room, even if I'd wanted, short of standing him up inside the door and having him fall out when it was opened. No, I needed somewhere else. I looked around for a solution, and that's when I saw Big Charlie.

I always give my designs names when I'm working on them, and Big Charlie was an abandoned prototype for a large free-standing lighting unit. Little Charlie was a smaller version which had actually gone into production, being slightly more practical.

Big Charlie was basically a tapered, seven-foot-tall, brushed-steel tube, the end cut off at an angle like an old-fashioned coal scuttle. It threw light up from the top and there were smaller holes drilled in the sides to let more light out. It was way too big for the flat but I'd been keeping it here while I decided what to do with it.

Well, it had finally come in useful. As a casket. I tipped it on to its side and ripped out the lighting equipment inside, then I unrolled the rug.

Mister Kitchen had leaked into the sheet. It was soaked dark red in places. The body was still warm. In this heat, I wasn't surprised.

I slid him along the rug on the plastic bags and got him into the end of Big Charlie. It was a tight fit but I just managed to squash him in. It had a solid base so he couldn't slide out the other end as I hoisted it upright and rolled it back against the wall.

I had blood all over me now to add to the general filth, so I gunned into the bathroom, tore off my clothes,

45

shoved them in a bin bag and showered. As I dried myself off afterwards, I looked at the clock.

Almost five.

I ran up the steps to my sleeping area and dressed.

Five minutes later, when the door buzzer went, I was ready. Cool and elegant in a cream linen suit with a grey shirt and a pair of new tan deck shoes. I thought I looked suitably casual and relaxed, and the suit calmed me, slowed my actions. I had bottomed out nicely.

As I sauntered down the steps from the gallery I saw the rug in the middle of the floor, spotted with Kitchen's blood. I quickly plonked a table on it and went down to answer the door.

There were five of them there. The first to speak was a petite, black-clad, bubbly thing with cropped red hair who introduced herself as Nikki. I'd spoken to her on the phone a couple of times and she wasn't very different to how I'd imagined her.

She introduced the others. They were a photographer, his two assistants and a make-up woman.

The photographer was a tall Viking of a man called Dieter. He had a deep tan, a mane of golden hair, shorts and a white T-shirt. When he spoke he had an accent not too dissimilar to my own. The names of his two assistants, a harassed-looking boy and an Australian girl, I immediately forgot, along with the name of the make-up girl.

Leaving the two assistants to lug Dieter's flight cases in, I led the way upstairs.

I offered drinks. Dieter requested a mineral water and the make-up girl wanted tea, but luckily Nikki opted to join me in a beer, which was a relief as I don't like to drink alone in company.

While I sorted the drinks, Dieter looked around, nodding his head. He particularly admired the light, streaming through the big windows in the roof, and soon picked the area he wanted to shoot.

'Okay,' said Nikki, drinking her Beck's straight from

46

the bottle. 'We'll just pick it up as we go along, I guess. It should be pretty painless.'

Bill and Ben, as I shall call them, were now busy unpacking cameras and stands and lights, and God knows what, while Dieter roamed around with a light meter.

Downing my beer like it would save my life, I had a brief chat with the make-up girl about the requirements. She was only really there to cover up any spots and make me look vaguely normal under the lights. So I sat on one of my kitchen chairs while she fussed around me. Meanwhile, Nikki had opened her huge bag and got out a tiny tape recorder. She tinkered with it for a while then propped it up next to me.

'Okay,' she said. 'How long have you lived here?'

'About two years, maybe three . . . I can't remember. I could find out for you, but dates and times and that sort of thing aren't exactly my strong point.'

'I'll put two years.' She smiled at me. 'It doesn't really matter, does it?'

'Not really, no.'

I filled her in on a few more details and she made notes on a small pad.

For those of you who are not familiar with the item, 'A Room of My Own', I shall enlighten you. It's been running in the *Observer* off and on for as long as anyone can remember, and consists of a large photo of someone's room, with that someone proudly seated centre stage. They cram into the picture every item of significance or sentimental import that comes to hand. I suppose the idea is that this room, and the objects in it, sum up the man, or woman, featured. I don't know about that, but it was bloody good publicity, and I intended to get a lot of my own pieces well placed.

'And you're thirty-five, aren't you?' Nikki asked, scribbling in her pad.

'Nearly thirty-six,' I said. 'It's my birthday next week.'

'Well, happy birthday for then.' Nikki laughed. 'I'd better put thirty-six . . .'

I watched as Dieter lugged the long sofa into a better position for his lights. The spots of blood on it seemed to stand out as though they were illuminated, but of course he didn't notice them, or if he did, they meant nothing to him. Nor did the marks on the rug, exposed as either Bill or Ben shifted the table out of the way.

'Okay,' said Nikki. 'And you're a . . . What are you? A sculptor? A furniture-maker? A designer? How would you describe yourself?'

'I'm all of those things,' I said.

'What should I put?'

I shrugged.

'What does it say in your passport?' Nikki asked.

'Student,' I said. '. . . It's an old passport.'

'Where were you at college?'

'Cambridge, for about five minutes. We didn't take to each other.'

'And when you left you started making furniture?'

'Eventually. After the usual young fool's aimless wanderings and evasions, hiding from the inevitability of the real world. I actually learnt carpentry and metal work on a kibbutz.'

'Was it something you'd always wanted to do?'

'It's funny . . . I remember when I was a kid, we were on a family holiday in France . . . Dad took us to a museum in Rouen. Le Secq des Tournelles. A guy called Henry René d'Allemagne had collected examples of ironwork from all round the world. I guess most children would have been bored rigid by the place.'

'Oh, God, yes, bo-oring,' said Nikki.

'But it's not boring,' I said. 'That's the thing. Manufacture, making things. Nobody's interested any more, in industry, engineering, fascinating, important things.' I could see the shutters come down behind her eyes, but I wasn't going to stop. The death of industry was a pet beef of mine. 'I got the bug at Le Secq des Tournelles,'

I said. 'I wanted to know how these things were made. Who had made them. There was a whole world made out of metal. And it was beautiful. There were intricate Islamic pieces, heavy medieval pieces, grilles, handles, knives, doors. Metal, iron, steel . . . You can hammer it and melt it and cast it and bend it and cut it and punch it. You can make tiny little pieces of jewellery with it or you can make bloody great ships. After that holiday I don't suppose I thought much about it until I was in Israel, and there on the kibbutz was an old guy, Haim, who ran a small forge, and he made things and something clicked and I was hooked . . .'

'So when you got back to England you started doing it for a living?'

'Yes. One-off designs at first. People seemed to like them, so I started doing larger pieces. Built-in furniture, I suppose you'd call it, and that expanded into whole interiors, shops, offices, fancy apartments.'

'What, like putting cupboards in, and that?'

'The full monty . . . Doors, furniture, fireplaces, fittings . . . All tailor-made for each place. But I've always kept the other side going, the pieces, the *objets*, for want of a better word.'

'Like that thing there . . .' Nikki pointed to where Dieter was placing the candlestick next to the sofa.

'Yes,' I said, my throat dry. 'Like that.' Would he notice the bloodstains on the spike? Maybe they looked like melted wax . . . I was powerless to do anything. The make-up girl was painting my face, and Nikki was asking me these damned questions. I had to sit there and watch helplessly while the evidence of my crime was arranged neatly for a photograph.

'What is it exactly?' Nikki asked.

'It's a candlestick.'

'It looks like some kind of weapon.'

'Yes, I suppose it does, rather. Maybe I should resurrect it.'

'How do you mean?'

49

'Last Christmas, didn't you notice, it was the year of the candle. This year there's going to be even more of them out there. They've become the gift of the moment; candles, candlesticks, chandeliers. You can't move for them. I suppose because in this day and age they're essentially useless, so they make the ideal gift . . .' I was babbling, the words pouring out to hide my panic.

'So that's what you do mostly now?' said Nikki. 'Make candlesticks and things?'

'I have three main lines. The interiors, the one-off pieces which are sold in . . .'

'In galleries?'

'I suppose in the old-fashioned sense. In Europe they still call them gallerias. They're really just expensive shops. Then there are my production pieces; cheaper stuff, mass-produced. Well, not mass . . . and not cheap, either, really. But you know what I mean?'

'Like the T-back chair?'

'Yes, chairs, tables . . . and smaller pieces, of course . . . Lamps, dining room stuff, kitchen stuff . . .'

'A friend of mine's got one of your coffee pots which I've always coveted,' said Nikki.

'I can get you one trade price, if you're very nice to me,' I said, and she gave me an arched-eyebrow look.

On another day I might have made an effort to seduce her. Since leaving Carrie I'd had a number of meaningless but fun flings with a succession of empty-headed trollops who didn't have the good sense to slam the door in my greedy face. A bout in the sack with the petite Nikki was an attractive idea. But today I had other things on my mind.

'I beg your pardon,' I said, as I hadn't been paying attention to her.

'You did the reception area for TV-TV, didn't you?'

'Yes, and their boardroom.'

'It's brilliant.'

'Thank you. But to tell you the truth, I don't do so much of that side any more, too much like hard work. I restrict it to one, maybe two, major interiors a year now. Things are really opening up for me with my own shops . . .'

'You've got how many now?'

'Seven, but I'm on the verge of signing a deal with some Japs that'll really put me on the map. We're talking total global domination here.'

'You've got a reputation for being quite difficult to work with.'

'Have I?'

'Well, you're famously rude to clients.'

'I just speak my mind, dear. I don't suffer fools gladly. I find it saves a lot of time in the world of business. And I believe that serious people respect me for it.'

'Yeah, I've heard that clients get really upset if you're not rude to them. You're kind of one up if you've been insulted by . . .'

'I'm sure. But what's this got to do with "A Room of My Own"?'

'Sorry, nothing really,' she laughed. 'Now, what pieces do you want in the shot?'

'Must get this in,' said Dieter, slapping Big Charlie. 'It's wild. What is it?'

'It's not important. I'm going to get rid of it . . . It's too heavy to move . . .'

'It'll look great in the picture, man.' And he whistled to Bill and Ben, who began to heave it across the floor. All the time I expected Dieter to come out with something like – 'This weighs a ton. What have you got in here? A dead body?'

I was too jittery to stay sitting down any longer, so I checked with the make-up girl that she was satisfied and wandered around the room with Nikki, picking things out and explaining their significance.

I was anxious to cram as much stuff into the picture as possible, to distract from the incriminating items. So we moved chairs, plates, pictures, sculptures . . . every spare nick-nack, artefact and holiday souvenir in the place. But it still wasn't enough. I was all too painfully aware of the hideous remains of my struggle with Mister Kitchen.

'This is nice,' said Nikki, pointing to a sheet of steel mounted on one wall. 'Is it movable?'

'Sure.'

Cut into the steel was a poem.

'How did they do that?' Nikki asked, running a finger over the words.

'It's a laser,' I said. 'Friend of mine uses it for precision engineering. He did this for me as a Christmas present a couple of years ago.'

'What's the poem?'

'It's by Stephen Crane,' I said. Nikki looked blank. 'He wrote *The Red Badge of Courage*.'

She looked blanker still.

'It's from a piece called "The Black Riders".'

Nikki read it out.

> 'In the desert
> I saw a creature, naked, bestial,
> Who, squatting upon the ground,
> Held his heart in his hands,
> And ate of it.
> I said, "Is it good, friend?"
> "It is bitter – bitter," he answered;
> "But I like it
> Because it is bitter,
> And because it is my heart."'

She smiled. 'Cheery little piece . . . Dieter, can we get this in?'

'Sure.'

Dieter got Bill and Ben to shift it and placed me on the sofa.

There I sat, lord of all I surveyed. The king in his castle, the dog in his kennel, the imbecile in his own shit. And as the Viking danced around, taking more light readings, moving things, staring down into his viewfinder and adjusting focus, climbing on and off the set of steps he'd brought with him, fiddling his tripod up and down, all I could think of was Carrie's mystery puzzle. This would make a good picture for the armchair sleuths, wouldn't it? The murderer sitting surrounded by all the tools of his bloody crime. Yes, folks, all the clues are here, all you have to do is find them.

The sticking plasters on the murderer's knuckles. Are they perhaps evidence of a struggle with his victim? As is also the large piece of broken bottle, missed by the killer when he was clearing up and now glinting beneath a low table. And what about the sunglasses, neatly placed on a side table? Are they the victim's own, dropped in the fight? Aha, those red spots on the sofa, could they be blood? And is that more blood on the rug? What about that vicious-looking candlestick next to the sofa? Is that yet more blood smeared around the spike? Could it, in fact, be the murder weapon? And what about the dark shape inside the tall metal cylinder? Just visible behind the holes . . . Could that be the victim's body? Not quite well enough hidden.

My God! It is! It's the stiff, the corpse, Exhibit A. Mister Kitchen.

Yes, ladies and gentlemen, the killer was too arrogant, too cocky, he hoped to taunt the police with this picture, but Inspector Doom was too clever for him . . .

'Say cheese!' said Dieter, and I grinned like the idiot I was.

# FIVE

tribulation n. Great affliction, oppression or misery.
[L *tribulare* press, oppress, f, *tribulum* threshing-sledge]
  So what the fuck is a threshing-sledge?

The newspaper people were gone and I was trying to
kill the jitters. Shut down all systems and start over again.
This tribulation business had been weighing on my mind.
I really should have just forgotten all about it, but you
know how it is . . . When you've got one really important
thing to do, you find yourself obsessively doing ten
unimportant things. So now, although I knew what a
tribulation was, I had no idea what a threshing-sledge
might be, other than it was female and used by the
Romans. What for? Torture? Milling? Transport? I could
find no reference to it anywhere else in the dictionary,
or in my encyclopaedia.

In the end I told myself I'd better not waste any more
time fretting over threshing-sledges and I got out my
stash of coke to freshen me up a jot. Supplies were
getting dangerously low. I chopped up what was left
and organised it into two fat slugs. I hoovered them up
and opened another beer, sluicing the cold fizz down my
gullet. Then I put on some Lester Bowie, lit up a Marlboro
Light, and considered my options.

It was coming up to seven o'clock. I had a body and a
murder weapon to get rid of and I still had no money.
The banks would be shut tomorrow, and there would be
no chance of my getting any replacement cards before
Monday. I had to either borrow some cash, or sit it out
till then. Even if I borrowed some it would be late by

the time I got out of town. I'd be scrabbling about in the dark in a manner liable to draw attention to myself. And I was out of drugs, out of brain fuel. Don't get me wrong, I'm not an addict or anything, but at times like this I needed all the friends I could get, and powder and pills are sometimes the best friends a man can have; they don't answer back, they don't question you, and you're not beholden to them for any favours. This was a grade A stressful situation for me and grade A medicine was of prime importance.

My last blast would see me through the next couple of hours, but if I didn't get some back-up then the horrors would start to creep in. The one thing I could do now was ditch the Leveller, after that I needed to do two further things . . .

1) Acquire some drugs to help me get out of London.
2) Hit the clubs until I met up with someone I could ponce some money off.

Then all I had to do was sit out the night and come to the problem of Mister Kitchen fresh in the morning.

Good, that was a plan of sorts, wasn't it? It had numbers and everything. You couldn't accuse me of not taking the bull by the bollocks. The disposal of the candlestick was simple; as I've said, there was a furnace in my workshop in Battersea that would melt it down without any problem. Adrian, my dealer, lived not far from there, in Vauxhall, so I could pop round to his place afterwards.

You see? It made sense. There was a neat logic to it all. That was the sign of a good plan.

I dialled Adrian's number and listened to his ansaphone message . . . 'Hello. You have got through to Adrian Weeks. Unfortunately nobody is able to get to the phone right now, but if you leave your name and number I'll be right back to you.'

Now, this didn't necessarily mean that Adrian was out. He left his ansaphone permanently on, to screen calls. So, after the tone I spoke slowly and clearly, all the while

55

expecting him to pick up the phone. I hadn't got very far
with my message when his voice cut into the line . . .

'Hello?'

'Hello, Adrian. Would it be cool to drop round?'

'Yep. I'll be in till about nine. Or if you tell me what
you need, I can meet up with you later.'

'No, I'll come and get it now. Oh, and Adrian?'

'Yep?'

'I'm short of cash. Some cunt ripped my wallet off
earlier. Is it okay if I owe you . . . ?'

'Yep. Sure. No problem.'

'I'll be there in about an hour,' I said, and Adrian
hung up.

Now I know what you're thinking: if I could get a
shit-load of drugs on tick, why didn't I borrow some
money off Adrian? Well, you can get drugs on credit, if
you've got a good relationship with your supplier, but it
just would not be done to borrow money off him. There's
etiquette involved here. A strict code. You piss off your
dealer and that's that. Find yourself another source.

Feeling relaxed and back in control I finished the beer
and the fag in quiet contemplation, letting the mad bleeps
and squawks of Lester's trumpet smooth out the wrinkles
in my psyche.

I closed my eyes and let it plug into my system. The
piano and bass were punching out a rhythmic figure,
round and round, the saxophone and trumpet were
doodling about on top of it, mysterious and eastern-
sounding in some minor key, then suddenly Lester's
trumpet sounded a blast and out of the chaos of the
disjointed jazz ramblings they all fell into a tune together,
loud and raucous and joyful.

Let the good times roll!

Lester hitting notes to the right and left of the written
ones, slurring, stuttering, sputtering, a crazy mix of jazz,
New Orleans brass bands and rock and roll. I jumped up
and danced around, and when the voices came in I sang
along . . .

56

'Come on baby let the good times roll . . .'

Let 'em roll, indeed. Let 'em roll and roll.

I danced over to my airing cupboard and got out a sheet, then I shimmied back to the Leveller and wrapped it up, securing the bundle with gaffer tape. Then I picked out a couple of tapes for the journey and went down to the Saab.

The Leveller wouldn't fit in the boot so I put it in the back of the car, the point sticking out between the front seats. Then I climbed in, snapped the front on the tape player and set off.

Assuming that at the weekend traffic would be no problem, I decided to take the direct route south, not skulk about in the back streets like I would normally do. Sometimes you just wanted to say 'I live in London, I shall bloody well drive through it'. But I soon discovered that the streets were busy with Saturday night traffic: young people on their way to places, rutting in their shiny automobiles, old people on their way home, rotting in theirs.

But I kept mellow. I drove with my window down, elbow out, Rachmaninov pounding from my stereo.

Edgware Road was slow going, and when I reached Hyde Park things got slower still. I got completely snarled in traffic down Park Lane. Horns left, right and centre, cars dodging in and out of lanes, big coaches hissing and fuming. I tried not to let it get to me. The effects of the last lines of coke were still with me, and though my head was hot and my palms dry and itchy, I was determined to remain mellow. I tapped my fingers on the car door and hummed along to the melody of the piano.

A car-load of yobs drew up alongside me. Four of them, all raring to go, on some plebeian night out in their Golf turbo. The driver jammed on the horn, freaking out an elderly couple in the car in front and causing them to stall.

'I don't think that's helping,' I said to the boy in the

57

passenger seat, whose window was wound down. He turned towards me, slack-jawed and dull-eyed.

'What did you say, mate?'

'I only said, that's not helping.'

Before the boy could say anything else, the traffic freed itself up a bit and we began to move. A minute later, though, it was back to a standstill. I heard a shout and looked round to see the Golf barging into a space next to me.

'Oi, wanker,' said the boy in the passenger seat, and his friends laughed. I ignored him. 'Oi, you, you ponce, are you deaf?'

I turned to the leering idiot and smiled. Just to show him no hard feelings, just to let him know that he couldn't get to me.

'What you looking at, you fucking ponce?' he asked. Ah, the intellectual prowess of the proud British bulldog. The backbone of the nation, the burly warrior of working stock, the fighting man in his car, the troll-king of the lower orders. Unsullied by learning, unencumbered by vocabulary, here was a product of millions of years of evolution. A descendant of Newton, Milton, Bacon and Darwin. Yes, scum will rise. Here was the fittest to survive.

To hail me and then ask what I was looking at. What an inspired piece of moron logic! But I didn't bother to point it out to him, I was on too good a roll to let him spoil things.

'Any other time I'd have taken you up in a battle of wits,' I said. 'You're obviously a very interesting young chap. But today, I'm just not in the mood. So don't bother trying to irritate me, okay?'

'Fucking ponce,' he said again, and again his friends laughed, as if this was the funniest thing they had heard all day. Oh, the simple joys of being stupid.

'If you're trying to wind me up,' I said, opening my car door and getting out. 'You're not going to succeed.'

I opened his door and pulled him over sideways by

the hair. Then, holding his head in place, I slammed the door into his face.

'I will not get angry,' I said. 'Mellow, mellow, mellow.'

Then I got back into the Saab and pulled ahead into a gap which had opened up in the traffic. The Golf tried to follow but they got stuck and I didn't see anything more of them.

It amuses me sometimes to hurt the proletariat. They're always so startled that a man who talks with a plum can fight like a pig. So many of them make the mistake of assuming that accent is an indicator of violent potential. At my dreary minor public school I was taught boxing, rugby and bullying. A considerably better introduction to the world of pain (imperviousness to and infliction of) than the rather effete and namby-pamby sports taught in inner-city comprehensives – such as football, skiving and playing fruit machines. I'm not saying I derived any great pleasure from shutting the boy's head in his door; it was just something that had to be done, you understand.

Thankfully, the rest of the journey to Battersea was uneventful.

My workshop is in a forty-year-old riverside ex-ball-bearing factory which will never be turned into luxury flats. It's a square red-brick affair with metal-framed windows which stands on a small estate among a dead-end collection of industrial buildings between the Battersea and Albert bridges on the south side of the river. There wasn't much else around here: an old bus garage that had been turned into a go-kart track, a handful of small houses, a newsagent and the Empire Tandoori, a sad little Indian restaurant which never seemed to have any customers.

I parked at the front of the building, on the blistered tarmac forecourt, and got the Leveller out of the car. I lugged it over to the entrance doors, unlocked them and went in. Then I began the long climb up the stairs.

I had the entire top floor, and beneath me were various

59

artists' studios, a clothing sweatshop and some guys with a room full of computers who did something or other which I could never fathom.

The computer guys had been broken into once, so the place was well secured now. As well as bars on all the lower windows and a plethora of complicated locks on the big iron doors at the front, there was a newly fitted alarm system and a guard dog round the side. It was a Rottweiler, a devil dog, huge and mean and ugly. It barked incessantly day and night. Some old geezer fed it and took it for walks, but nobody else dared go near it. It lived in a bunker in a concrete hell-hole at the bottom of the old iron fire escape that went up one side of the building. By law we couldn't have the fire escape removed, so the computer guys had built the concrete pen and installed the devil dog. God knows what we'd do if there ever was a fire, it would mean climbing down the iron stairs and into the shit-filled trap at the bottom. I should imagine most people would rather be burnt alive than torn to pieces by the black monster in the pen.

As I trudged up the stone steps with the Leveller on my shoulder, I could hear the dog barking outside, but as I climbed higher the sound faded. There were only three floors in the building, but each one was about twice the height of a normal floor. It was hot and stuffy and still in here, and by the time I reached the top I was dripping sweat. I was surprised to find our door unlocked, there shouldn't have been anybody in. I employ six staff in the workshop, where I make my one-offs and prototype designs, but they were all supposed to be up at my other factory near Leeds which handles all the production line stuff. The guys in Leeds had got behind on an order and my London lot had gone up to help out.

So, who was it? Who was rattling around in my workshop on a Saturday night? I opened the door and went in. It was Terry.

Terry is a Scottish lesbian, reasonably attractive in

a sort of short-haired, rings-through-the-nose, strong-featured kind of way. She was the only woman I had working for me, and it suited me that she was a dyke. I knew from past experience that if I had any straight women around it was an unwanted distraction. I wasted half my time trying to fuck them. When I work I work bloody hard. Sometimes for days at a stretch without sleeping. So I don't need anything that's going to get in the way. I'm focused and industrious and quite frankly good at what I do. It's the intensity of concentration and effort that I have to maintain that means I need to unwind as many ways as possible when I'm not working. I need to wipe the tape, blow the circuits and shut down.

There. I'm sorry about that. I'm sorry if it sounded like some kind of justification, but I wanted to get it straight. I suppose, deep down, I'm just like anyone else.

I want to be liked.

Terry is about twenty-four, I think. At work she wears a boiler suit and big boots, and at home I'm sure she wears something even more butch.

'Oh, hi,' she said, when I came in. 'I didn't expect you in today.'

'What are you doing here?' I asked. 'I thought you were up in Leeds with the others.'

'No, I told you, remember? I was coming down tonight to sort some stuff out. Some stuff of ma own. Christ, your memory's like a sieve.'

In return for the paltry wages I paid her, Terry had free use of the space and equipment in her spare time. She'd studied sculpture at the Slade and had aspirations in that direction. She built oversized, violent, confrontational pieces and was starting to make a name for herself. It wouldn't be long before I lost her, which was a shame as she was good.

'What are you working on?' I asked, unable to see any obvious evidence of work.

'I'm just waiting on a delivery, actually. Something

I've been knocking up at home, but I'm running out of space. I did ask if I could store it here for a while?'

'Yeah, sure. How big is it?' I asked.

'It's about eight foot high, but I'll keep it out the way in the storeroom.'

'Yeah, fine.'

'It's all under control in Leeds. I'll go back up in the morning, but quite frankly I'm not really needed.'

'Whatever, as long as we meet the deadline.'

The workshop was a good space, roomy and light, painted white throughout. It had a concrete floor and a lot of metal structuring. The high ceiling was set with roof lights down the entire length and there were hundreds of little square, metal-framed windows along the whole of one wall. It was divided into three main areas: the storeroom, the tool room, where I had various machines – lathes, saws, drills and the like – and the furnace room. The furnace was a small industrial model I'd got from an iron foundry in Sheffield which was going out of business. It was useful for casting small items and for heating metals so they could be forged. Most of the forging was done by Old Mick. Mick was about seventy-odd and had been a blacksmith in his time, in the olden days when such crafts still existed. He was a marvel with iron and steel and I was trying to get him to train as many of my workforce as possible before he kicked the bucket.

Although we kept the furnace running all the time, it had to be turned up to get hot enough to melt iron. My plan was to adjust the temperature now, then come back and feed it the Leveller after I'd visited Adrian. So I stashed the candlestick on a pile of iron and metal rods, turned the various dials on the furnace and left it to it.

When I went back through to the tool room Terry was opening the loading hatch. It had been here when I bought the place and had proved invaluable as it had an electric-powered winch for hoisting up heavy items.

'Do you need a hand?' I asked.

62

'If you don't mind,' said Terry. 'If you can operate the winch, I'll go down and supervise that end.'

'Sure.'

I went over and looked out. Down below were a transit van and two monstrous bull dykes in combat gear. They were manhandling a big, ugly construction out of the van.

I pressed the down button and watched the big iron hook on its twisted steel rope drop down to the forecourt below. By the time it was there so was Terry, and she helped her two pals get the sculpture in position. She then fixed the hook to it and signalled up to me. I pressed the up button and slowly the sculpture was cranked aloft.

Once it was up I stopped the engine and left it dangling in mid-air. All I had to do now was push out the short metal platform for it to come down on to, but this was no easy task. The platform mechanism was half rusted and badly needed replacing. It squealed and groaned as I shoved it out, adding my own grunts and gasps to the ear-grating metallic concerto. I eventually got it into place, however, and was just lowering the sculpture on to it when Terry returned.

'Jesus, that bloody platform's worse than ever,' I said. 'Nearly broke my back.'

'I know,' said Terry, fetching a set of wheels. 'It's not been the same since the winch slipped that time and Barry dropped those marble slabs on to it. I think it got bent. It'll be a hell of a job straightening it out.'

'Can you get on to Coleridge and Porter first thing Monday morning? See if they can send somebody round.'

'Okay.'

We fixed the wheels under the sculpture and moved it into the middle of the room.

'What is it this time?' I asked.

'It's part of my Disney series,' said Terry proudly.

'So who is it?'

'Can't you tell?' She smiled at me.

I stood back and looked at the thing.

It was constructed largely of wood and rusted iron, and looked like some very stern gargoyle. It had two long protrusions from its head which could have been ears or horns, it was hard to tell. It had huge, unforgiving, staring glass eyes and teeth which looked like scythes. As far as I could tell it was an animal sitting up on its haunches.

'Is it Goofy?' I said.

'Close,' said Terry. 'It's Pluto.'

Now she mentioned it, I could see some resemblance, though it was a vicious, rabid Pluto, not the faithful mutt of the Disney cartoons.

'Very nice,' I said.

'Its not finished yet,' said Terry. 'I'm going to put an engine in it. It's going to clank and clatter and give off noxious fumes.'

'I see you've kept a dog in your time, then?'

'It's more of a comment on Disney than dogs.'

'I'm sure it is,' I said.

'You're not getting reactionary in your old age, are you?' she asked.

'I've always been reactionary, darling.'

Terry's two formidable lady friends arrived, suddenly shy and awkward in these unfamiliar surroundings.

'Anyone fancy a beer?' I asked, and they all said yes. I sent Terry off to the fridge in the little kitchen to get some bottles.

'Lovely evening,' I said, and one of the shaven-headed muff-divers mumbled something.

'I beg your pardon?' I said.

'It was supposed to rain today,' she said.

That was the end of the conversation, and as we fell silent I wondered if I should hit Terry for some cash. But I was fucked by etiquette again, wasn't I? It wasn't done to be borrowing cash off your employees. Especially not in front of her friends. But it didn't really matter, I'd be bound to meet up with someone later, somebody who would positively enjoy lending me money.

'D'you know where the opener is?' asked Terry, emerging from the kitchen with a handful of bottles. 'Somebody's swiped it from in here.'

'No idea,' I said. 'But I've got one on my knife.'

I had a Swiss army knife attached to my keyring. I took it out, pulled out the bottle opener blade and gave it to Terry. She prised the caps off two bottles, gave me one, then passed the opener and the remaining two bottles to one of her friends. They sorted out their beers and we drank in silence for a while, contemplating Terry's Pluto sculpture and watching the early evening sun as it filtered through the tiny windows, turning the floor into a swimming pool of skittering light.

After a while Terry's mates relaxed and they started to discuss what they were doing that night. I wasn't paying much attention, but it involved meeting in a bar on Old Compton Street and going on from there.

Well, I wasn't going to stand around here all evening listening to their fascinating arrangements, I had things to do. I finished my beer in about two gulps and set the bottle down on the floor.

'Right,' I said. 'No peace for the wicked.' Then I bade them farewell and set off for Vauxhall.

# SIX

It only took me a few minutes to drive to Adrian's. Apart from one or two black spots, the roads in south London always seem to be quieter. Adrian lived in a quiet, elegant square of tall Victorian houses within spitting distance of the Oval. I'd been to a couple of test matches with him down here. Lazy afternoons with a beer cooler and marijuana.

He lived alone. He didn't have a wife or girlfriend. In fact I'd never seen him with an obvious partner, male or female. If he had a sex life of any kind it was completely hidden and secret. He was one of those people you can never imagine undressed. He wasn't a physical person. He never hugged anyone, never kissed. He always wore a suit and tie and was very self-contained. He was friendly and polite to everyone, yet was always, somehow, alone, somehow separate. He was a person you talked to about cricket, or fishing, or furniture or politics, but never anything personal, never anything intimate. Never sex. It was like he'd shut himself off from that world, had said to himself one day that it wasn't for him. Of course, I may have been wrong. He may have had a depraved private side he kept hidden, a life of prostitutes, toilet antics and ritual humiliation. But I doubted it.

I parked easily and rang his doorbell. Adrian answered with a smile and took me inside. He was solidly middle-class and unashamed of it and looked like an architect or a doctor. He was balding, his remaining hair cropped very short, and he wore big round spectacles. His owlish

66

eyes had obviously seen a thing or two in their time, but they didn't show it.

As far as the authorities were concerned he was a financial adviser, and in fact he did have a lot of dealings with the City. He'd even invested some funds for me a couple of years back which had done very nicely. But that was a front for his real business, as a 'Drugs Baron'. I had no idea of the number of devious ways he had of processing his money, but he'd never had any trouble with the law. My payments to him for 'financial advice' were tax deductible; he gave his earnings the semblance of being above board and it all worked out very nicely, thank you. Okay, so somewhere down the line there were drug-crazed lunatics with Uzis and machetes, drive-by shootings, kidnappings and assassinations, but in Adrian's house it was all very civilised indeed. It was elegant and tasteful, formal in a manly sort of way, with a mixture of antique and modern furniture, including several items of my own which he'd acquired in various transactions.

All around his walls were framed pictures – prints, paintings, drawings – some large, some small, and they all depicted the same subject: hell.

On the way in I looked at a new arrival, a big, heavy-framed oil in the hallway. It was a dark nineteenth-century piece, highlighted with flashes of vivid orange fire. It showed naked sinners, mostly rather curvaceous young women, being herded into a flaming sea by burly, sweating demons.

'A warm welcome to your visitors,' I said.

'It's rather kitsch, isn't it?' said Adrian, opening the door into the sitting room. 'Only place I could put it. I'm running out of wall space.'

'Do you never think it might be nice to buy a picture of something else?' I asked.

'A man's got to have a hobby,' said Adrian, going over to an antique writing desk and opening one of the drawers.

'You need an excuse for collecting,' he went on, as I stood in the centre of the polished wooden floor wiping sweat from my face with a sleeve. 'A focus. To a certain extent what you collect is irrelevant. Though some of my pictures are worth a small fortune, that's just a useful by-product. It could be toy cars, cigarette cards, comics, matchboxes, guns, the Impressionists. Things are only valuable because people want them.'

He offered me a couple of neat lines of coke from a small mirror, and I eagerly snorted them up. He followed suit while I studied his art collection, hung on the expensive striped wallpaper.

'It's a male thing,' he said. 'Men love to collect. They're hunter-gatherers.'

'How did you start?' I said, arching my back and feeling the buzz down my spine.

'Some years back I was doing a deal with some Japanese and I ended up with a couple of rather valuable prints of Emma-Hoo judging the dead. It sort of grew from there.'

'Emma who?'

'The Japanese ruler of hell . . .'

'Does everyone have a hell?' I asked, studying a tiny and very violent Persian painting of marauding demons.

'All religions deal with the future,' said Adrian. 'That's their main selling point. They all feature an afterlife of some form or another. There's usually a kingdom of the dead, a guide of some kind to take you there, and a whole local government department of chaps to look after you when you arrive. The features are different, but usually you'll have to cross over a desert or a river or a sea to get there. Then there'll be an entrance, often guarded by a monster of some kind. And once inside, that's where they judge you.'

I sniffed and a gob of coke slid down my throat.

'How's the charlie?' said Adrian. 'Satisfactory?'

'It's a cheeky little number,' I said. 'But it's got a good

nose on it. I'll take five grams. And I don't suppose you've got any sulphate, have you?'

'I've got tons, why?'

'I have special needs this weekend.'

'You want to watch yourself on that shit, an old fellow like you.'

'I'm not as old as you, pal, and don't you forget it.'

'You sure you want sulphate? What about something a little hipper? I've got ice, meth, E . . .'

'No. I can't keep up with all these modern drugs. At heart I'm just an old-fashioned guy. I want what I used to have when I was a teenager, good old-fashioned sulphate. Actually, you know what would be really nice? Some blues . . . But that's not going to happen, is it?'

'We've moved on since those days.'

'But you have got sulphate?'

'Sure. I mostly sell it to guys who want to mix it with other gear . . . I tell you, don't buy shit on the street, you don't know what you're getting.'

'A gram'll do me. I'll pay next week . . .'

'Don't worry. I trust you.' Adrian left the room, and I continued to examine his pictures. It struck me that most of them were simply an excuse to show a lot of nubile, naked women being given a hard time.

Soon Adrian returned with a small, neatly wrapped package and a handful of unframed prints.

'Have a look at these,' he said, spreading them out on the table.

As I looked at the pictures I picked up the package and put it in my pocket.

'I've just got hold of them,' said Adrian. 'Pricey. But you can't have a collection of hell without some Dante. And these are the definitive illustrations; Gustave Doré, original plates from the 1861 French edition of *The Divine Comedy*.'

'Comedy?'

'Well, I guess the definition of comedy must have changed a bit since Dante's time.' Adrian passed a hand over the prints. 'Hell, purgatory, paradise, the whole enchilada mapped, in every bureaucratic detail. It's a complicated place, is hell. There's levels and tiers and circles and God knows what. Like, if you can imagine the zones on the underground map being the nine circles of hell, and all the stations being different sins. You see, every kind of sinner has a strictly allocated place, and a clearly defined punishment. It's a very literal hell. Look, here's one for you: Pride.'

He showed me an endless line of naked middle-aged men toiling up a slope carrying huge slabs of rock on their backs, watched by two gloomy robed figures, one in Roman gear, the other in kind of Italian Renaissance garb. The Italian looked pinched and snooty.

'Who are these two funsters?' I asked.

'That's Dante with Virgil, his guide through the inferno.'

I looked at another print; this time Dante and his pal were pestering a handsome, muscly figure who was standing in a sort of fiery pit.

'What's going on here, then?' I asked.

'The fellow in the tomb is a heretic.'

'He looks a lot more fun than Dante and co.'

'Dante does look a bit of a miserable git, doesn't he?' said Adrian. 'But it's a miserable idea, sin. Somebody waiting to analyse all the fun you had, then slap you down.'

Adrian poured a couple of large Scotches and we sat in comfortable armchairs.

'Is there always a judge?' I said.

'Always. That's the one thing all hells have in common. Your soul gets judged, then it's punishment or reward. Tartarus or the Elysian fields. Rebirth as a king or as a worm.' He picked up the TV remote control and pushed a button. 'I just want to catch the news,' he said as the screen was filled with naked black bodies, skeletal and infected, quietly waiting for the end on some desolate, dying piece of wasteland.

70

'Poor buggers,' said Adrian. 'I've been thinking of sending some money.'

'What's the point?' I said.

'They're human beings,' said Adrian.

'So what?' I said, and Adrian laughed.

'You really are a pitiless son of a bitch, aren't you?' he said.

'You want to know my philosophy, Adrian?' I said. 'My attitude towards the human race? My feelings about the numberless hordes of starving and bloodied peasants who make up the bulk of homo so-called sapiens? I go along with the pundit in *Airplane* . . . They bought their tickets, they knew what they were getting into. I say let 'em crash.'

Adrian laughed again. He probably thought I was joking. Then he suddenly became serious and gestured towards the screen with his glass.

'There's hell for you,' he said. 'Not all this.' Now his glass swept around the pictures on the walls. 'These are just cheap porno entertainments.'

'We all go to Africa when we die, do we?' I said.

'You know,' said Adrian, shaking his head. 'There are some things you shouldn't be too flippant about.'

'How will God punish the unjust among that lot?' I said, as a mother hugged her dead baby. 'What punishment could be worse than that?'

'So maybe they'll all go to heaven.'

'Even the sinners?'

Adrian shrugged. 'I'm not an expert on heaven.'

'You see this,' I said, pointing to the screen. 'You see this and you can't believe in anything. Except maybe Darwin. Compost, that's all we are. Compost for our children to grow in.'

'But you've got to do something,' said Adrian. 'They're human beings.'

'Of which there's not exactly a shortage,' I said. 'You look at them dropping like flies in Africa and think, that's it, curtains for the African. But the population in Africa is set to double in the next twenty-five years. The world

71

population is rising at a rate of ninety-four million a year. When is somebody going to offer us Death Aid? Cull the World. What was the American version? "We are the world." Fucking right, we are. There's not lot of room for anything else. War doesn't even scratch the surface. Two per cent of the world's inhabitants died during the Second World War, you know, but after just nine measly months of peace the world population was back to its pre-war level. The Khmer Rouge killed twelve per cent of the Cambodian population, but within four years of Vietnam invading and sorting the place out, the population had overtaken pre-Khmer Rouge levels. They're now about four million up.'

'Yeah, yeah, yeah,' said Adrian. 'But you can't look at these pictures and just think statistics . . .'

'Then turn it off,' I said.

'You're a bad man,' said Adrian. 'You'll go to hell when you die.'

'Do you believe in hell?' I asked.

Adrian looked at me and smiled. 'Do you believe in hell?'

'As everyone knows, Sartre said hell is other people. I think hell is yourself.'

'You think everything is yourself,' said Adrian. 'You've got the biggest ego of anyone I've ever met.'

'You never answered my question,' I said. 'Do you believe in hell?'

'Well, your modern Christian would do away with the idea of hell altogether,' said Adrian, refilling our glasses. 'They reckon it's incompatible with the idea of God being a God of love rather than the Old Testament rampaging bastard figure.'

'Farewell the Punisher,' I said. 'I'll tell you what the modern Christian requires of his hell. First and foremost it shouldn't be for punishment, but rehabilitation, to retrain the sinner into becoming a useful member of dead society. There's probably a gym, and TV, and the option to study Open University degrees in basketwork.

Then maybe they'll let the dead back up to earth to do community work.'

'Hell is the absence of God,' said Adrian. 'That's the modern concept . . .'

'But do you fucking believe in it?' I asked.

'I don't know,' said Adrian. 'I'm not like you, I'm not certain about anything. I go to church every now and then – weddings, funerals, Christmas. I like the singing . . . I mean, I believe in God, but what type of God, I don't know. And as for hell . . .'

The weather forecast came on. '. . . and today was another hot and sunny one, with temperatures reaching the high eighties in London and the south-east.' Look at that! No mention of the fact that they'd forecast the opposite. No mention that they'd been completely and utterly wrong, just the bland smile and the dull delivery. 'As you can see from the satellite picture, things are not so settled on the Continent, it's stormy and very wet. There's a band of rain sweeping off across the Channel and into northern France, and bad news for you gardeners, I'm afraid, it looks as if it's going to completely pass us by. Tonight will be warm and sticky, and on to tomorrow's chart, another scorcher, hot and dry, maybe a bit of cloud in northern parts and . . .'

On and on and on, it was like the news, the proliferation of newspapers and magazines, the constant white noise of chatter on the radio, the experts, the analysts, the forecasters, the writers of fat books about the end of history, about the future of capitalism, about time and the universe, none of it meant anything. It was all just there to reassure us, to give us the impression that we could know what was going on, that everything in the world had been neatly labelled and placed in a glass case for us to look at and not feel threatened by. Yes, we could all sleep easy in our beds, safe and secure in the knowledge that we had all the facts, that we *understood* . . . That is the news and weather, we are closing down now, good night.

'I'd better give my lawn a squirt before I go out tonight,' said Adrian. 'It's getting a bit parched.'

He turned off the telly and started his CD player with another remote. Noisy English rock music filled the room. Adrian always kept up with music, but I'd stopped bothering a few years back. I'd retreated into the world of CD re-releases and nice boxed sets with more music in them than any man could possibly need in a lifetime. There was something refreshing about the sounds spilling out from Adrian's system, though. The music was lively and full of youthful energy. I guess Adrian fed off it, used it to charge himself up before going out for the night. He wouldn't be back home till it was light, having serviced his various clients in bars and clubs around the capital.

He pulled himself up out of his armchair and, singing along quietly with the music, went over to a shelf and picked up a vase.

'Care for a little weed to smooth out the wrinkles?' he said.

'Don't mind if I do,' I said, suddenly aware of the effects of the coke; my dry mouth, my dancing teeth, a sore patch where I'd been chewing the inside of my cheek, my National Health eyes which didn't quite fit properly.

Adrian brought the vase over to the table and fished a joint out from inside it.

'It's skunk,' he said. 'Quite a kick to it.' He took a lighter from the vase and lit the joint. Its end flamed and billowed before settling down.

I looked at the vase, it was ancient and cracked, Greek-looking, black figures on a red background.

'Is this genuine?' I said.

'Mm,' said Adrian, holding a lungful of smoke. He let go of his breath with a sigh. 'Don't drop it, will you? Should be in a museum, really.'

He took it from me and turned it slowly in his hands, pointing out the various people on it.

74

'This is Hades, you know who he is, of course, and these are his attendants, the three brothers Thanatos, Hypnos and Morpheus. Death, Sleep and Dreams.'

He passed me the joint and I took a long pull. The smoke was light but it burned like steam. It hit me instantly. Sometimes dope can be a relaxant, sometimes it can make you mellow, sometimes it can make you laugh and sometimes it can give you the creeps. Feed you an instant dose of paranoia and fear.

This was a paranoia joint. Suddenly I was struck dumb. I couldn't speak. I picked up a book of matches from the tabletop and moved them an inch to the right, then I moved them back again. I clasped my hands together and ice formed around my spine, my brain fizzed. I couldn't speak, I couldn't move, the walls were closing in on me. I looked at Adrian sitting there, passive, smiling like a cunt, studying his vase. Death, Sleep and Dreams.

He put the vase down and took the joint off me. Then he cupped his hand around the end and filled his lungs. It seemed to take forever, then he carefully put the joint down on an ashtray, or had he done it a hundred times? It was such an impossibly time-consuming action. The music was horribly loud and grating. Adrian turned to me and suddenly I knew that he wanted to kill me. I had to get out of there. But how could I when I had lost the use of my body?

'What's the matter?' said Adrian. 'Heebie-jeebies?'

I nodded. I think I nodded. I had certainly intended to nod, but whether that was what had happened, I couldn't be sure.

He turned off the music. 'Let it go,' he said without looking at me, and I closed my eyes.

I was in free-fall, spiralling down, I was nauseous, my head spinning, I was inside that crazy orchestra at the end of 'A Day in the Life' by the Beatles, louder and louder, din, din, din, out of control, and then, BANG, I let go and hit the big chord at the end.

I eased the breath out from inside of me, and all the

75

poison went with it. I opened my eyes and saw Adrian taking the top off a bottle of beer. He handed it to me and I poured a freezing gulp down my dry throat.

'Adrian?' I said. 'If you wanted to get rid of a body, how would you do it?'

'A body?' sitting down and taking another toke. 'Best way's to burn it. Get a fire hot enough to burn it all – bones, teeth, the works. If there's no body you can't be done for murder. Why? You killed someone?'

'No.' I took the joint from him and inhaled.

'You planning on killing someone?'

'No. I was just wondering. I saw this thing on TV the other night, some guy trying to get rid of a body. I just wondered what I'd do in the circumstances.'

'Burn it. It's the only way. Unless you've got some powerful chemicals that'll dissolve it. As I say, you can't be tried for murder without a body.'

'Are you sure?'

'I'm pretty sure. Unless there's loads of people saw you do it, of course, or it's on film or something, but even then, with a good lawyer you might get away with it.'

Fire. Of course. Why hadn't I thought of that? I'd planned on melting down the Leveller, why not Mister Kitchen as well?

'This is good skunk,' I said.

'Long as you don't fight it,' said Adrian.

# SEVEN

I wanted to check the furnace before I went home to pick up Mister Kitchen. If it was hot enough I could bung in the Leveller and melt it down. It would be one thing out of the way.

The car pretty well drove itself back to the workshop. I cranked up the volume on the stereo and whacked in a John Lee Hooker tape, letting his ancient voice yell sweet nothings in my singing ears . . .

'I woke up early one morning, Mister Lucky was standing by my bed . . .'

I was floating on a sea of bliss, my brain chrome-plated, with a song in my heart and a plan in my head. Man, it was no wonder music and drugs had been used in religious festivals ever since the invention of God.

'Mister Lucky was standing by my bed. Yes he was . . . That's right. You know what he said? He said, "You were born for good luck. Bad luck can't do you no harm . . ."'

Morpheus, god of dreams, had spoken to me through Adrian Weeks. He had shown me the way, he had lit the runway lights on the shining path, he had given me the tools, he had instructed me how to boot Mister Kitchen straight to hell, and he had french-kissed me deep into my soul, breathed his hot sweet breath into my lungs, poured his itching, electric blood into my veins. I giggled. Happy days are here again, let the good times roll, and all that shit . . .

'Call me Mister Lucky, because bad luck can't do me no harm. Everything I touch, it turns to gold . . .'

The sky was nearly dark, a full moon fighting the

streetlights for dominion as I glided on to the forecourt outside the works and danced out of the car. There was a slight numbness in my legs and the blood must have drained from my head, because I stumbled giddily across the tarmac like a Tennants-addled dosser. I sniggered and slapped some life back into my legs, then went over to the big double doors, but before I could get my keys out I noticed that they were ajar. I pulled one open and went inside.

The light wasn't on in the stairwell, but an orange warning beacon started spinning in my head. Were we being burgled? No doubt under normal conditions my heart would have started to pound and my palms to sweat, etc., but tonight, apart from the lights in my head, nothing happened. I was detached, aware of danger but unfazed. I was calm, superhuman, untouchable. I was stupid.

I quietly climbed the stairs. As I neared the top I could hear music and a simple explanation came to me. Terry must still be working here. That was a hitch but not the end of the world. I still had to get back up to St John's Wood and back; by then she might have left.

I thought I might as well go in and ask her how long she'd be, to save any arsing about later, so I carried on up. The door to the studio was open but there was no light coming from inside. Well, I say no light; there was a weak flickering, just not the full neon glare I might have expected. The music was heavy and insistent, the same trance heartbeat, over and over, with the occasional subtle changes in the noise. Drug music.

I pushed the door open.

I wasn't quite prepared for the scene I was presented with.

The workshop was lit by big white candles, several stuck to convenient points on Terry's Pluto statue, one on each upper paw, one on his nose and one on his dick. Next to him was the Leveller, primed with a candle on each of its three spikes. Terry must have found it on the stack of rods and unwrapped it.

Talking of unwrapping, there were clothes strewn around the floor, and Terry herself was in the middle of the pool of light, on a white sheet with her two friends, stark naked and mid-sex. Now, of course the first entry on page one of the Big Boys' Book of Sexual Fantasy is 'girl on girl action'. But the girls in the fantasies are not real lesbians, they are red-blooded man-eaters, rabid heterosexuals who simply fancy a bit of experimentation, which, let's face it, usually concludes with the man joining them for the big finish. Real lesbians are a different matter entirely.

Furthermore – real sex is no great spectator sport. You need professionals to lift it out of the embarrassing and ridiculous. Sex is a pretty clumsy and sordid affair when viewed from the outside. The real fun is in the head.

You ever notice in porn films, there's some guy, he's humping two of the most achingly beautiful girls you're never likely to meet, they're involved in the most wicked and depraved sexual acts, but to make himself come he closes his eyes? Always at the last moment the eyes close . . . He has to think of some other act, some other woman, some other position to make himself come. He's in our fantasy, and he's off having his own fantasy, and the people in that have their eyes closed, like mirrors going to eternity, a dream within a dream. But what I'm trying to say here is that the bizarre spectacle in my workshop did not in any way arouse my prurient interest. It wasn't just that Terry's friends were large and unwieldy, it wasn't the whiteness of their bodies, the awkwardness of their postures, the spots and blemishes, the rings in unusual places. I mean, I'd fucked stranger-looking women than these in my time. No, it was a private thing. It wasn't for me. I know there are some types who get their kicks from watching unseen, but it has never appealed to me. I like there to be some sort of contract between voyeur

79

and voyee. I like a watched woman to know that she's being watched, but to pretend that she doesn't.

This lot had made the place their own. A sacred circle marked out with beer bottles. I was utterly excluded from it. It looked like some kind of nutcase religious rite. As the candlelight glinted in the cold eyes of Pluto, his acolytes – the temple girls, his shaven-headed virgins – forecast the weather using only their bodies, summoning up isobars with fingers and tongues. The overnight, the short term, the long term, European and world weather. Pluto's muff-divers could predict it all.

I pulled the door shut and crept back down the stairs.

I sat in the car for a while and it was like I hadn't seen what I had seen, that it hadn't happened. It was a blip, a vision, something I'd peered at on the television late at night in a semiconscious state.

The whole day had been a bit like that.

What had I done? I'd got up, had breakfast, killed a guy who'd come to buy my car, been robbed by some homeless twats, helped my ex-girlfriend give birth to an alien, had my picture taken for the *Observer* and bought some drugs.

I think I'd handled it okay. A lot of lesser men might have cracked, might have fractured under the pressure, but me, I'd handled it; everything that they could throw at me I'd fielded.

I'd behaved like a gentleman. Like an Englishman. I'd stayed calm and rational. It was types like me who had built the British Empire, who had gone out into a strange world, among strange people, and kept their underpants clean and their smiles fixed. They had invaded the heart of darkness and behaved at all times like they were at a village fête on the green outside the pub. We'd strolled our way around the world, hands in white flannel pockets, and we'd shown the cowering peons and goat-herders, the trouserless heathens and painted medicine men the benefit of good manners, sang-froid and a clean rifle. We'd strapped men over the muzzles of cannons and blasted their guts to kingdom come, we'd bought and sold and whipped and branded them, we'd turned the Chinaman on to opium, we'd sold smallpox to the Indians and always we'd shaken hands, held the door open for ladies and never spoken with our mouths full. And I think that's important. It was good to have a straight back and speak in a clear and confident manner. These days England is a shabby little place, a place of corduroy and pissy American beer.

Actually, let's face it, that's all bollocks, isn't it? All that stuff about the stiff-upper-lipped gentleman subduing the evil savage. The Empire wasn't built by white-flannelled croquet players, it was built by skinheads, and hooligans, bullet-headed squaddies, red-faced drunken jocks and big-boned farm labourers, cockney wide-boys and Geordie psychotics, the ignorant mass of the brute working classes. The morons we see bloated with alcohol destroying some foreign shopping centre were the very morons the Hottentots saw charging towards them across the battlefield. The boots that smash the faces of Asian kids in city parks were the very boots that trampled over Africa and India and anywhere else that had anything worth nicking.

I cursed Adrian. The weed had turned me philosophical. And thinking is not what the English mind is best equipped for. Poetry and philosophy do not sit well in the Anglo-Saxon armchair. We like bricks and beer and pies. Concrete. But the skunk had set my mind adrift, wandering from thought to thought, until here I was dreaming of empire on this dull and dreary industrial estate, surrounded by ugliness and pointlessness. England had shrunk to the size of a council dump. It had lost its flavour. Give me a rifle and a map covered in red any day.

It was time to do something.

The sky got about as dark as it was going to get and I started the engine and drove slowly back north. It was getting on for half nine now; with any luck, by midnight

I would have burned all the evidence and would be out on the town celebrating. Then I could systematically consume enough drink and drugs to pass out in my bed and wipe all the events of today from my memory. Start afresh tomorrow as if nothing had happened. Just as I had done last night and the night before and every night before that for as long as I could remember (or, rather, couldn't).

There was a parking space right outside my flat and I slid across the road and slipped the car into it like an ice skater, like a fucking ballerina. I got out of the Saab and looked at the space. There was only about an inch to spare at either end. It was impossible. You could not park a car in that space. But I had done it. I had defied all the laws of parking.

I went over to my front door and was fumbling for my keys when somebody opened the door from inside and I leapt back about three feet.

'Where the bloody hell have you been?' said a bowel-freezingly familiar voice.

It was my father.

'Jesus, Dad,' I said. 'You scared the shit out of me.'

'It's not clever to swear.'

'It's not clever to ambush people on their doorstep.'

'Have you any idea what time it is?' he said.

'About half nine. Why?'

'Why? Why? Your mother and I have been waiting here for you since eight o'clock.'

'Why?' I said.

'Because we are supposed to be going out for dinner.'

'Why, Dad, why? Help me out here.'

My mother appeared in the doorway now and gave me a big weak smile.

'Happy birthday, dear,' she said.

'What do you mean?' I whined. 'My birthday's not till next week.'

My father gave me one of his patent withering looks.

'You're kidding,' I said. But it seemed horribly plausible. I never knew what date it was. It was hard enough getting the hang of what day it was.

'I can assure you,' said my father. 'Today is your birthday. You might forget it, but I never could. It's a black date forever seared into my brain.'

So that was what the 'birthday dinner' message on my Psion meant. My birthday dinner – the family's annual penance.

'It's lucky your mother still has the key from when she stayed with you last Easter,' said my father. 'Or we should have been standing out here on the pavement like a couple of burglars.'

'Why the hell should a burglar be standing out on the pavement?' I said. 'Surely burglars skulk in the shadows.'

'That's not the point,' said my father. 'The point is we've been waiting an hour and a half for you.'

'Well, I'm here now,' I said. 'And I'm sorry, but I just forgot. Okay? I seriously thought it was next week. I've been very busy lately, I had no idea of the date. I'm a bit disorganised. I've been . . .'

'Oh, save the excuses, lad,' said my father, and we all went inside.

# EIGHT

My father was a tall man, with wiry black hair streaked with grey which he wore flattened down across his head and slightly curling over the ears. In the late sixties and early seventies he'd had it long. I've got photographs; him in a suit with his long hair, like fancy dress. With heavy black-rimmed glasses, a style which he still sported. In the photographs, the suits had wide lapels and the ties were fat and gaudy, but these days he favoured suits of a classic English design and cut, and sober club ties. Tonight he had on a dinner suit with ruffled shirt and bow tie. He'd once been in advertising, but he was now a writer. Under the butch name of Robertson Carter he'd turned out a string of phenomenally successful books on how-to-succeed-in-business. You know the sort of thing – *The Ten-Point Management Plan*, *Delegating For Fun and Profit*, *Be Assertive Make a Million* and *Shit on the Weak*. Actually, not so much a writer, more of a guru, an astrologer. A leading weather forecaster in the new religion of business.

Mother did nothing. To my knowledge she never had worked. She was involved with various pitiful charitable organisations, but that was a social thing, not a vocation. She was wearing a once elegant and expensive but now slightly worn evening dress. She hated to spend money. Something to do with being brought up during the war. She bought all her Christmas presents from second-hand shops.

The image of my mother in those old photographs disturbed me, because she was young and slim and

84

pretty and full of life. Quite sexy, in fact. Growing up I'd just thought of her as 'my mother', but looking at those pictures I could see she had been a person. A young girl, like the young girls who entertained me.

Talking of young girls, there was one in my flat. A teenage girl with long blonde hair, part of it woven into a pigtail down one side and topped off with a black floppy hat like an overgrown beret. She had tight black leggings, big black boots and a baggy black velvet top. She had a pale, pretty face and a silver ring through her nose. She was sitting on a sofa and reading a Japanese style magazine from one of my piles. She glanced up at me as I came in, nodded and went back to the magazine.

'This is your cousin Gaia,' said Mother. 'You remember? Uncle Graham's girl.'

'Gaia?' I asked.

'Jill,' said my father.

'I'm not called Jill any more,' said the girl, without looking up again. 'I'm called Gaia. I changed my name.'

'Well, that should save the whale, eh?' I said, and she glared at me.

She was rather cute in a pierced, gypsy sort of a way. Young and unwashed. I tried to remember whether it was illegal to sleep with a first cousin.

'She's staying with us for a few days,' said Mother. 'Getting to know London. She starts college in September – North London University,' she added, proudly.

'Where are we eating, then?' asked my father.

Now, you can imagine how I felt. I did not need this. I shut everything down and retreated into a dark corner of my mind to think. As I did so, I kept my body running. Maintaining all visible signs at a sustainable level. I wandered around sorting drinks and handing out nuts, that sort of thing.

Father wasn't to be diverted, however.

'I said, where are we eating?'

And then it came to me.

'A little Indian place,' I said.

85

'Not too spicy, I hope,' said my mother.

'No, Mum,' I said. 'It's one of those Indian places that doesn't use any spices at all.'

'Oh, good.'

'Of course it's spicy,' I laughed. 'But you don't have to order anything hot.'

Mother made a small, disappointed sound.

'Where is it?' said my father.

'Down near where I work. Nothing fancy, you know? But fantastic food. The best in London. Not many people know about it yet, but it's starting to get a real reputation. Get in now before they ruin it.'

This appeal to my father's snobbishness appeared to work, as he asked no more questions for the time being.

All I had to do now was manoeuvre Mister Kitchen out of Big Charlie and into the boot of the Saab. But my brain was fired up and no sooner did problems present themselves than they were solved.

'Let's go out on to the balcony,' I said. 'It's a lovely evening. We can look at the sunset.'

'The sun set an hour ago,' said Father.

'Then we can look at the bloody stars,' I said.

'It's not clever to swear,' said my father.

'Fuck off, Dad,' I replied.

'Very funny.'

'Come on,' I said and led my reluctant little herd up the stairs to my sleeping deck.

When I'd had the roof rebuilt I'd had the balcony added. It wasn't very large, just comfortable for four people to sit out on. I sometimes ate breakfast out here, or sat in the evening getting stoned and watching the jets. I pulled open the sliding glass doors and took my family out.

It really was a lovely night, warm and clear and scented with evening flowers. Stars twinkled, the fat moon glowed, you know the sort of thing. We overlooked some communal gardens and a few trees, but this high up one's attention was inevitably drawn upwards to the sky.

'I should have brought my coat,' said Mother. 'I shall get chilly.'

'It's the hottest night of the year,' I said, but I guess Mother was brought up never to go out without a coat.

'But they said on the weather forecast . . .'

'They changed their minds . . .'

'Oh.'

'I'll go and get some more drinks,' I said.

'We don't want any more drinks,' said Father, looking at his chunky wind-up watch. 'It's getting late. We should be getting on.'

'I think I've got some champagne in the fridge,' I said. 'We can have a toast, or something.'

'That would be nice,' said Mother, and Father sighed.

I went back inside and slid the door shut, first making sure that I slipped the lock.

They were stuck out there now and I could get on with things undisturbed.

Ignoring my father, who was tapping on the glass and shouting something, I went downstairs and tipped up Big Charlie. Then I reached in and took Mister Kitchen by the feet. With some difficulty I dragged him across the floor, out of the room and down the stairs to ground level, his head bouncing off each step.

I opened the front door and looked out. There was nobody around, and I was getting reckless now, anyway. I felt in a funny way protected, invisible, I hardly cared if anyone saw me any more. So I dragged him over to my car and popped the boot. It took an age to manhandle him up and over the rim, and the string which was securing the sheet in place caught on the latch, snapping and coming unravelled, but at last it was done. I slammed the lid shut and wiped the sweat from my face. My whole body was drenched and my throat was painfully dry. I swallowed what saliva I could summon up and leant against the car, shaking slightly, as if my frame had become too weak for a huge, bloated and pounding heart. There was only one thing for it; I took out my cigarettes, lit one up and enjoyed a long, slow smoke.

Calm. Peace. Hope. O, sweet Marlboro.

So, Mister Kitchen was in my boot, the furnace was fired up and ready to rock. Let's go.

I was just about to get into the car and drive off when I remembered my parents and nubile cousin trapped on the balcony.

I stamped out the cigarette and went up to rescue them.

'Where the hell have you been?' asked my father. 'And why did you lock us out here?'

'Did I? It must have locked itself when I shut it. I've been trying to find some bubbly. No luck, I'm afraid.'

'Well, maybe we can go out and eat now.'

'Yes, good idea,' I said.

'You've got a nice flat,' said Gaia on the way down.

'Thanks,' I said. 'It got photographed for the *Observer* today.'

'Yeah?'

'They're doing a piece on me. Where do you live?'

'Bromley, but I'm getting a squat in Camden for when I start college. Actually I've spent most of the summer with the Dongas tribe.'

'Are they that traveller bunch who try to stop new roads being built?'

'We do a lot more than that. We're trying to establish a whole new way of living, of looking at the world. We're pagans.'

'Well, hats off to you,' I said.

By now we were all downstairs and getting into the car. Mother, as usual, was last, fussing about, dithering. She offered to lock up and I let her. She still had a strong mothering instinct.

'Are you sure we shouldn't take a cab?' said my father. 'You've had a drink or two.'

'I'm okay to drive,' I said.

'Well, you'd better not have anything to drink with your meal.'

'I know my limits,' I said.

'Here,' said Mother. 'I almost forgot. We got you this.' She handed me a bottle of expensive wine. 'Happy birthday.'

'Thanks, Mum.' I kissed her.

'You'll not drink it tonight, if you're driving,' said Dad.

'You're not still on about that, are you?'

'If you get into trouble, don't expect me to help you out.'

'Perish the thought.'

Luckily the conversation couldn't progress any further, as a man who had been watching us from the other side of the road came over and interrupted us.

'Excuse me,' he said. I nodded but said nothing. Even though he was smartly dressed in a corduroy suit and looked harmless, I was on the defensive. Nobody came up and talked to you in London unless they were:

a) mad
b) a beggar
c) intending to rob you
d) a Christian
e) a policeman
f) all of these.

'Is this your car?' he said.

'Yes,' I replied, ushering Mother into the front passenger seat.

'I'm sorry to bother you,' said the man. 'My name's Peter Kitchen. My brother was supposed to see you this morning about buying your car.'

'Oh yes?' I said.

'It *is* for sale?'

'Yup. I've had a couple of people round to look at it today . . .'

'Did my brother . . . ? Andrew, his name is. Andrew Kitchen . . . ?'

'No,' I said. It seemed the safest bet. Stop the trail before it even got to my door.

'Well, I'm sorry to have bothered you.'

Peter Kitchen smiled and blinked. He seemed a pleasant enough guy, softly spoken, shy. His arrival had answered one of my questions about the body in the boot. The dead Kitchen was definitely chip-on-shoulder material. Middle with lower pretensions, rather than the other way round. That fitted.

Peter was still blithering on. He obviously had a need to talk, but I hadn't been listening; I'd spotted part of his brother's winding-sheet sticking out of the boot . . .

'It's just I . . . he seems to have gone missing. In so much as. We were supposed to be going to the theatre tonight and he's just vanished. His girlfriend doesn't know where he is. She's worried sick. I'm . . . The last anyone saw of him was this morning, when he set off here to buy this car.'

'Have you told the police?'

'Yes . . . But he doesn't officially become missing before twenty-four hours.' He gave a little laugh. 'They said, you know, tomorrow, if he still hasn't shown up, they'll look into it. They didn't really take me very seriously, as a matter of fact. This sort of thing must, I mean, he'll probably show up. I just thought I'd better at least ask.'

'Sure,' I said and opened the car door, but Kitchen *frère* hadn't finished.

'His girlfriend didn't know the address. Andy had it on him. She just remembered the name of the road and the type of car . . . listen, if . . .'

'Look,' I said, 'I'm sorry to appear rude, but it's my birthday and I'm going out with my parents for a meal.'

'Sorry. Yes, sorry.' He fumbled in his pocket and brought out a small tatty photograph. 'He definitely didn't come here this morning?' He showed me the picture. It didn't look much like the Andy Kitchen I'd topped, so I had no guilt about saying I hadn't seen him.

I got into the car and drove off round the corner,

90

leaving Peter standing there on the pavement looking at the photo of his brother. Searching for a ghost.

Once we were out of sight I stopped the car and jumped out, waving the bottle of wine and shouting, 'I'll just put this in the boot.'

I sorted out the dangling sheet and dumped the bottle on top of Andy Kitchen, then got back in and started the engine.

'You're not selling your lovely car, are you?' asked Mother.

''Fraid so,' I said, pulling away from the kerb.

'Can't you afford to run it any more?'

I laughed. 'I'm buying a new one.'

'A new Saab?' asked my father.

'No. A Typhoon. Direct from the States. Bright-red GMC Typhoon turbo. It was supposed to be here earlier in the week, but it's been held up, should get it Monday.'

'What do you want with an American car?' asked my father. 'A Saab's much more sensible, they're very safe cars.'

'Dad. There's nothing to discuss here, I've bought the Typhoon.'

'You should have sold this one first. It'll be very expensive running insurance on two vehicles.'

'I'm trying to sell it. But I'm getting the Typhoon direct from a dealer in America, so I can't take part exchange. The insurance company know what's going on.' Why did I bother? Why was I trying to explain?

'Do you have a good insurance company? It's stupid to try and cut corners.'

'Yes, they're good. They're not cheap.'

'I could have a word with my company, if you like.'

'Dad. It's sorted.'

Where did they train fathers to have the special ability to make you feel like a child again? I was thirty-five, for Christ's sake . . . Thirty-six! I didn't have to justify anything to him.

'I always thought this Saab was a very sensible car for you,' said my father relentlessly. 'Despite being a turbo. They're very safe cars.'

'I don't want a safe car,' I said. 'I want a Typhoon. I want a Typhoon because it's impractical, the steering wheel's on the wrong side, it's an invitation to car thieves and it does hopeless mileage. Okay?'

'Now you're just being silly.'

'That's half the point, Dad.'

'Yes. Very clever. And how much will this "Typhoon" cost you?'

'More than your BMW.'

'Are you sure you can afford it?'

'The money's not important.'

'Money's always important, lad.'

'What I mean is, I can afford it.'

Dad sort of harrumphed.

'You won't ever be able to forgive me for earning more money than you, will you?' I said, watching his sour reaction in the rearview mirror. 'For as long as I can remember you've nagged me about getting a "proper" job. You've told me I've got to grow up and stop messing about wasting my life. And then one day you wake up and my Mickey Mouse job makes me more money than yours. Sticks in your throat, doesn't it? Because you were wrong.'

'We'll resume this conversation in ten years' time,' he said. 'You have to stick at it, you have to prove it's not just a flash in the pan. Which reminds me. Have you arranged a private pension plan? I've seen so many people make a quick buck and think it's going to last forever.'

'Let's change the subject,' I said. 'It's my birthday. The rules state that you have to be nice to me.'

Dad snorted.

Mum started telling some story about a charity lunch involving a lot of people I assumed I was supposed to remember. But it acted as a convenient white noise, which enabled me to think some more.

Think, think, think.

My poor brain was getting worn out with thinking. Kitchen's brother had gone to the police. Tomorrow they would start looking for him. He'd set off to see me and was never seen again. Well, it would be easy enough to keep up my story, that he'd never turned up, as long as I didn't have his fucking corpse hanging around, stinking the place out. It had to be done tonight. I had to dump him tonight. Before dawn he had to go into the burner. He had to become soot.

My thought process was interrupted when a couple of people stepped out into the road ahead. I prepared to slow down and steer round them when I realised it was the two jerks who'd robbed me at the garage.

A gift from the Gods, Karma, sweet luck, happy days are here again. Revenge, served cold on a plate with mayonnaise. I could have kissed my steering wheel, only I didn't have time. Lumberjack Jock was in front, laughing, swaggering, expecting traffic to stop for him. Well, I had news for him. NEVER ASSUME ANYTHING. I put my foot down and he saw me too late, he tried to jump back but I swerved and knocked him flying, there was a terrific bump and Mother screamed.

'Have you gone mad?' yelled my father.

'He stepped out in front of me,' I said, accelerating away.

'You must stop. You knocked him down.'

'He'll be all right. Hardly touched him. Teach him to be more careful in future.'

'I demand that you stop this car. You might have killed him.'

I stamped on the brake and we stopped with a jerk. I turned round in my seat.

'It wasn't my fault,' I said. 'He stepped out and I couldn't avoid him.'

'You deliberately tried to hit him.'

'They were drunk, probably hooligans.'

I checked the mirror. Lumberjack's lanky pal, Rhubarb, was chasing down the street towards us, waving his arms.

'I lost control,' I said. 'Now let's go or we'll never get dinner.'

'You're a bloody maniac,' said my father.

'Now really, Dad,' I said. 'It's not clever to swear.'

I put the car into gear and we got off just in time.

'Hopefully he'll be all right,' I said, putting my toe down.

'I doubt he'll be very hopeful,' said Father.

'Eh?'

'That was a complete mis-use of the word "hopefully".'

'I thought the sentence was perfectly clear.'

'But "hopefully" means to do something in a hopeful manner. If you mean you hoped that he would be all right, then that's what you should have said.'

'That's what I did say.'

'No. You said, "Hopefully he'll be all right", implying that he would be all right, and, not only that, he would be all right whilst optimistically looking forward to something in the future.'

'You didn't really think that, though, did you? I'm sure you understood exactly what I was trying to say.'

'That's not the point,' said Dad. 'The point is, you completely mangled the English language. A language that I happen to think is very beautiful and precise. There are rules. You can't just use a language willy-nilly.'

'Well, I'm sorry, but I always thought that the basic point of language was to easily be understood.'

'That was a split infinitive. You mean "to be understood easily".'

'I mean exactly what I say.'

'But there are rules. The English language isn't just an arbitrary collection of words and phrases . . .'

I grinned. I'd accidentally managed to divert the old fool from what had just happened. Mother was in a state of silent shock. And Gaia? I sneaked a peek at her, but it was impossible to tell what she'd made of the whole thing. As for me, I had a nice warm glow inside. I'd got the fucker.

94

Dad was still whingeing on about grammar and semantics when we got to Vauxhall, but the sight of the estate and the dingy little Indian restaurant soon made him shut up.

'Is this it?' he said. 'Don't tell me your mother and I have dressed to the nines to come and eat here?'

'I didn't ask you to dress up,' I said.

'It's your birthday, we always go somewhere nice.'

'Trust me,' I said.

I parked and we all trooped into the restaurant. I'd never been inside before, and it was truly grim. A cheap Indian restaurant of the old school. Red flock wallpaper, formica tables, plastic flowers and virulent pictures on the walls.

There were no other customers.

A very short middle-aged waiter came over to us, smiling.

'Table for four,' I said, and he indicated a table, then fussed about sliding chairs in and out and generally making the act of sitting down twice as long and complicated as it needed to be.

'You like drinks?' he asked, once we were settled.

'Champagne,' I said, and he grinned and went away.

Now, personally, I'm very fond of Indian food, but it was plain that this place was not really up to scratch. I doubted if they'd had any other customers in all week. They'd be out of business by the end of the year. But that really wasn't my problem. My problem was how to get Kitchen into the furnace.

The waiter returned with a bottle of sparkling German wine and ceremoniously filled our glasses.

'Yes,' I said when he'd finally gone. 'The wine list's nothing to write home about, but the food's what people come here for.'

'Doesn't look like anyone does come here,' said my father.

'It was probably packed earlier,' I said.

'I doubt it.'

95

'A toast, then,' I said. 'To me.'

'Happy birthday,' said my mother. Dad mumbled something, and Gaia shrugged.

I took a gulp of the sweet, warm wine and tried to smile.

The waiter brought over some small photocopied menus, but I didn't look at mine. 'I'll just go and check the car,' I said. 'I'm not sure I locked it.'

'You did lock it,' said my mother.

'I'll just check,' I said. 'You can't be too careful round here. If the waiter comes back, order me an onion bhaji, chicken tikka massala and a channa massala, pilau rice and a plain naan. Oh, and a plain poppadom . . . two plain poppadoms.' I said all this on the move, covering my exit. 'Two poppadoms' was said halfway out the door.

I pulled it shut and hurried back to the car. I'd deliberately parked a little way from the restaurant so they wouldn't see me drive away. I jumped in, gunned it round the corner and skidded to a halt in front of my workshop.

The doors were locked shut, so that meant Terry had gone home.

Excellent.

I could lift Kitchen up with the mechanical hoist, feed him to the fire and be back in the Empire before the starters arrived.

Let me just pause for a moment to tell you a joke.

Q: How do you make God laugh?

A: Tell him your plans.

I put my hand in my pocket and it was then I realised I'd lost my keys.

96

# NINE

Well now, as I've said before, a lesser man might have
been stopped in his tracks by this fresh turn of events;
he might have thrown in the towel, retired and become
an alcoholic. But not I. Pausing only to curse whatever
bad luck had brought me to this pass, I re-engaged my
tired and aching brain and pondered the situation.

When had I last had my keys?

Mother had locked the flat. Father had let me into the
flat. Second time I'd been to the workshop the door had
been open. First time I'd used my keys definitely. I'd
given them to Terry so she could use the attached Swiss
army knife to open the beer.

Fuck it to hell. I'd left them there, hadn't I? With Terry
and the bull dykes. That's what came of waking up too
early. My brain hadn't been fully engaged.

I rattled the doors to the workshop, more to release my
frustration than to try to somehow magic them open.

I looked up at the building, but of course all the
windows were shut.

Nothing. Nothing. Nothing.

I went round the side.

The only possible means of entry, other than by the
front, was the fire escape. There was a door at the top
of an iron ladder which could only be opened from
the inside. You could climb the steps and smash one
of the windows, but to do that you'd have to get past
the devil dog.

At night he was let out to roam the little yard at the
bottom of the ladder.

Well. Maybe he wasn't there tonight. Maybe he was asleep. Maybe I could slip past him up the ladder, smash a window, put my hand through and open the door. Maybe . . .

Maybe not.

I backed the car over to the wall and clambered on to the bonnet and then the roof. From there I could see over the wall, and as I put my head up there was a fearsome growling. I found myself looking down into the eyes of the devil dog.

Black, dead eyes like a shark.

Well, fuck that for a game of soldiers.

I heard an engine and turned to see a beat-up old van pulling to a halt on the forecourt.

I jumped down off my roof and tried not to look suspicious.

Then the driver of the van cut the engine, the passenger door opened and someone got out. Oh, joy of joys, it was Rhubarb, the cream of the begging cream. Another man got out the driver's side, a little squat fellow with thick glasses.

This was not a good thing.

I watched as Rhubarb came towards me. What else could I do?

He looked at the front of the Saab, where there was a small dent, and raised his eyebrows. 'Had an accident, did you?'

'Someone stepped out in front of me,' I said. 'Couldn't stop.'

'Oh yes? Is that what happened, is it?'

'Well, no, actually,' I said. 'Now you come to mention it, that's not what happened.' I could no longer bother to lie to this fool. 'What actually happened was that some stupid cunt didn't have the good sense to get out of my way when he saw me coming.'

Rhubarb hit me in the stomach and I sank down the car to the ground, breathless and blind.

'You think you can just go about running people over,

98

do you?' he said and kicked me in the ribs, sending a pain burrowing across my chest. I looked up to see him extract my wallet from his pocket and begin to take the contents out one by one and flick them down at me.

'If you want to act like an arsehole,' he said, 'you shouldn't leave your card.'

One of my business cards, with the address of my workshop on it, spun down and bounced off my nose. Luckily, to my knowledge, my home address wasn't on anything in the wallet.

'Credit cards,' he said. 'Cancelled 'em, didn't you?' He kicked me again.

'So you're going to beat the shit out of me, are you?' I asked. 'That'll be a nice birthday treat for me.'

'You shouldn't have run over Mike, then, should you?'

'Surely you can appreciate it was a simple act of revenge for you robbing me.'

The squat toad came over now, propping up the lumberjack Jock, Mike, who obviously couldn't walk on one leg.

'That wasn't a robbery,' said the Jock, his voice sounding dry and hoarse. 'It was a political statement.'

'Bollocks,' I said.

'Redistribution of wealth.'

'Why can't you just admit that you're bandits and be happy?' I said, still too winded from the punch to move.

'Because we're not,' said Rhubarb, propping the lumberjack up at his other shoulder. 'Everything we do is politically motivated.'

The Jock winced. From the look of it, his leg was broken. The other one, however, was in good working order, as I discovered when Rhubarb and the toad brought him over to me, suspended between them, and he began to kick me.

'Your days are numbered, shit-head,' said Rhubarb. 'This is the future. The boot of the people kicking you into history.'

'This isn't the future, you idiot,' I scoffed. 'This is just today. Just another bad day.' I stopped talking then as the lumberjack's boot connected with my mouth and burst open my bottom lip.

'England's a new country now, brother,' said Rhubarb. 'New forces control it. This is the dawn of a new paganism.'

I'd quite frankly had enough of this. It wasn't the assault, it was the sixth-form lecture I couldn't stomach.

'You think the times they are a changin'?' I said, dribbling blood. 'You think the old order has toppled? You think Joe Public's got rid of Lord Snooty? You think that pop stars, boxers and comedians own this green and pleasant land, do you? Well, think again, you dumb, grade Z cretin.'

With this, I heaved myself upwards with all my force and barrelled into the trio, sending them sprawling across the tarmac.

Mike the lumberjack yelped as they dropped him, and I gave him a swift, vindictive kick in his bad leg.

'You've believed the hype,' I said, swinging a wild punch at Rhubarb as he got to his feet. I connected with the side of his head, which probably hurt me as much as it hurt him. 'You've swallowed their dope. You've bought the hook, rented the line and had the sinker shoved up your sorry arse. You think that just because you're allowed to run around dressed like a red Indian and sleep in shop doorways, then it's the birth of a new Utopia.'

Before I could say any more, the toad grabbed me, rugby-tackle style, and we crashed into the car. Rhubarb came over, and as he belted me, I jerked my head to one side, causing his blow to wind up very similar to the one I'd got him with.

'A free country for the common man!' I yelled, struggling to throw the toad off. 'God's kingdom right here on earth!'

We slipped and slammed to the ground, me face

downwards, which meant that the toad's hands were crushed beneath our weight. He let go and I rolled free. Rhubarb kicked me again but I managed to grab his foot and bite him hard in the calf. He went hopping and swearing away and I was up again.

'The people haven't won,' I yelled, charging head first into the toad's gut like a mad bull. 'The people haven't won shit.'

He grunted as he hit the wall and we separated once again.

I was now in the centre of three wounded men.

Mike was trying to pull himself up on one of my door handles, Rhubarb was nursing his leg and the toad was getting his breath back.

'Now listen,' I said. 'This is stupid. The aristocracy may own less of this country than they did a hundred years ago, but they still own more than you and I ever will.'

Rhubarb and the toad both came at me together now and we went down in a tangle.

'The top ten individual landowners of 1894 were all aristocracy,' I groaned. 'Earls and dukes and lords. The top ten now, they're all still toffs.' We were too bunched up to really fight. We just sort of rolled about flailing at each other, and in the confusion we must have rolled into Mike because he shrieked in pain and fell on top of us.

This diversion allowed me to wriggle free. Pausing only to kick the toad in the head, I scrambled clear.

'And these ten people own a sixteenth of Britain,' I shouted at them, pleased with my ability to remember statistics under pressure. 'A sixteenth! One out of every sixteen square miles of Britain is owned by these ten toffs. So don't tell me the people have won!'

Rhubarb flung himself at me and took me down. He managed to get on to my chest and sit there smacking my head back on to the ground.

'Why don't you shut up?' he said.

'Because it's about time you heard the truth,' I replied,

101

and flipped him over on to his back before he knew what was happening.

It was now my turn to slam his head on to the ground.

'Let's consider the hit parade,' I said. 'Who was at number one in 1894? I'll tell you, it was a fellow by the name of the Duke of Sutherland. Well, he's come down in the world a bit since then, I grant you. These days the Sutherlands are only at number six.'

The toad hit me from behind and I lurched forward, temporarily stunned. But I was up before they could inflict any more damage and the two of them chased me round and round the forecourt like little kids playing tag. I needed an edge, or this could go on all night.

'Whereas the number two hit of 1894,' I went on, 'the Duke of Buccleuch, is now at number one, with the big, big sound of money. My, how the status quo has changed. Buccleuch, Seafield, Athol, Sutherland, all in the top ten a hundred years ago. All still in it now. And if you think names like Farquharson, Westminster and the Duke of Northumberland sound like the names of plebs, then, pal, you are one misdirected moron.'

At last I hit on a plan. I managed to get to the lumberjock, flatten him, and grab his bad leg before the others could stop me.

Mike went white.

'Now back off,' I said, sitting there with Mike's leg in my lap. 'Or I'm going to break this leg some more.'

They stopped, and there we all were, panting and filthy.

'This won't take a minute,' I said, slowing my breathing. 'So just listen.'

They eyed me with utter hatred.

'Of course Buccleuch isn't the biggest landowner in Britain *per se*,' I explained. 'No, he's only the eighth. The biggest landowners are institutions. So who are these institutions? Is it the Animal Liberation Front? Class War? The Druids of Stonehenge? The Dongas tribe?

You know, I don't think it is. How does the Ministry of Defence, the Crown Estates, Oxbridge colleges and the Church of fucking England grab you? Wise up, Einsteins. You don't exist. As far as these people are concerned, you're just rabbit shit. Listen to that . . . Listen!'

We all stopped and listened.

'Hear that noise?' I shouted. 'That's the sound of you lot pissing in the wind. So you can beat me up, you can insult me, you can rob me, but never again try to tell me about social changes in Britain in the twentieth century, okay?'

'Let me go,' whimpered the lumberjack.

'You shouldn't have come here,' I said. 'You should have taken him to hospital.'

'This isn't over,' said Rhubarb. 'We know where you live.'

'You don't know where I live, you nitwit. You know where I work, which isn't the same thing at all.'

'It's a saying,' said Rhubarb.

'So is piss off,' I replied. 'So will you piss off and leave me alone?'

The toad sniffed and Rhubarb shrugged, but it was clear we'd all had enough.

I let Mike go and they helped him up. Then the three of them limped back to the van.

'I'll concede there have been some changes in society,' I shouted after them. 'But it really doesn't matter to me one way or the other that there aren't any saloon bars left in pubs.'

They drove off into the night and I probed my face and body for bruises and cuts. I felt soft and tender all over, but luckily the only blood seemed to be coming from my mouth. I studied myself in my reflection in the car window. My split lip looked like a burst sausage. I was ugly but not a casualty.

I adjusted the windscreen washers and gave myself a good squirt in the face. It stung like hell but washed off the worst of the blood and dirt. I brushed down my white

103

suit. It was beyond repair, but would see me through the rest of the evening. The worst thing was I'd lost a shoe in the fight. I searched all round the forecourt and surrounding area, but could find no trace of it. There was only one thing for it. I opened the boot and unwrapped enough of Mister Kitchen to get at his legs. He'd stopped bleeding and the sheet was stuck to him in places. He'd cooled slightly but wasn't yet stone cold. His feet had swollen somewhat so it was a bit of a struggle removing his boots, but by undoing all the laces I eventually got them off. I sat in the car and got into them. They were big and clunky, steel-toe-capped Caterpillars, and it took me forever to do up the laces through all the holes and eyelets. They were slightly too large for me and didn't go with the suit, but were otherwise fine. I lobbed my spare shoe in the boot and locked it.

I badly needed something to deaden the pain so I chopped up a couple of lines of coke on my bonnet and snorted them through my battered nose.

Feeling almost refreshed, I headed back to the Empire Tandoori and my waiting family.

When I got there the three of them looked at me like I was something out of the Day of the Dead.

'What happened?' quavered Mother. 'Are you all right?'

'I'm fine . . . I caught someone trying to break into my car. Lucky I went out to check, huh?'

'Yes, you look very lucky,' said Dad with irritating sarcasm.

'Mm, well, he didn't take too kindly to me trying to stop him.'

'Are you hurt?' said Mother. 'You should get to hospital.'

'I'm fine, I'm fine. Looks worse than it is. It was just a scuffle, really. So, how's the food?'

There were a variety of dishes on the table. Overcooked mush floating in grease, mostly. It had hardly been touched.

'It's very nice,' said Mother gamely.

'You like it, don't you, Gaia?' I said. Although it looked as if she hadn't exactly got stuck in.

'I can't really eat this,' she said. 'I'm vegetarian.'

'Some of these are vegetarian dishes, aren't they?' I said, sitting down and piling my plate.

'Yes, but I don't know what they've been cooked in. I don't really eat out, usually, I like to prepare all my own food. It's the only way I can ever be really sure what's in it. That way I can avoid toxins and additives and animal substances.'

'Suit yourself,' I said. 'But you're missing a treat.'

'Is this whole evening some sort of elaborate joke at the expense of your mother and me?' said Father. 'Because, if so, it's been very successful.'

'Not to your taste, then?'

'This is possibly the worst food I've ever tasted. God knows how long they've had it sitting out the back waiting for a customer.'

'I think it's rather good,' I said, forcing down a heaped spoon of glop. 'It's authentic.'

'Hah! Then I suppose we shall all get dysentery, shall we?'

'Now, now,' said Mother. 'Let's not argue. It's his birthday.'

'I'll drink to that,' I said and gulped down some of the warm German fizz. 'Here's to us all,' I said. 'A happy family. Now, hopefully, we can enjoy the rest of our meal in peace.'

'How can we enjoy something hopefully?' said Father.

'Oh, well spotted. I see we're all going to fully enjoy tonight, aren't we?'

'To enjoy fully.'

'Ah, right. Split infinitive. Listen, Father, for your information, there's no earthly reason why an infinitive shouldn't be split. It's a quite pointless rule made up by a bunch of bored Victorian academics one wet afternoon when they had nothing better to do.'

'I agree,' said Gaia. 'All those rules, all that grammar stuff, it was all invented by the ruling élite to keep the ordinary people down. It's like the Queen's English is a little club that only the powerful can join. Like a secret code.'

'Well, your lot,' said Dad, 'the socialists, have mangled the language worse than anyone, total jargon, total gobbledygook, what with chairpersons, and refuse collection operatives, and all that claptrap about agendas and workshops and differently abled people that they put in their propaganda. If you want to talk about codes, that is a code, my girl, council speak, the code of religion. Those leftie-liberal pronouncements are sacred writings, they are caballa.'

'And what about your books, Dad?' I said. 'They're just the same. There's as much jargon in them as anywhere else. Learn the secret language and success will be yours, name things to have power over them.'

'I suppose you might have a point,' said Dad. 'But it doesn't mean that we should be allowed to use English sloppily. It's part of the general decline in standards that is destroying our society. Like the beggars you see on the streets everywhere . . .'

'They're there directly as a result of government policy,' I said.

'Ah, here we go,' said Dad. 'Let's hear it from my son, the communist.'

'Their benefits are cut,' said Gaia. 'They can't afford housing, there are no jobs.'

'Then they should stay at home.'

'A lot of them are abused at home,' I said. 'They can't stay.'

'But they're abused on the streets,' Dad snorted. 'Most of them are prostitutes.'

'So what do you suggest?' I said.

'Well, I'm sorry, but in my book you're better off being abused by your parents than by total strangers.'

I laughed. 'So you think, Dad, that all our problems

would be solved if we could all just speak English properly.'

'I agree,' said Mother. 'I can't understand a word anyone says on television any more . . . It's all that background music they put over everything. It ruins it. Why does it have to be so loud?'

'That's a very useful contribution to the conversation, Mother,' I said.

'Don't be rude to your mother.'

'Oh. Would you prefer that I totally ignore her, like you do? Is that more polite?'

'Please don't fight,' said Mother. 'It's the same every time you two get together. You just argue all the time.'

'We are not arguing, we are having a civilised discussion,' said Father.

'Well, can't you discuss something nice?'

'Like what?' I said.

'Well, while you were out, Gaia was telling us about the environment.'

'I'll bet she was,' I said.

'It's not something to joke about,' said Gaia. 'Pollution is the most important problem facing mankind.'

'Oh, I thought we'd covered that,' said Dad. 'I really am fed up with listening to the whines of the so-called environmental lobby. I mean, did you know that the whole Lloyd's fiasco was triggered by outrageous environmental claims in America? Claims that won't be settled until well into the next century.'

'They deserved all they got,' said Gaia. 'They were just greedy idiots . . .'

'Oh, you can laugh at them, but it hits everyone. Why is it so difficult to make a claim on your house insurance when you get burgled? Why is car insurance so hard to get and so expensive when you do get it? I'll tell you why, because of the Green movement in America.'

'What's your point, Dad?' I said. 'That they shouldn't have made the claims, or that they they shouldn't have caused the pollution in the first place?'

'This is so-called pollution going back decades,' said Dad. 'Nobody thought to question it until these bloody Greens sprang up, banging on about mother earth and the legacy of our grandchildren.'

'We've only got one planet,' said Gaia.

'And what would you do?' asked Dad. 'Ban the motor car? Close down all the factories? Destroy all the fertilisers? Plunge us all back into the dark ages?'

'Yes,' said Gaia, her eyes alight with youthful evangelism. 'If it meant I could breathe clean air and eat clean food and not give birth to deformed children.'

'My God,' said Mother. 'You've not had a handicapped child, Jill?'

'Of course she hasn't,' said Father. 'Life expectancy is higher than it's ever been, people are healthier, the chance of having a handicapped child is lower than ever . . .'

'Have you got any Nurofen?' I asked Mum.

'I think so, dear.' She rummaged in her bag.

'Don't try and change the subject,' said my father.

'I've got a headache,' I said.

Dad humphed and took out his cigarettes. Gaia shot him a disapproving glance, but he chose to ignore her. 'Well, all I can say,' he said, lighting up, 'is thank God your birthday comes but once a year.'

'Listen,' I said. 'I'll admit this meal hasn't been a total success. I think, to tell you the truth, they've changed the chef. So I'll pay, okay? . . . Actually, bollocks, no, I haven't got any money on me.'

My father sighed and got some money out of his wallet.

'Here,' he said, dropping two fifty-pound notes contemptuously on to the table. 'That should be more than enough.'

'There,' said Mum. 'I knew I had some.' She passed me a packet of Nurofen. I took out a couple and downed them with a swig of wine.

'Now, how about another drink before we go?' I said, rubbing my hands together.

'No,' said Dad, getting up. 'Your mother and I are going home.'

'I'm going to stay out and celebrate a bit longer,' I said. 'It's only half past ten.'

'You can do as you please,' said Father. 'Come along, Jill, we'll get a cab.'

'Actually . . .' Gaia looked at me. 'Do you mind if I hang about with you for a bit?' She turned back round to Dad. 'I can get a taxi later.'

'Sure,' I said.

'You will not get a taxi later,' said my father. 'It's not safe.'

'I'll bring her home, then,' I said.

My father thought about this, but realised he was on to a loser.

'As you please,' he said. 'But don't come back too late. I promised Graham I'd look after you.'

'She's in safe hands,' I said, and my father gave me one of his looks.

'Good night,' he said. 'And happy birthday.'

I kissed Mother and saw them out the door. As Dad strode off down the street in search of taxis I asked Mum for my spare door key back and she fished it out of her bag for me. Then I kissed her again and sent her off after Dad.

When I came back in, the little waiter had reappeared.

'You want sweet? Ice cream?'

'Bring me two brandies and the bill,' I said, and sat down with Gaia.

'Thanks for that,' she said. 'I haven't had a night out since I got to London. I was going crazy . . . I mean, your parents are very nice, but you know . . .'

'You don't have to be polite for my sake,' I said.

'Well, your dad's a bit right-wing, isn't he?'

I laughed. 'Just a bit.'

'I think it's good the way you stand up to him.'

'Don't get me wrong,' I said. 'I'd argue with him whatever he said. That's what fathers are for.'

109

The waiter brought two brandies in ridiculously large glasses and two imitation After Eights. I gave him one of the notes that Dad had left and told him to keep the change.

'Here,' I said, passing one of the glasses to my cousin. 'You *do* drink?'

'Yes.' She smiled at me. 'When I can afford it.' She gulped down the brandy and grimaced.

I'd have grimaced too if I'd had the energy. It really wasn't the best brandy in the world.

I tried to imagine her body underneath her clothes, but couldn't concentrate.

'So what are we going to do?' she said.

'We're going into town,' I replied. 'To try and track down a lesbian.'

She frowned at me but said nothing.

# TEN

As we were getting up to leave I suddenly felt weary. Sore, dense, aching, torn, tired right down to my bones, like an old man. Shattered. Plus there was a giddiness in my head, a singing in my ears and I had a sudden loss of peripheral vision.

'Would you excuse me a moment?' I said to Gaia. 'I have to go and vomit.'

I stumbled to the back of the restaurant and through a door marked 'Toilets'. There were two tiny cubicles here, off a dark corridor. I went into the one with a cheesy metal plate on the door showing a man in a Quality Street chocolate soldier's outfit.

The toilet stank of cleaning fluid, a fierce, burning and sickly sweet chemical stench that tipped me over the edge into full-blown nausea.

I knelt at the bowl and vomited copiously into the blue water. A scalding mixture of hydrochloric acid and undigested Indian food, laced with beer and cheap German wine whooshed out, as if from a fireman's hose.

One mighty squirt and it was over. Once emptied, I washed myself properly at the sink. The cold water on my face brought me back to life with a spasm of ecstasy. I closed my eyes and sighed with pleasure. Then I dabbed at my suit with some moist paper towels, and within a few short minutes I felt respectable again. But puking had left me even more limp than before.

I lined up a small slug of sulphate on the top of the plastic cistern – just a little pick-me-up to get me out

111

of Battersea – and hoovered it up with Dad's fifty-pound note.

I'd have a headache in the morning, but desperate times called for desperate measures. I hadn't had any speed for a couple of years and the dirty taste of it was comfortingly nostalgic.

I sniffed and swallowed and sniffed, then rubbed some more cold water into my eyes and went back out to my little cousin.

She sat there in all her black and blondeness, soft and warm and studded with jewellery. I wanted to hoick her up and fuck her right there on the table, while the short Indian waiter stood patiently nearby, waiting to clear away the mess, with an all-enduring smile on his dark features.

'You all right?' she asked with a child's concerned frown.

'Never better,' I said.

'You looked green.'

'I think I might have some kind of a bug,' I said. 'Now, let's go find a taxi.'

We walked down to Battersea Bridge Road and waited. There was a huge car advert on a billboard, a gleaming German monster on an expanse of white, a clear invitation to defacement, and, sure enough, Gaia got a big marker pen out of her bag, climbed up on to a low wall and began to write in the white space. There was an expression of childish concentration on her face, and she looked like nothing so much as a naughty schoolgirl.

I read what she had written – 'Go out and commit a senseless act of beauty'.

'Very good,' I said. 'But doesn't that rather depend on your concept of beauty?'

'Beauty is beauty,' she said, jumping down from the wall.

'Is it?' I said. 'I find cities beautiful, I find motorways beautiful, I find cars beautiful, I find guns beautiful, they're quite exquisite pieces of machinery, have you ever held one in your hand? I find medical photographs of operations and diseases beautiful, I find Kylie Minogue beautiful . . .'

'Kylie Minogue? You're joking.'

'And pills, those plastic two-tone pills.'

'But natural things are so much better,' said Gaia. 'The countryside, isn't that beautiful?'

'Yes, but it's not natural. Our lovely English countryside is a product of thousands of years of human management.'

'But it was balanced, man has always lived in harmony with nature. That's what we're trying to get back to, the Dongas, the Rainbow tribe. We're trying to change people's perceptions. This society has nothing to offer millions of people in this country.'

'But equally there are millions of people in this country who think you're just a bunch of dirty, hippy troublemakers . . .'

'We have no enemies,' she said, with the sanctimoniousness of a teenager. 'Only confused friends. Yeah? We believe in Community, not Communism. There were these people in Cromwell's time called the Diggers . . .'

'Gerrard Winstanley,' I said. 'Set up an alternative community on St George's Hill in Surrey.'

'That's right . . .'

'Believed in the principle of no land ownership. Agrarian communism.'

'Yes. How do you know about him?'

'I believe a man should always know what he is talking about, Gaia . . .'

I couldn't elaborate any further, because a black cab stopped for us and we piled in, the driver happy to be going back into town.

We crossed the river and headed up through the back streets of Chelsea. London was busy with people, the weather creating a continental twenty-four-hour atmosphere. Everywhere there were cafés with tables on the pavement, bars spilling out into the night, and young

113

people, so many young people, drinking and eating, happy and laughing. And so little trouble. There was a soft, good-natured spell over the city. When I'd been growing up there'd been hooligans of every type. Mods and rockers, skinheads, teds versus punks, mods again, skinheads again . . . Everywhere the threat of violence, gangs of youths, drunk and ugly, looking for a fight. These days it seemed like one long, happy party.

'Nobody does anything any more,' I said, looking out of the window. 'Nobody makes anything. All anybody wants to be is a television presenter.'

'People do things,' said Gaia. 'Some people care. I spent all summer with people who are really trying . . .'

'Digging holes and making tree houses,' I said. 'That's just not what it's all about. A country has got to make things. Britain was once the greatest manufacturing nation in the world, we made things that the world wanted. Bridges, boats, furniture, machinery, clothing. We made it, the world bought it. This was once a nation of busy mills, crowded factories, working mines, foundries, teeming docks where you could walk from one harbour wall to the other across the decks of ships. That was what made Britain great. Now we have nothing. The factories and warehouses are luxury apartments, the mines are museums, we import everything. But nobody's interested. Nobody's interested in industry, in manufacture, it's not considered glamorous, we're becoming just one big nothing. That's what we need to be angry about, to be fighting for. Not a return to Christian values, not the wonder of wildlife, but to have a point, to create a product that somebody else needs. And it's vital we do something about it. I'm doing something about it. In my own tiny, insignificant way I'm at least trying. I make things. Useful things. Some, admittedly, more useful than others. I make chairs and tables, beds, doors. I make things that people need, and that people want. I'm in the middle of finalising a deal with the Japs. I'm reversing the national trend. Usually they sell things

114

to us. If an idiot like me can do it . . . This country – it's this huge elaborate structure, this fun palace, built on nothing. All we have left is the arms trade. It's our only surviving industry. We're being propped up by sales of missiles and tanks and mines and torture equipment to the warring nations of the world. Take that away and what have you got? We'll fade away, open the atlas and there'll be just sea where the British Isles once were, and people will scratch their heads and they'll say . . . "England . . . ? Yes, I vaguely remember . . . Didn't they used to make Beatrix Potter tea towels and marvellous wildlife documentaries? I often wonder what happened to the place." We'll never have an empire again,' I said, turning back to look at Gaia.

'So?'

'We've grown soft and self-indulgent.'

'It's better than charging around the world putting people into slavery and stealing all their natural resources,' said Gaia earnestly.

'Probably,' I said. 'But sooner or later some bunch of marauding foreigners are going to come over here and obliterate us.'

'Oh, *really*. That's so xenophobic. We should be working for world unity, everyone helping everyone else.'

I snorted. And it was my father's snort. I felt ashamed, but excited, unable to stop myself.

'It's not funny,' said Gaia.

'Oh, but it is,' I said. 'You talk like a hand-out, one of those leaflets you get given outside tube stations and throw into the nearest bin. Ban fox hunting, McDonald's is bringing about the end of the world, peace in Bosnia, open our hearts to our friend the Eskimo . . .'

'But those are all good things,' said Gaia. 'There's no need to patronise me, just because I'm younger than you. Did you never have any ideals?'

'Hundreds,' I said. 'But a bit of cash soon cures you of that.'

'You need to get back in touch with your spiritual side.'

'What?'

'You've lost touch with yourself, with the planet. We're all part of nature, all part of the same . . .'

'May the force be with you,' I said.

'Call it what you like.'

'I'm afraid I call it bollocks, Gaia.'

'Well, you're wrong,' she snapped. 'You're so pseudo-cynical, you pretend to have all these views when really you're just scared.'

'You know your problem?' I said. 'You can't believe that anyone who thinks differently to you really means it. You think the only kind of ideals you can have are leftie-lovely-liberal-let's-all-be-friends-money-is-evil ones. What you can't grasp is that somebody can hold equally passionate, equally fervent and equally genuine views of a completely opposing nature.'

The speed was starting to talk for me now. It was powerful stuff and I was pretty cranked, beginning to babble, my mouth dry and sore from the puke. Gaia, on the other hand, was getting sullen and petulant.

'Well, Hitler had strong views, didn't he?' she said.

'Yes,' I said. 'He was a good old mystic, vegetarian, tree-hugging kind of a guy, wasn't he? I'll bet he was into crystals and astrology. You see, ideals can get fucked. They're not necessarily a good thing, *per se*. Once you start believing in something you start to lose your belief in yourself. Then anything can happen. The best intentions can go screwy; pro-life, animal-loving, fluffy-cardigan types can end up sending nail bombs to the daughters of scientists who use rats to find a cure for cancer. Christians burn Jews, Jews burn Muslims, Muslims burn Christians . . .'

'But that's what I'm saying,' said Gaia. 'You shouldn't have these labels, these partitions, these false walls between people. We're all the same, we're all part of

116

one energy, we're all children of one mother, the earth mother. Gaia.'

'And we're all children of one father, too,' I said. 'Darwin. The weak will always get crushed, the stupid will always get fucked, the rich will always win.'

'What are you talking about?' said Gaia.

'Darwin. I'm talking about Darwin. I'm talking about a great big cosmic steamroller made by Darwin and co.'

'Survival of the fittest?' she said.

'Something like that.'

'But that's such an old-fashioned concept,' she said. 'Nobody believes in all that fascist stuff.'

'People don't really still use that word, do they? "Fascist"? It's like something off *The Young Ones*.'

'What's that?'

'An old TV programme.'

'Oh, yeah. I think I might have seen some of that. Was Rick Mayall in it?'

'That's the one.'

'Well, it doesn't matter what words I use. The main thing is, all that Darwin stuff doesn't work any more.'

'Doesn't work? What do you mean, it doesn't work? What the fuck are you talking about? Show me one incident in history when a bunch of ignorant savages haven't been utterly annihilated by a more advanced society? Tell me, have I missed something, or is Neanderthal man still knocking about the place? Running multinational corporations and inventing manned space flight?'

'You talk as if it's a good thing,' said Gaia, 'destroying the planet. We could learn so much from other societies, from the Indians in the rain forest, from the aborigines in Australia. Have you ever read *The Songlines* by Bruce Chatwin?'

'Have you ever read a history of the world?' I said. 'Have you ever read the *Financial Times*? It's all there. Darwin, fucking Darwin. Don't give me all of that shit about losing touch with Mother Earth, losing touch with our soul, with the spirit world, because now we've got

117

Nintendo and cinema-sound home speaker systems, and ABS. We've got the microchip, we've got Darwin. You can rub your crystals, earth-woman, but the bomb is dropping. Yes, the yanqui is coming and he's got a badge pinned to his hat and it says, "Darwin, survival of the fittest". What happened in Africa? What happened in India? What happened in America? We had stronger magic, stronger medicine, we had Darwin, and smallpox and fire water.

'Why didn't they see it coming? The shamen? Why didn't they see it written on the wind? Sung out of the earth? Why didn't any of them see it coming? It's no good being able to dance with wolves when you can't stop a bullet. Why didn't any of them see Darwin riding over the horizon on his iron horse, with his six-gun in his hand?

'Well, I hear Johnny Apache cry, we don't need all that, white man. We don't need your bad medicine, because we can talk to the dead. Hell, you can talk to the dead, can you, pal? Well, find out what they've got to say because pretty soon you're going to be joining them. I've got electricity, I've got stone-washed cotton for the worn look, cheap cotton, mass-produced by faceless slaves in sweat shops in Hackney, in Bradford, in North Korea and South Korea, in China, in India and the Philippines. Go tell the slaves about Gaia, tell them about the wonders of nature, tell them about tantric yoga and holistic medicine and acupuncture and aromatherapy. You've got Anita Roddick and I've got big Arnie with a pulse gun. BY CHRIST, WHAT ARE YOU GOING TO DO? Save the world with shampoo and face scrub? Don't give me your crap about spirit guides. Don't give me your shit about the songlines, about walkabout and the dreamtime. What good is a painting of a lizard on a cave wall when the white man turns up with his bulldozers, his cranes and his fucking tanks? All made by Darwin and co. Stamped with the company name. Let them dream, let them drink themselves into oblivion, because here comes Darwin

118

on a white horse, here comes the future, here comes television, and who the hell needs telepathy when you've got the fucking telephone?'

'But the old ways are stronger,' said Gaia, trying to control the hurt in her voice. 'The old magic is reappearing. Native Americans are getting their power back.'

'Yes, they're saved. But what saved them? What power gave the force back to the original niggers of North America? What saved the Cherokee, the Sioux, the Yellow Feet? What saved Sitting Bull and Geronimo and Crazy Horse? Was it the Dog Spirit, Hoochie-Coochie? Was it the ghosts of their ancestors? Was it the great Sky Buffalo, Bull-Shit? No, it was Bingo. Bingo, bingo and bingo. Licensed gambling on the reservations. Bingo for all! Christ, money'll cure the evils of society quicker than prayer, woman. Money will sort out your problems with crime, famine, pestilence and a sick spirit quicker than anything. The great god Moolah. Just pray that he shows up with his pockets bulging and a smile on his face. Yes! Give 'em bingo and their world is saved. The mystic prayer goes up, "Housey-housey!" And all's well in the world. And what company makes the bingo halls? Whose name is stamped on all those little dancing balls? It's Darwin and co. Yes, they eventually grasped the concept of progress and it was called bingo!'

'Is that what you believe in?' said Gaia, her voice high-pitched with suppressed emotion. 'What do you believe in? What?'

'I believe in beer,' I said. 'I believe in beer and Nurofen. I believe in concrete.'

We reached Old Compton Street and got out of the cab. The driver tried to protest about the fifty-pound note I offered him, but he very quickly realised that I was not a man to be argued with and he accepted it grumpily.

I pocketed the change, tipped him and he pulled away.

Soho was more packed than ever, a noisy, carousing rabble of young hipsters.

119

'You think white is right, then, do you?' said Gaia angrily, standing bullishly in the middle of the pavement. 'Racial purity . . . the Englishman's God-given right to rule the world?'

'Fuck, no,' I said. 'I mean, it's happened to us often enough; Darwin's paid us enough calls in our time, like when he came over with Caesar, and we didn't know better than to run around in the nude like a bunch of twats, living in mud huts and painting our arses blue. So let's welcome the new bunch, whoever they may be and whenever they may come. It's about time we had some fresh blood, it's about time we were shaken up again.

'Because what's saved us Englishmen down the years? I'll tell you. There's no such thing as an Englishman. That's what's saved us.

'Shit, we've had Darwin come over with the Romans, the Angles, the Saxons, the Vikings, the Normans . . . And, let's face it, there'd be nothing worth eating in this fucking country if it wasn't for the Indians, the Chinese, the Thais, the Jews and every other fucker who's turned up on our doorstep with their pots and pans. They've all taught us a thing or two, every better-armed, better-equipped, better-organised and generally more advanced invader, they've all taught us that nothing'll finish you off quicker than racial purity. You give me the choice between central heating and painting my arse blue, I'll plump for the orgies, the wine and the vomitorium every time. It's Darwin, it's progress, it's the future. Fuck getting back in touch with nature, fuck Celtic mysticism, fuck church on Sundays, I'm not interested in juju, magic, voodoo or morris dancing . . . All I want is to be allowed to bury my body and go in peace.'

I was ranting. I stopped. It wasn't really fair on poor old Gaia. She stood there, staring off down the street, hating me.

'Excuse me, can you spare any change, mate?' said a voice nearby which I ignored.

'I think I want to go home,' said Gaia quietly.

120

'I'm sorry,' I said.

'You're a bully,' she said.

'Yes. I probably am.'

'You're just like your father.'

'Right again,' I said. 'That's the tragedy of growing older. You realise that you gradually turn into your own father – the man who, when you were a teenager, you wanted to hang, draw and quarter. You get to his age and you realise he had a point. And now you're stuck with some snotty, ungrateful teenager, who . . .'

'Oh, thanks.'

'I don't mean you.'

'Don't you?'

'JUST FUCKING LIGHTEN UP, WILL YOU?' I shouted. 'You're young. Enjoy yourself.'

'I can't when other people are starving, begging, homeless, dying of AIDS . . .'

'Oh, for fuck's sake.'

'I'm going back to your parents,' she said and pushed off down the street towards Cambridge Circus.

# ELEVEN

I followed Gaia down Old Compton Street, calling her name, but she sped up and I had to run. I finally caught up with her on Charing Cross Road and put a hand on her shoulder. She shook it off.

'I'll take you back,' I said.

'I'd rather you didn't.'

'Well, at least take some money for a cab,' I said and offered her a twenty-pound note. She looked at it for a few seconds before snatching it.

'I'm sorry,' I said. 'Look. Let me take you back, I promised . . .'

'I don't want your help.'

'Listen. It's not that important. I was like you when I was younger. I did believe in something. I used to think, "Why can't everybody just be nice to each other?"'

'Yeah,' she said stroppily, 'and now you think, "Why can't everybody just be happy?"'

'Right,' I said. 'Because sooner or later you'll realise that all this . . . It's not your fault . . .'

Somebody held my elbow and said, 'Excuse me.' I turned and punched them as hard as I could in the face. When I turned back Gaia was gone. I looked up and down the road, but she was nowhere to be seen. She must have run, or jumped on a bus, or something. I looked round to see who I'd hit and saw a stunned student, Spanish or Italian, sat on the pavement clutching a map of London, surrounded by a startled group of his friends sporting little coloured backpacks and Benetton outfits. They were looking at me as if I was a dangerous madman, so I hurried back down the road and into Old Compton Street.

Fuck it, at least they'd have something to put on their postcards home.

All this running about hadn't done me any good. My stomach lurched and the nausea and tunnel vision returned with a vengeance. I forced myself on, each step an effort. The crowds surged around me, buzzing and grotesque like a dream crowd. Like a psychedelic carnival sequence in a bad film.

I stopped. I couldn't carry on. I couldn't walk another step. I seized up, becalmed on this busy pavement. I pictured myself frozen, as people brushed past me on either side, another city burn-out, another casualty. I'd slump to my knees, crawl into a doorway and stay there for ever; people would offer me ten pence, the odd scrap of food would be donated to me, vagrants would stop by and give me swigs of Special Brew. My shoes would be stolen. Drunken louts would piss on me. Pigeons would shit on me. Shopkeepers would abuse me. I'd stay there and eventually forget who I'd been and how I'd got there and what the point of it all was. Then, one cold winter, I'd be found dead and they'd take me away and that would be that.

I looked around for a solution. Then I saw it. Salvation! My kind of church. A sex shop, and in the window a sellotaped and fading sign which read, POPPERS SOLD HERE. Flashing next to it in purple neon, SEX SEX SEX. And in red, LIVE SHOW. What a package. What a combination. I staggered in, fighting my way past the snake's embrace of dangling plastic strips which hung in the doorway.

It was brightly lit inside, the shelves lined with huge, shiny plastic dildos and vibrators, blow-up dolls with hideous gaping mouths, shrink-wrapped magazines with stickers over the unshowable. And there – a line of small brown bottles. I picked one up and read the label – 'KIX

stabilised amyl nitrate, ventilate well, highly flammable'.
Oh, bliss. Kill or cure.

As I paid for the amyl I saw a small dark staircase
leading up to the LIVE SHOW area. That was just what
I needed.

Upstairs there was a man reading a newspaper in an
armchair, and a row of booths. I went into one and closed
the door. It was perfect, my own private confessional.

I took out my gear and chopped up a mixture of coke
and speed. I snorted it, then put a pound coin in the slot.
As the window slid open, I unscrewed the poppers and
stuck the bottle to my left nostril, then, holding the right
one shut, I inhaled.

The whole lot hit me at once, nearly knocking me off
the stool. My head swelled up, charged with poisoned
blood, my brain expanded, forcing my eyeballs out of the
front of my skull. My lips pulled back from my clenched
teeth, into a wide stupid grin. BANG BANG BANG. Like
an earthquake. Rocketing down the tunnel. Out of it. Out
of everything. I was there and not there at the same time,
a spectator of my sordid state. I grunted, the sick amyl
gas swilling inside me.

I looked at the girl and she looked in my general
direction, naked except for a suspender belt and red
high heels, skinny, with a big arse and black eyes. Blue
veins beneath her troglodyte white skin.

There was an electric fan in her little cubicle, a wooden
chair and a small bed covered with a fake-fur tiger-skin
cover. She sort of posed around it, half dancing, occasionally lightly rubbing her nipples then turning to waggle
her buttocks at me.

My eyes were fucked; it was like watching some
old flickering film. It all started to recede from me.
Then . . .

Three things happened at once.

The shutter slid shut, I sniffed and something snapped
in my left cheek. It could have been the drugs, corroding
my skull, it could have been my tiredness, a trapped

124

nerve in my cheek, a paralysed muscle, but whatever it was, the whole side of my face froze up. There was numbness, and behind that a distant pain, a pain which I could sense would grow, consume my head with agony. I rubbed my cheek, trying to massage some life back into it, but it was stuck. I needed something stronger.

I left the comfort of the sweaty little booth and went out, blinking, into the light. The man in the chair looked up.

'For twenty quid you can have a private show.'

'What happens?' I asked, talking out of the side of my mouth, slurred like a drunk, or a man coming back from the dentist.

The man in the chair shrugged. 'It's your money.'

'Twenty quid?' I croaked.

He nodded.

I groped in my pocket for my money and handed over two tenners, the last of my notes.

The man went to a door and opened it. 'Leah? You're on.'

He held the door open and ushered me into her cubicle. Leah had wrapped herself in a dressing gown and was stubbing out a fag as I entered. She closed the door and I sat in the chair.

She took off the dressing gown. 'Well?' she said.

'Hit me,' I said.

'I don't do kinky stuff,' she said with a Welsh accent.

'What do you mean, you don't do kinky stuff? You dance naked and pretend to masturbate for strangers, for Christ's sake.'

'That's dancing. I don't do kinky stuff.' She started to put the gown back on. 'If you want S&M go to a specialist. You'll find one in the phone box.'

'I don't want S&M. I want you to hit me in the face.'

'Well, it's M, even if it's not S.'

'I've got a trapped nerve in my cheek,' I said. 'It's doing me in. I think you might be able to jump-start it, shock it back into action, but I need someone to belt it.'

125

'Are you serious?'

'I'm desperate.'

'You're not doing it for fun?'

'What difference does it make? Just fucking hit me.'

'Where?'

'Here. Just here.' I pointed to my cheek and closed my eyes.

Then she hit me. Well, she tapped me. A delicate, ladylike little thing, hardly more than a caress.

'Not like that,' I said. 'Thump me. Give me a good crack, let me . . .'

I never got the rest of the sentence out; suddenly I was flying backwards into the flimsy wall. My head whiplashed back and I blacked out for a moment.

I woke up sliding down the wallpaper towards the floor. The sting in my cheek told me that her punch had fixed things.

'How was that?' she said.

Before I could answer, the door was wrenched open and the previously bored man came in brandishing what looked like a truncheon.

'What's going on?' he said.

'It's all right,' said Leah. 'He had a trapped nerve.'

'A trapped what?'

'Nerve,' I said, rubbing my aching jaw.

The man stared down at me with practised contempt. 'Get the fuck out of here,' he said. Then, to Leah, 'You okay?'

'I'm fine. Honestly.'

'Could you help me up?' I said. 'I'm feeling rather fragile.'

The man made no move to assist, so Leah pulled me to my feet.

'Thank you for your help,' I said.

'Fuck off,' said the man, and I got out of there.

# TWELVE

Old Compton Street has become the gay heart of the capital. Where there was once a colourful mixture of sex emporiums and funky little immigrant endeavours – restaurants, delis, and quirky old shops – there are now expensive clothes stores and shiny new European-style bars and cafés. And, oh, the beautiful people! Boys with beatnik facial hair, girls with no hair, caps and hats and all in black. Shoulder bags, bottled beer and cups of coffee . . . In the words of Julius Caesar when invited to dine with the barbarians, 'Scena mea non est.'

All I knew was that Terry and her mates had talked about coming here for a drink. It was a long shot, but it was all I had to go on. I started at the Charing Cross Road end and worked my way down, checking every joint on the street and in the streets off it. The entire range of bang-up-to-date bar design was represented, from ersatz art nouveau to modernist, post-modernist, industrial, ethnic and American trash. There was even one establishment entirely fitted out with a range of my own steel tables and chairs.

I pushed my way through heaving knots of bright-eyed drinkers, scanning the tables inside and out, scouring the none-too-diverse faces for Terry.

Halfway down I struck lucky, or half lucky, or half unlucky, or unlucky, depending on how you want to look at it.

In a white-tiled, brightly lit, ostentatious-Penguin-classic-reading type of a place, I saw Terry's two lesbian

127

stormtroopers from the workshop. I wormed through the closely spaced tables and said hello.

They greeted me politely enough and I asked them if Terry was with them.

'No,' said the one on the left. 'You've just missed her.'

'She's gone to a party,' said the one on the right.

'Do you know if I left my keys in the workshop?' I said wearily. 'They had the bottle opener on the keyring.'

'Oh, yes. You left them, didn't you?' said the other one. 'I think Terry took them with her.'

'I thought she was going to leave them there,' said the one on the right, taking a swig from a bottle of Belgian beer. 'Hang them on a hook, or something.'

'She said she was going to, but I don't know if she did,' said Leftie. 'I think she changed her mind.'

'But they were definitely there?' I said.

'Yeah. Yeah. She tried to ring you.'

'Where's the party?' I asked. 'Is it nearby?'

'Nah. It's up in Highgate.'

'We didn't fancy it,' said Righto. 'Sounded really poncy, some architect or something. I think maybe Terry was gonna try sniffing around after some work.'

'Whereabouts in Highgate?' I said. 'Do you know the address?'

'Nah,' said Leftie.

'Something Park,' said Righto. 'Fitz? Fitzrovia? Fitzroy . . . Something like that.'

'Yeah, something like that,' said Leftie.

Joy! What a marvellous night this was turning out to be. I was basically left with five options.

i) I could go home and forget about the whole thing. Get some sleep, get my strength back. Tackle it in the morning.

ii) I could try to get some money together for petrol and get out of town.

iii) I could go up to Highgate and try to find the party.

iv) I could go to Terry's flat and wait for her to come home.

v) I could go to the workshop and try to break in through the fire escape door.

There were drawbacks to all these options. Option one, the home option, was very enticing, but I knew that the police would be bound to pay me a visit sooner rather than later. I could always refuse to answer the door to them, but it was risky still having Mister Kitchen in my boot. I knew I wouldn't properly rest until I'd got rid of him, or at least hidden him somewhere.

The 'get out of town' option was tempting but again risky. I really didn't know how far I'd be able to drive without passing out, going crazy or being stopped. I could only risk a long drive after getting some sleep, which took me back to option one. Plus I was down to a handful of change again after the taxi, the money I'd given to Gaia and the shenanigans in the sex shop. What a twat I'd been; I'd had the cash, but I'd been diverted by Gaia's young body.

So, option three, then. The problem with this option, finding the party, was that I might not find it, and even if I did find it and found Terry still there, she might not have either my keys or her own keys to the workshop with her.

The 'go to Terry's flat' option was okay, but it was too static, too passive. I had to keep doing something or I'd fall apart, and besides, she might be out all night, or meet someone and stay out all weekend.

I've already been over the problems with option five, breaking in. Facing the devil dog had to be a last resort.

My only choice, then, was option three – finding the party. If that didn't work out I could always move on to option four and go round to Terry's flat.

Highgate it was. And for that I needed a car. I didn't want to drive around in a cab all night looking for a party. So, etiquette be blowed, I had to swallow my pride and beg.

129

'Listen,' I said to Leftie. 'The keys to my flat were on that keyring . . .'

'Bummer.'

'Exactly, bummer. So I need to find Terry, but I'm totally broke, all my money's at home. You couldn't lend us any cash, could you? I can give it back to Terry on Monday.'

'I can spare a bit,' said Righto, and I felt like kissing her but didn't think she'd appreciate it.

'Is five enough?' she said, getting out a note. 'Only we're going clubbing, and . . .'

'That's very kind of you,' I said. 'Five's great.'

I thanked them profusely and went back outside.

With the change in my pocket I had just over six quid, probably not enough for a black cab but it might be enough for a minicab. I certainly couldn't face public transport, the state I was in. Actually, to tell you the truth, I never use public transport. Occasionally, in an emergency, I have to take the tube, but I can't remember the last time I got on a bus.

There was a minicab place on Greek Street I remembered, and sure enough there was a clump of black guys, Africans mostly, hanging about on the pavement, negotiating fares with young clubbers moving on to pastures new and fresh-faced student types returning home after a night on the town.

I went over and tracked down the guy in charge, a busy little Nigerian with a loud voice.

'You want a cab?' he said.

'Yes,' I said. 'I've got six pounds and I want to get to Battersea.'

'Whereabouts in Battersea?'

'Just the other side of the bridge . . .'

He thought about this for a while then grinned. 'Okay, my friend. Six pounds.' Then he turned and shouted to a fat white bloke who was standing apart from the others drinking coffee from a polystyrene cup.

130

'Passenger for you, Graham.' He pronounced the 'H' in Graham, so that it came out 'Gray-Ham'.

The Blob took a last drink from his cup, wadded it and chucked it in a bin, then he came over, walking slowly and deliberately, a look of disdain on his face like he was better than all this.

He got into his car, a big old Ford Granada saloon, without saying anything and did his belt up.

The operator hustled me into the back then explained the conditions to Graham. Graham shrugged and started the engine. The syrupy sound of Melody Radio filled the car. I gave him the name of the street and we set off.

The car stank of air freshener but was clean and had the smooth ride of an automatic. I didn't pay much attention to our route at first, I was lost in thought, my speeding mind chasing round and round, trying to untangle tonight. It was only when we were halfway across Westminster Bridge that I took in where we were.

'Which way are you going?' I said.

'South Bank. Avoid the traffic, mate.'

'Oh. Okay.'

Graham seemed to take this as a cue to start a conversation

'What about Charlie and Di, eh?' he said, his voice high-pitched and strangulated. 'What do you make of it?'

'I can't say I've ever given it much thought,' I said, hoping to kill the discussion before it got started.

'He's a mug, isn't he? I mean, Di, she's a lovely lady, isn't she?'

'She's a cunt,' I said.

'What's that?'

'A cunt,' I said, hoping this would shut him up.

'So you're on Charlie's side, are you?'

'Charles is a prick.'

'You don't like either of 'em, then? Reckon we should get rid of the lot of them, do you? What about the tourists, eh? I'd be out of a job.'

131

'I told you, I don't care about them. I have no feelings towards them one way or the other.'

'You just said that Princess Di was a cunt.'

'Let me tell you something, Graham,' I said politely. 'There are only two types of people in this world, cunts and pricks. The cunts are the nasty ones and the pricks are the stupid ones. Cunts and pricks, that's all there is. You may think there's more, but, believe you me, that's it. Now if you want to know how to work out which somebody is, it's easy. You might think it's tough, you might think you know someone who isn't either, and you say to yourself, "Jesus, I don't know . . . are they a cunt or a prick? Maybe they're something else." YOU'RE NOT PAYING ATTENTION! There isn't anything else. But if you want to know what they are, just ask yourself one simple question. Are they a cunt? If the answer's no, then they're a prick. See? Simple. Lady Di – cunt. Prince Charles – prick.'

'What are you, then?' he said. 'If you're so fucking clever?'

'I can't work out whether I'm a tragic hero, a comic villain or just one of those born fools in farces who keep losing their trousers.'

'What you talking about?'

'I'm probably a prick, Graham, like you.'

I saw him look at me in the rearview mirror.

'Are you having a go?' he said.

'Perish the thought,' I said. 'I'm merely making conversation.'

'Because, if I thought you were having a go . . .'

'I'm not having a go. It was a joke, all right?'

I don't know whether he was distracted by our argument or just incompetent, but, at the – admittedly confusing – junction of major roads and one-way streets around Vauxhall Bridge, he ended up on Wandsworth Road instead of Nine Elms and Battersea Park Road.

'Which way are we going?' I said. 'I want Battersea not Clapham Common.'

132

Graham realised his mistake, swore and made a rash right-hand turn into a side street.

'You can't get through this way,' I said. 'You'll get stuck behind the railway. You have to go further down.'

'Yeah, yeah, all right,' he said. 'I know where I'm going.'

He made a couple more wrong turns and failed to get us either up on to Battersea Park Road or back on to the Wandsworth Road. We were now heading down a street of semis with drives and front gardens.

'Go right here,' I said.

'Here?'

'Yes.'

With that he pulled off the road and into someone's driveway.

'Here?' he said.

'Very funny,' I said.

'You said "right".'

'I meant where the road turned right, didn't I?'

'Oh, did you?'

'I was only trying to help.'

'Get out of my cab.'

'What?'

'GET OUT OF MY FUCKING CAB.'

'Oh, for fuck's sake.'

He jumped out of his door with surprising speed, wrenched mine open and pulled me out. He was trembling with rage and, all things considered, for once I didn't say anything or do anything, I just stood there and watched the fat fuck drive off.

I sat down on the kerb and rested my head in my hands. I would have wept but my eyes had dried up, so I just stared at Mister Kitchen's Caterpillar boots. I cursed the bastard, I cursed the dead bastard with all my heart for putting me through this. If he hadn't impaled himself on my candlestick none of this would have happened.

But there was no point in sitting here feeling sorry for myself. It was onwards ever onwards for me, into

133

the never-ending night. Towards what? Towards that conflagration. Towards that fiery pit.

I kick-started myself with a blast of amyl, and then marched down the road like a machine, some barmy out-of-control robot, my head pounding and all the bruises on my body singing.

It took me about a quarter of an hour to get back up on to Battersea Park Road and I tramped along it keeping an eye out for black cabs or a bus, or anything, but it was just one of those nights. Nothing showed. I might as well have been walking through a fucking ghost town.

Halfway there I stopped and leant against a lamppost to rest. I was desiccated, as if all the liquid had been drained out of me. The lamplight was faulty, flickering on and off, sending me dazed and confused. I felt like I was being tortured in one of those sixties spy thrillers.

I looked up to see a derelict hobbling towards me on crutches. He wore a long coat, a wide-brimmed hat and a dirty patch over one eye. He stopped when he got close and stared at me.

'What do you fucking want?' I yelled. 'Ten fucking pee? Leave me alone, for Christ's sake. Why is everybody picking on me?'

He shook his head and came closer. 'Are you all right?' he said, his voice soft.

'Here,' I said, slinging some coins at him. 'Go and drink yourself to death.'

'I'm not begging,' he said and I grabbed him by the lapels of his filthy jacket and shook him. 'Why not? Why the fuck not? What's the matter with you? Why aren't you begging?'

'I've got all I need.'

'You smug bastard,' I said and took a swing at him, but as I did so I stumbled on the edge of the kerb, turning my foot and losing my balance. My punch went wild and I swiped the air. As a searing pain shot up my leg, I fell awkwardly into the road.

134

I gripped my ankle and rolled about in the gutter, moaning and muttering. I tried to stand but it was agony. The tramp came to help me and got me back on to the pavement. I tottered a couple of paces, hopped, tripped and fell again.

Again the tramp helped me up, and that was the final straw; he was asking for it now. I wrestled his crutches off him and pushed him away from me.

He didn't protest, he didn't say anything, he just sat down and watched me with his one, deep-set, dark eye as I clicked away up the road.

Well, I guess this was about as fucking low as a man can get, stealing the crutches off a cripple, but his fucking sanctimoniousness had really got on my wick.

I ended up walking on those crutches all the way to the workshop. Towards the end, as I rounded the park, I was passed by a couple of cabs, but by then it wasn't worth it, they'd only give me a hard time for taking them round the corner.

By the time I got back to my car it was half past twelve and I was a shell of a man. My body ached all over from the various pummellings I'd received. My eyes hurt, my leg hurt, my teeth hurt, my guts hurt, my feet hurt, my lungs hurt, my blood hurt, running sore in my veins. I was ripped, sacked and sick as a dog.

I looked at the factory building – salvation, but salvation denied to me. Inside was the furnace, no use to me at all without the keys to get in. Tantalising, mocking . . .

I got in the car, turned on the engine, closed my eyes, and went to sleep.

I don't know what I dreamt, if I dreamt at all, but I woke when my head fell forward and hit the steering wheel, sounding the horn.

So this was what it felt like to be woken from the dead, this is what it felt like to be one of those crazy flesh-eating zombies in a zombie film. No wonder they were always so fucking pissed off.

I got out my A to Z and looked through it until I found

135

Fitzroy Park in Highgate. It wasn't that long a road; it shouldn't be too difficult to find a party there. But the effort of putting the car in gear and moving forwards seemed almighty, like climbing Everest, like cleaning the stables of Augeas, like eating three Shredded Wheat.

There are cases of people with brain damage, people who've had strokes and can no longer function, where they find that if they play music it gives them a thread to hang their lives on. With a soundtrack they can cope, the music does their thinking for them, they can dress and eat and go about their business; but if the music stops they stop, stranded, washed up.

I was in need of some music therapy right now. I opened the glove box and sorted through the tapes until I found what I needed – Wagner. That was the stuff to put some fire up a man's arse. I slotted in the last act of *Götterdämmerung* and turned the volume up. That was more like it.

Act like a god, man.

Forge your own destiny.

Strike down Mister Kitchen and burn his body on a funeral pyre, burn down the fucker, burn down Valhalla.

And so, with Siegfried's funeral march feeding me, I drove north.

# THIRTEEN

Hiayoho! Hiayoho! Face fixed straight ahead. Neck rigid, teeth gritted, eyes bulging, trying to ignore the pain in my foot, my left foot, the clutch foot. Eyes on the road. Hands on the wheel. Fierce concentration. Red light means stop, green light means go. I just wished it all didn't look and feel so much like a damn video game, because one slip and GAME OVER would be plastered across my cracked windscreen.

Ah! You are neighing! Lured by the fire, the light and its laughter? I too am yearning to join him there; glorious radiance has seized on my heart. I shall embrace him, united with him, in sacred yearning, with him ever one!

Hiayoho!

Oh, those Krauts, those gloomy death-wish romantics. *Liebestod*. The love death. Going out in a blaze of glory, like Butch and Sundance, Thelma and Louise, Tristan and Isolde . . .

Slicing through the city and the night in the mighty black Saab, turbo-charged, my chariot, my warhorse, Grane. Ah! You are neighing! I was Brünnhilde, taking Mister Siegfried to his destiny. I was Wotan, Hagen and Alberich, and all the dwarves and giants rolled into one. Except the Wagner kept slipping into various themes from *Star Wars*, and suddenly I'd be riding the Millennium Falcon, at any moment I expected the streetlights to smear and slide and do that sexy hyperspace thing where they stretch out and bleed away to infinity and POW! I'd be ejected into another dimension.

137

Body, don't fail me now. Let not my soul desert me in my hour of need. I could do it, I could do it, I could do it, I know I can, I know I can, I know I can. I was delicately balanced here, on the very knife edge, I was the proverbial man sliding down a razor blade using his balls for brakes and all because dear sweet Kitchen couldn't get it into his stupid head that it really doesn't matter how a man talks, that the working classes couldn't possibly despise the middle classes as much as the middle classes despise themselves. All right, I'll admit I do have my faults, but, hey, nobody's fucking perfect.

Jesus Christ. Some days you just can't get rid of a body.

The stupid thing about all this was that it had happened to me once before. In as far as I'd been stuck driving around with a body in my boot. I mean, I don't want you to think that I made a habit of it or anything, but it was something that I had a little bit of experience of.

It was about five years ago, maybe six. Anyway, it doesn't matter how long. In those days Carrie had still been working as an interior designer, and I'd still been going out with her. She'd got this major job in Lincolnshire. Remember Lincolnshire? That's where I'd been heading all those long hours ago. Why? I'll tell you why . . . But that's getting ahead of myself.

So Carrie was in Lincolnshire, doing up some country pile that had been bought by an advertising exec. She was staying in the house while she did the work, supervising her gang and getting her hands dirty with paint and paper.

I went up to stay with her for a couple of weeks in the middle of the summer. I think the idea was that I might build some stuff, but I never really got round to that.

The house itself was pretty impressive but the general area was bleak and flat and empty. I wouldn't recommend Lincolnshire for a sightseeing holiday, and I should know. During the days, while Carrie worked, I took to exploring; driving around the countryside, trying to get myself lost. I soon got to know the place pretty well, and bombed around like a local. I had a Range Rover then, used it to lug around materials and finished product. It was useful being so high on those country roads, I could see round bends and over hedges.

One day, in the middle of nowhere, I came across an extensive fenced-off area, with large yellow and black signs festooned with skulls and crossbones, hazards, poison, every evil symbol you could think of, warning people to keep out.

I skirted round trying to see what might be inside, but there was no way in. There were a couple of big steel gates, but they were chained and padlocked, razor-wired and spiked.

Well, of course, this only served to arouse my curiosity even further, and I decided I had to get in there and see what it was all about.

I came back the next day with some tools, wire snips and bolt-cutters and the like. I found a convenient, secluded spot and set to making a hole in the fence. Then I cut a flap, folded it back and scrambled through.

Inside there was nothing. Just grey, dry ground, dotted with a few scrawny brown weeds struggling for survival. It didn't look like anyone had been here for years.

I trudged around for half an hour or so before I came across a torched and bulldozed site that had presumably once boasted buildings; impossible, now, to tell what they might have been. Possibly a small factory or a storage area. Nearby there was a dump, a pile of old rusted containers which had obviously once held chemicals of some sort. A little further in, the vegetation died out completely, the ground became black streaked with yellow, and I knew I had reached the heart of this barren and blasted place.

There was an ungodly stink here. A sulphurous, electric smell that burned my nostrils. I covered my mouth and nose with my hand and forced myself on until I came to the very centre.

It was a lake, filled with a virulent orange chyle, Fairy Liquid green in places and streaked with oily rainbows. The surface was almost covered in a thick layer of foamy ochre scum and a sort of jelly-like stuff, sticky and viscous. Occasional bubbles came to the surface and slowly popped as if in a slow-motion film, and as they did so they released the foul gas.

It's hard to describe the atmosphere – the desolate place, the dead land, the evil lake, the unholy stink. I was appalled and fascinated at the same time. It was a glimpse of hell – of hell on earth.

Maybe they'd tried to clean it up, tried and failed, and they, whoever 'they' were, had in the end just abandoned it, sealed it off, in the forlorn hope that with time nature would take a hold again and disperse the poison.

Driving away I felt sick and dizzy, feverish. I was worried that the fumes might have seriously affected me in some way. I was hurrying to get back to Carrie and so I suppose I might have been going too fast; I was certainly driving erratically, like the worst sort of drunk, with double vision, hot flushes and giddy spells. I was used to the roads and the high vehicle gave me a false sense of security. I could see quite easily if any other cars were coming, but anything lower was hidden. So it was that, coming too fast round a bend, swerving drunkenly, I hit a dog.

It was a labrador. I saw it too late. A big, fat, old yellow bitch. It tried to jump out of my way but I knocked it with the side of the car.

I pulled over on to the verge and jumped out. The labrador wasn't cut or obviously injured in any way but it was lying in the road, unmoving. Now, I'm something of an animal lover and am particularly fond of dogs. I'd had one as a boy, a labrador, very much like this one, except it was a male. This was before we'd moved to London. I had many happy memories of wandering around the countryside with him and had been desolate when he'd got cancer and had had to be put down. I've always wanted another one, but it's not fair on dogs living in London.

So you can imagine how I felt, standing over this lifeless bundle.

I didn't know what to do. I tramped a little way down the road to see if there might be someone around who could help me.

And it was then that I saw him. The dog's owner. A boy of about twelve. He was walking along whistling and calling for his dog. He had on wellingtons, jeans and a battered old canvas jacket, and he had floppy blond hair.

I knew that I couldn't face him. I was a coward and a fool and the lowest kind of creeping scum, but I couldn't tell that boy what I had done to his dog. I turned and ran back to the car, opened the boot, picked up the dog and put her in. Then I reversed away from there as fast as I could.

I was shaking with panic now, and almost in tears, but nothing could make me go back. As soon as I was able, I turned the car around and sped off.

I knew what I had to do, I had to get to the nearest big town and find a vet, explain what had happened, leaving out the boy, of course, and let them sort it all out. There was a decent-sized place about twenty minutes back the way I'd come, but as I drove I thought, and as I thought I sweated, and as I sweated I became chilled. I was still nauseous and fuzzy-headed and perhaps I shouldn't have risked thinking at a time like this, but I couldn't stop myself. I'd never felt so guilty and degraded in my whole life. I really, really didn't ever want anyone to know what a bastard I'd been, but I had to do something, didn't I?

Ten minutes later I was passing the fence and I stopped.

I found the hole I'd cut, then carried the dog out

141

of the car and pushed her through on to the wasteland.

I remembered seeing an old wheelbarrow at the dump
and I hurried to get it. It was just about serviceable and
made the task of shifting the dog a damn sight easier.
However, by the time I reached the lake's edge I was
sick and faint, barely able to put one feeble foot in front
of the other.

Nobody would ever find the dog again. Nobody would
ever swim in this lake, nobody would ever drag or drain
it. Besides, I didn't know what corrosive muck was in
there, but I felt sure it would eat her away in a matter of
moments, and then I'd be okay, because nobody would
ever know what I'd done.

Gasping and wheezing, swallowing bile, I tipped the
barrow up and the dog tumbled down the bank towards
the mess. But she snagged on a lump of concrete halfway
down and stayed there on the bank. I went to look for
something to push her in with, cursing myself the whole
time for the spineless imbecile I was.

I found a long piece of rusted metal but as I tried to
lift it the life drained out of me and I blacked out.

I was in a state of delirium, neither awake nor asleep,
confused and frightened. I became convinced that the
boy was me, that it had been me strolling along that
country lane, and that it was my dog which had been
killed. Killed by some demon, some terrible, pitiless
fiend. It was so unfair, I was only a boy. I sat by the
side of the road and burning tears fell down my face,
all the unjustness of the world hit me, all the pain that
children are vulnerable to. I wanted to die, to sit there
by the road until I fell asleep and never woke again . . .

God knows how long I lay there, or would have
continued to lie there, if the dog hadn't revived me.
I came round to find her licking my face and barking
feebly in my ear.

Once I had worked out where I was and what was
going on I thanked her and stroked her soft ears. She

142

had probably saved my life. Just the sight of her happy face made me feel a lot better. I tried to stand but was too weak, so I sat there, hugging the warm dog and getting my strength back.

So I hadn't killed her. Everything was all right. I must have just knocked her out. This thought gave me the strength to stand, and then I started to walk. I called the dog and she tried to follow, but her back legs were useless, they hung behind her. It looked like her spine was broken. She tried to pull herself along the ground, and I saw a long trail where she'd dragged herself from the edge of the poisoned lake all the way to where I had lain. I went back to her and tried to lift her, but I was too weak, and she whimpered in pain. So I tried to get her into the wheelbarrow, but it was no use. I had no strength, and was growing weaker by the second. I held her around the neck and cried into her fur.

'I'll come back,' I said. 'When I'm stronger. I'll come back for you. Don't worry . . . I'll come back . . .' She barked, and carried on barking.

I headed for the car. Behind me I could hear her howls growing quieter. I never looked back, and by the time I got to the fence she was silent. Then I got in the Range Rover turned the AC on full and drove away as carefully as I could.

All the way home I was pursued by phantom demons, dark shapes in my mirrors, police, boys with floppy hair, shapeless monsters . . . I meant to go back, I did, but I was sick for three days after, feverish and pukey, I couldn't get out of bed. Carrie had wanted to get a doctor but I was scared and talked her out of it, told her it was a flu bug.

Eventually I did feel well enough to return. I found the dog where I had left her, stretched out as if asleep. I put her in the barrow and wheeled her to the lake, and this time she went in. I watched as she slowly sank beneath the surface, which closed around her, bubbling and hissing. In a few seconds the lake was still and smooth, like nothing had ever happened here.

I found a diseased and stunted bush, uprooted it and used it to smooth out the three sets of tracks. Mine, the dog's and the barrow's. I reversed all the way to the fence, brushing and wiping as I went. Once there I repaired the hole and pushed vegetation up against it. I still felt terrible about the whole episode, but I was sure that once I got away from this hell-hole I could convince myself that it was all just a rotten dream.

Indeed, until tonight, I hadn't ever really thought about it. But the thing is, you see, I feel worse about that boy and his dog than I do about Mister Kitchen, and if I'd had a full tank of petrol this morning, I'd have been there, I'd have disappeared the little oik and would be back home by now.

I could have had a civilised meal with my parents. I could have behaved, I could have been nice to Gaia, I could even now be bouncing her naked body up and down on my thighs, instead of driving my black Saab towards oblivion, my body punished, my brains on the verge of a MASSIVE SHORT CIRCUIT.

I took a squirt of whisky from my flask and the Wagner ended. I passed through Kentish Town in silence and floated on up into Highgate.

# FOURTEEN

Coming into the top of Fitzroy Park was like leaving London and entering some small, rich village in the heart of the country. It was a narrow, secluded road which wound down the side of Highgate Hill overlooking Hampstead Heath. There were big trees and grassy verges and a string of expensive houses. I couldn't imagine how much money one would need to live here; each building was huge and individually designed in a striking variety of styles: from thirties villa, to sixties modernist bunker, to eighties post-modernist Lego house. There were security gates, posh cars, high walls, it was like a small-scale, less vulgar, English version of Beverly Hills.

I opened my window and drove up and down, stopping now and then to peer at likely houses. Any one of them could have fitted the dykes' description of a posh architect's gaff, but none of them had any obvious signs of partying.

Meandering along, gawping at the buildings and not paying much attention to the road, I was suddenly startled by a leather-clad figure on a giant Japanese superbike. The mighty Honda roared round a corner and swerved past me at the last moment, but not before I'd twisted the wheel in panic and sent the Saab skidding off the road and crashing through a line of bushes into someone's garden.

I came to a halt half in a flowerbed, half on the lawn. A spotlight flicked on and the garden was instantly lit up, bright as day.

I got the crutches and stumbled out of the car to survey the damage. Apart from the plants nothing was harmed, there were no obvious new dents in the car.

'You arsehole!'

I looked round to see a big man coming out of some sliding doors carrying a rifle. I stood and waited for him, getting my first proper look at the house. It was a dazzling construction of glass and concrete; angular and starkly modern.

'You arsehole!' the man shouted again. 'You've parked in my hydrangeas.'

As he got nearer I saw that he had a bloated, red, drinker's face and a big fat nose on him. His grey hair was untidy and he wore jeans and a colourful short-sleeved shirt, which was straining to contain a massive beer gut. I guessed he was about sixty.

'What are you doing?' he said, his voice slurred. 'Why? What's happening?'

'I'm afraid I lost control,' I said.

'Ha, ha!' he laughed theatrically. 'Lost control?'

'Of my car,' I explained.

'I don't know who you are,' he said and grabbed me by my lapels with one hand, pulling me close to his great beery head. There was a mist of alcohol around him and his eyes were watery and unfocused.

'I don't know you . . . What are you doing here?' His voice was loud and cultured.

'No, you don't know me,' I said, patiently. 'I was looking for a party.'

'Oh.' He let me go and sat down hard on my bonnet. He looked up at the sky and took a long, deep breath through his nose. 'What a lovely evening,' he said.

'Yes,' I said, propping myself up on my crutches.

He took out a packet of Camels, removed a cigarette and offered me one. I took it and he lit them with a silver lighter.

'They bollocksed up the weather forecast again,' he said, exhaling a cloud of blue smoke.

146

'They always do.'

'Arseholes,' he said. 'Fuck 'em. Fuck 'em in the arse.' Then he grabbed me round the neck and, holding me tight in the crook of his elbow, crushed my head to his chest.

'You're one of us,' he said. 'Would you care for a drink?'

'Sure. Why not?'

'MARGARET!' he bellowed, his voice echoing in the still night air, and presently a very thin woman came out of the house, walking slowly and carefully as if every step might shatter her frail body.

'Margaret, bring us a bottle,' said my host. 'There's a man in our bushes who wants a drink.'

Margaret turned and disappeared back into the house.

'So, Johnny,' said the big man, 'you lost control?'

'Is that an air rifle?' I said, and he belched.

'I use it to keep the cats off the lawn.' He nodded. 'Fucking cats. There are so many cats round here, cats, cats, cats, can't stand the fuckers. Ha! Did you think it was John Wayne coming for ya? Did you, Johnny? Did you? Ha!' He pointed a nicotine-stained finger in my face and fixed me with his griddled, egg-white eyes.

'I know who you are,' he said. 'I know you.'

'Do you?'

'You are Raffles the cat burglar, Gentleman Jim the sneaky thief, you are a flower fairy creeping from my shrubbery, Mister Thunderbolt, the bolt from the blue. Why have you come for me tonight, Wee Willie Winkie? Who sent you?'

'Nobody sent me, it was just bad luck.'

'No such thing, old sport.' With that he flung me to the ground and stuck the barrel of the gun in my eye, pushing it in so that it hurt.

'You see, you're looking down the barrel of my gun,' he said. 'You're looking at the future and you're thinking, how much damage could that pellet do? Well, from this range, Johnny-boy, it would sure as shit put your eye out

147

– your evil eye – and possibly, just possibly, penetrate into your brain. And you're thinking, "What bad luck". Well, let me tell you, Raffles, there's luck and there's bad luck and they're both the same thing. You can't have bad luck, because if it was bad it wouldn't be luck. All you can have is luck. And if things are bad, well then, that's just tough shit. But you see, Johnny, you see, you can't do anything about it. That's the whole point . . . Are you familiar with patience? The game of patience?'

'The card game?' I said. 'Where you play by yourself?'

'That's the man. Now a good patience player will always do better than a poor player, an inexperienced player. A good player will know tactics, strategies, when he's faced with a choice he'll make the correct decision, but if the cards fall a certain way even the best patience player in the world won't be able to finish the game. That's luck. And in patience there's only one point, to get all your cards out. So if the cards fall a certain way, a good player won't be any better than a bad player. There's nothing you can do about that. Except cheat. But what's the point in that? You're only cheating yourself . . . Or the cards, and they're just dumb cards. So what I'm saying is . . . What I'm saying is, get some music on. You're looking for a party, we'll have a fucking party. Let's dance!'

He hoicked me up and, rubbing my eye, I hopped into the car and turned the ignition key. I thought about making a break, driving across the lawn and out, but there was a silver BMW blocking the driveway, so I thought better of it and instead put on the first tape that came to hand and turned the volume up. The cracked tones of John Lee Hooker spilled out across the lawn.

'Ah,' said the big drunk, grinning. 'Mister Hooker, the singing pensioner. Shit-kicking music for the middle classes.'

Margaret suddenly appeared next to us, carrying a

148

champagne bottle and some glasses on a tray. The big man jumped and shivered.

'Bloody hell, woman,' he said. 'You give me the spooks!'

She said nothing, just started to pour champagne into the glasses with the same slow, fragile dignity with which she did everything. She'd obviously once been very beautiful, but her beauty was ravaged by drink and fags.

'Let me do that,' said the big man impatiently and he grabbed the bottle from her trembling hands and took over.

'This is Johnny,' he said, passing me a glass.

'Johnny isn't my name,' I said.

'As if Margaret fucking cares,' he said. 'As if anyone cares. As if it really mattered . . . I'll tell you who you are. I'll tell you. You're Mister Lucky, because bad luck can't do you no harm. Here's to you, Johnny Luck.'

We drank.

'What a great party!' he yelled and flung his arms out, catching Margaret a great clonk on the side of the head with the champagne bottle. Soundlessly, she fell over flat on her back in the flowerbed and lay very still.

'God, I'm sorry, Margaret,' he said. 'It's the old backhand.' He grinned now and jabbed me in the belly with the bottle. 'I'll tell you what,' he said. 'Let's have a game of tennis.'

'Is she all right?'

'I should imagine so. Come on . . . Tennis.'

'Listen, I'm going to have to move my car at some time . . .'

'We're having a fucking party, you can't go now.'

'I have things to do . . .' I said, lamely.

'You're a dark horse, Johnny. Dark. You have a dark secret . . .'

'I just lost control.'

'There you go again. Christ, Johnny, we none of us

149

have any control. Now come with me, for fuck's sake, and let's play tennis.'

He strode away across the lawn, yelling about tennis. I drained my champagne glass and looked forlornly at the parked BMW blocking my exit, then I reluctantly picked up my crutches and followed him.

Behind the house, at the top of a sloping lawn, was a tennis court. As he got to it, the big man switched on some lights. 'I'll just get changed and get the necessary requirements,' he said and disappeared inside a small pavilion.

What the fuck? I wandered on to the court and waited for him.

Presently he came out of the pavilion, stark naked apart from a pair of brand-new, gleaming white tennis shoes.

'It's a warm night,' he explained. 'Look at this body, it's decaying.' He chucked me a racket.

I put down one crutch and, leaning on the other, readied myself.

'We all come to this, Johnny,' he shouted to me. 'Sagging, yellow, dead flesh. Naked we arrive and naked we go . . .'

He didn't have a racket for himself, instead he tried to hit a ball to me using the empty bottle. The ball pinged off to one side. On his second attempt the ball flew out of the court altogether, but on his third try he managed to get one over the net. I slammed it back at him and he missed it.

'Sorry,' he said, retrieving the ball. 'I'm a little bit drunk. Do you know why? Do you know why I'm this shambling fucking excuse for a man? Do you know why I'm drinking myself to death?' He tapped a ball over to me with the bottle and I sent it hissing back, knocking the bottle out of his hand as he tried to return it. But I was put off balance by the swing and I tumbled on to the hard court.

'Do you know what the matter is, Johnny? The matter is . . . Do you know? There is nothing the matter. I have

150

no excuse. It's just that the world is so full of fucking arseholes. Look . . .'

He came over to my side of the net, then he picked me up and led me to the end of the court where there was a view out over London between the trees.

'Some nights I come out here,' he said, 'and I look at that view and all I can see is arseholes. Arseholes, as far as the eye can see, ranked arseholes, arsehole upon arsehole . . . And then I get scared, scared to go back into the house because I know it'll be full of them, I'll be stepping in them, swimming in them. I won't be able to get across the floor for arseholes. It's a world of arseholes, Johnny. When I look in the mirror last thing at night, what do I see? An arsehole, smiling at me, winking with its one wrinkled eye, an eye like a fresh bullet wound. Yes . . .' He turned and stared at me. 'Your eyes. One, two. Bang, bang.' He formed one hand into a pistol and shot me twice, right between the eyes.

'I know people, Johnny,' he said. 'I see them with my third eye, my magic arsehole. You've come for me. I know who you are. You're Ed Gein the devourer, you're Death, Johnny. Cold Johnny Death come for me at last. You've got my name in your big black book. Roger Bigelow, your time's up. Roger Bigelow, you'll say, I've brought what's coming to you, the pocket-sized apocalypse, close of play, game set and match. You have the smell of death about you. Sweet and sticky. Why, I wouldn't be surprised if your whole car wasn't full up with dead bodies. Bring out your dead! Johnny's here! I know about these things, you see. I've got my eye, the eye in the pyramid, the winking arsehole of destiny. Come on, let's look in your boot!'

'I've got to go, Roger.'

'We've all got to go. But not before I see what's in your boot.'

'There's nothing in my boot.'

'Oh, come on, everyone's got something in their boot. Let's go and take a little look.'

151

Before I could stop him he was off again, barrelling across the tennis court, then back round to the front of the house. It took me a while to get crutched-up and follow him, and when I got there he was trying to wrench open the Saab's boot with his hands.

'Open it,' he said.

'No.'

'Open it, you arsehole . . .' He began to kick it with the heel of his tennis shoe, his low-slung bollocks swinging in their sac.

'Open the boot and let's see your collection. Let's see what poor fuckers you've got in there.'

The last thing I needed was for him to bust the lock and me not be able to get Mister Kitchen out. So I opened it for him. Besides, I didn't think it would make much difference. He was too addled to take in the implications of what was in there; the two of us had gone way beyond the clutches of reality.

'Ta-daa!' said Roger, pulling the lid up, and there was Mister Kitchen, wrapped in his dirty sheet. Actually, he was only really half wrapped now. What with me getting his boots off, and all the jostling and bouncing about he'd had to put up with.

'Ha, ha!' said Roger. 'Let's shoot him in the arse! That's the only thing to do with a body in the boot, don't give it the time of day. Shoot it in the arse!'

He fetched his air rifle from where he'd dropped it and went back to the boot. He aimed at Kitchen and pulled the trigger.

There was a phoot sound and a lead pellet thwacked into one of Kitchen's buttocks.

'Bull's-eye!' Roger punched the air triumphantly. 'Let's shoot him in the arse again. No, wait. Wait here . . . I need my hat.' So saying, he stumbled across the lawn towards the house.

I got in the car and started the engine. The back wheels spun for a moment in the loose earth before they got a grip and I jumped across the lawn. Then Roger was in

152

front of me, waving the gun and sporting a huge stetson with a silver sheriff's badge pinned to the front of it. I could either run him down or stop.

I stopped.

'Ha ha!' he yelled. 'It's arse-shooting time again. I only found this hat again this evening . . . I was doing a spot of spring cleaning. Now get that boot open, the sheriff's in town and arses will be shot.'

I opened the boot, he reloaded and fired at poor old Kitchen's nether regions once again.

'Don't let the arseholes grind you down,' he said.

Roger suddenly clutched his chest and, shouting, 'Good fucking Christ,' fell over sideways into a bed of delphiniums.

I went to him. His face was twisted in pain.

'Are you okay?' I asked.

'No. To tell you the truth, I think I've just had a heart attack.'

I knelt by his side, he looked already dead. 'The party, Roger,' I said. 'The party I was going to . . . Somebody on Fitzroy Park is having a big party tonight, an architect, do you know where it is?'

'It's next door,' croaked Roger. 'They didn't invite me. There was a bit of trouble last year . . .' He was evidently having difficulty talking, but he wasn't about to stop. 'But I watched them through the fence getting ready . . . I bet they were worried about the weather. They were supposed to be having it outside . . . And the forecast, first they said it would rain, then they said it wouldn't . . . let it rain, I say.'

I stood up.

'We're the same, you and me,' he said.

'Roger,' I said. 'I need you to do one last thing for me.'

'What?' he said.

'Where are your car keys, Roger . . . The keys to the BMW.'

'Inside, in the kitchen, hanging on a hook by the door . . . Are you taking my car, then?'

153

'No . . .'

'Take me instead.'

'No.'

'The key for my boat's there as well. We could have gone sailing, you and I. You know what? You know what I am? Nothing. A big bloody nothing. I knew you were coming tonight. I was waiting for you. Release me, Johnny, let me go . . .'

I left him there and went into the house.

Inside was carnage, the place was wrecked, it had been systematically destroyed: the big paintings on the walls were ripped, the expensive leather furniture was slashed, books torn to shreds, glass shelves shattered. The debris crunched under my feet as I picked my way across the polished wooden floor.

The kitchen was off the sitting room, and it too was destroyed, everything breakable was broken, anything bendable bent, and, smeared in dripping foody letters across one white wall, was the slogan 'Happy Birthday'.

I'd never know what had gone on here tonight, who Roger Bigelow was, what his story was. He was just one more crazy fucker I had to deal with.

Amazingly the keys were still there, hanging neatly on their hook. I plucked them off and went back outside.

I could hear Roger all the way across the lawn to the car.

'It's all just talk, Johnny, it doesn't mean anything. They tell you things and they talk about it and then they don't happen, and they talk about that . . . They're all arseholes . . . If it snows instead of blazes, if night replaces day, if the entire economy of the western world collapses and gravity no longer works, then it doesn't matter, they'll just report it and talk about it and analyse it, and show us how it was inevitable, and tell us how it affected things and what will happen tomorrow, and all will be well in the world . . . But in your black book, Johnny, the truth's in there. It's not a forecast, it's not

154

analysis . . . It's the truth . . . Release me, Johnny!' he cried out. 'Take me with you!'

'I can't . . .' I said. 'There's no more room in my boot.'

I unlocked the BMW and moved it away from the front of the driveway. Then I went back to the Saab.

As I drove across the lawn past Roger he was still lying in the flowers. I couldn't see if he was moving or not.

I pulled out of there and things were back to normal. It was just another Saturday night and I was once again footling along this agreeable road looking for a party.

I turned into the driveway next door. There was a gravel parking area with several expensive cars sitting on it, and four people carrying bottles of wine were just approaching the front door.

I had arrived.

One of the guests pressed the bell, and presently the front door was opened and they were greeted by a tall guy with a glass in his hand. The hum of voices and the thud and whack of dance music briefly spilled out into the heavy night air, then the new arrivals went inside, the door closed and all was quiet again.

The house was one of the older ones on the road, a beautiful, classically English nineteen-twenties' creation, large and elegant and tasteful. All I had to do was get in there.

I got out of the car and decided to be bold. I just had to hope it was a large party and the host wouldn't necessarily be the one who opened the door. Even then I had a good chance of bluffing my way in. I knew from experience that a certain amount of confidence could get you into most parties. Then, as I was locking the car doors, I remembered the bottle of wine that Mother had given me and I knew that some things are meant to be.

Providence.

I opened the boot. The bottle had rolled under Kitchen, and I had to shove him about to get at it. I tried not to look at his pellet-riddled arse in the process. Then I slammed the boot and crutched awkwardly over to the front door.

# FIFTEEN

I was just about to ring the bell when I noticed that there was a gate at the side of the house leading to a back garden. I peered round and saw lights and a few people wandering about. This was better than a frontal assault.

I opened the gate and went down the side of the house. It seemed to go back for ever. It was a huge place, much added to since it had been built. The garden was huge as well, informal, with many mature trees and shrubs. The sort of garden you could get lost in.

There were several flaming torches stuck into the ground, as well as night-lights in coloured glass containers. There was a barbecue glowing on a small terrace, though it looked as if it was on its last legs. There were a couple of drunks, however, tending to some sausages. It was either a late supper or an early breakfast.

I said 'hi' to a few strangers, gave my bottle to a black-clad girl who appeared to be in charge of drinks out here, and did my best to mingle. Though it did seem that I was getting some funny looks. I put this down to paranoia. It had been one of those days. One of those days where everyone seems to be against you, one of those days you realise in retrospect you should have spent in bed watching daytime TV. Of course my drug intake hadn't helped in the 'Oh-shit-everyone's-looking-at-me' department, and I was still shaky from the skunk that Adrian Weeks had foisted on me and the incident at Roger Bigelow's.

I wandered around for a while trying to ascertain if

this might be the right party and checking out the other guests. Most of them were about my own age, some younger, one or two older. It was an arty, media sort of a crowd, and I thought I might be in luck. It didn't take me long to scan the faces in the garden. None of them belonged to Terry so I decided to go inside.

There was a large modern conservatory leading on to the garden and I went via this. It was tiled with rustic terracotta tiles, and lush with large tropical plants and impressive cacti.

Indoors, the party was still going strong with all the usual themed rooms and cliques. There was, of course, the dancing room, where the more energetic/extrovert/drug-crazed/I-wish-I-was-still-sixteen types threw themselves about with gay abandon to the latest hip dance sounds mixed with nostalgic seventies disco classics. Then there was the kitchen, packed with people who all knew each other, talking loudly and drinking, the quiet room with people chatting more seriously and the drugs room where people sat and smoked dope and giggled. There was the hallway contingent, the people on the stairs, the room upstairs with only two people in it, one of whom was crying . . . And so it went on. It was a big, rambling place, interior-designed to within an inch of its life, and on the crutches it took me twenty minutes to do two complete – and fruitless – circuits.

Coming down the big wide stairs for the third time my bowels were suddenly gripped by a chain-mail fist. My whole body went into a spasm of shivering. I gripped the heavy wooden banister and closed my eyes. Cold, greasy balls of sweat seeped out of my forehead and ran down my nose; there was a hammering in my brain. Great gurglings and volcanic bubblings shook my guts and an aching bolt of pain connected my arse to my stomach – temporarily, for I knew that any second now the bolt would snap and all hell would break loose.

I clenched my buttocks tight and pulled myself back up the stairs, step by painful step.

Like a thousand-year-old man I crept towards the bathroom. I knew it was empty because I'd just checked it. The crutches helped slightly as I could lift myself up on them and relieve the weight on my lower parts, but it was desperately slow going. I got there, though, somehow or other. I went in, turned the key in the lock behind me and leant against the door for a few seconds before crutching, stiff-legged, to the toilet.

At last I was there. I dropped my trousers and pants and sat down.

It was always like this when I needed a shit. I was sure it wasn't normal but I'd sort of got used to it.

I let go.

First there was the rock. The hard, burning lump which had sat there in the gateway for ages. It was forced out, like a champagne cork, driven by the pressure from behind. Slowly, slowly it came, accompanied by a great rumbling . . . then – POW! Out it shot, and WHOOSH, out came the rest.

It was 'eye of the needle' time, a debilitating evacuation. What I extruded into the bowl was the usual gourmet slush, a green spinach purée dotted with toasted clots of blood and streaked with bright raspberry red, the whole thing bound in a mucous jelly. One day I would have to go and see a doctor, confess to him the poisons I consumed, but I feared it, feared that he would tell me that the only thing that kept me alive was slowly killing me. My insides were rotting away and falling apart. I was the disintegrating man.

I sat there for a long while, my anus opening and closing, gasping like a landed fish.

Then, bloop, bloop, gurgle, whoosh – the second wave.

And the third.

I hunched over, shuddering and panting until it was over. Gradually warmth returned. The life pulsed back into my extremities. The fuzz cleared from my head, leaving behind a dull buzzing.

158

It was over.

What I needed was another beer.

I cleaned up as best I could, squirted an ozone-destroying blast of air freshener to dispel the charnel-house stink, and got out of there.

I went back downstairs and fought my way through the chattering throng in the kitchen towards the giant American fridge.

'. . . well, I saw him the other day and he's working for A&M as a press officer . . .'

'. . . no, *Emmerdale*'s really good. I used to watch *Brookside* religiously, but *Emmerdale*'s fab . . .'

'. . . I don't suppose there's ever a perfect time to have children but, you know, we're going to be too old soon . . .'

'. . . well, I'm sorry, but I thought *Raise the Red Lantern* was boring shit . . .'

I got to the fridge and opened it with all the reverence of a dying man reaching the first-aid box. Oh, glory be, there's no more welcome sight at a party than massed ranks of cold beer in a fridge. I liberated a couple of silver and white cans of Asahi Japanese beer with the snazzy blue Samurai, put them in my jacket pockets, and battled my way out.

I sat on a wicker sofa in the conservatory, opened one of the cans and poured a nice cold slug down my gullet.

You can forget the poetry of Wordsworth, the sonatas of Chopin, Margot Fonteyn as a dying swan, Turner's landscapes, caviar, champagne, silk stockings . . . For the truly sublime you can't beat a cold beer on a warm night.

I closed my eyes and sighed.

'Hello there.'

I opened my eyes. It was Adrian.

'What are you doing here?' I said.

'Tony and Cleo are clients of mine. You might say I'm in charge of catering.' Adrian sat down next to me on the sofa and offered me a hit off the joint he was holding. I eyed it suspiciously.

159

'It's all right,' he said. 'It's good old-fashioned red Leb.'

I inhaled a lungful and rode out the giddiness.

'You look like shit,' said Adrian. 'What happened to you?'

'What hasn't happened to me?' And then the penny dropped. 'Oh, Jesus,' I said and slapped my forehead. 'That's why people have been looking at me strangely since I got here.' I grinned at Adrian and handed him my spare beer. 'That's a relief.'

'So, what's the story?'

'I've had one of those days. I've been knocked about a bit.'

'Need a pick-me-up? Some E or something? How about a downer?'

'No, no, no. I'm still cooking with the gas you gave me earlier. I am totally wired.' I raised my can in a toast. 'Here's to the chemical solution.'

'Just don't ever forget that it takes away as much as it gives. The happier you get tonight, the more miserable you get tomorrow. It's a Dorian Gray thing. You pay for every happiness. That's what hell's all about, and believe you me, I know.'

'I've got a theory,' I said. 'It's like there's a big book, with all your allocations, every orgasm you're allowed, and when you've used them all, your number's up. Man, you can fuck yourself to death.'

'There's a Chinese story . . .' said Adrian.

'There would be,' I interrupted, and Adrian smiled.

'"The Hundred And Ten Pills"' he went on. 'By a guy called Jin Ping Mei. It's about a rich libertine, a merchant, a trader in drugs and spices, called Hsi-men, who lives a debauched and merry life with his several wives. One day he meets an old monk who sells him these hundred and ten pills, for his virility. They keep him up for hours and he can come over and over again. But there's a catch.'

'There always is,' I said.

160    ⌐

'Quite. He can only take one pill every full moon. That's the idea, anyway, but after the first pill he's hooked and he starts popping them left, right and centre. Men, women, children, his wives, the local prostitutes, nobody is safe from Hsi-men's rampant sex-drive, but as he takes more and more pills they start to destroy him. By the end he's coming blood and air, his bollocks swell up to the size of footballs, his arse is hanging out, and one of his wives, not knowing the cause of his distress, gives him a triple dose of pills to keep him going, and, well . . .'

'He fucks himself to death,' I said.

'Yup. There's no such thing as a free wank. And the chemicals, they'll do for you quicker than anything.'

'That's rich, coming from one of London's major suppliers.'

'Hell, hypocrisy is healthy,' said Adrian.

'So where can I find me a monk with a hundred and ten pills?' I asked.

'Well, he'd be a very wealthy man, whoever discovered the ultimate aphrodisiac,' said Adrian. 'But most of them, they're worse than the monk's pills. Take one of the oldest drugs known to man, Cantharis vesicatoria, for instance.'

'What's that, then?'

'Fabricus, De Geer,' said Adrian. 'Spanish fly.'

'Does it work?'

'Hah! I wouldn't recommend it. It's a pretty little green beetle, lives in southern France and Spain. When touched, it releases a yellow acid which causes nasty blisters on the skin. Traditionally, you collect the flies at dawn when they're still sleepy, kill them with the steam from boiling vinegar and crush them. That's your drug, that powder. Swallow that and it'll cause irritation of the kidneys and bladder, which leads to increased sensitivity in the genital area. That's your aphrodisiac. When you itch you've got to scratch. Drives you crazy. The Marquis de Sade was said to have made full use

161

of it to achieve sexual frenzy. Bad stuff. Damages the kidneys. Take too much, and once you've had the joys of appalling abdominal cramps, burning pains in your mouth and throat, vomiting blood, diarrhoea and pissing blood, you're dead.'

'I know the feeling.'

'It's the perfect example of our relationship with the world of pleasure and chemical stimulation.'

'So where can I get some?' I asked.

Adrian laughed. 'You want to come outside?' he said, standing up. 'I'm with some people.'

'Sure.' I hauled myself out of the chair and followed him out.

A little way down the garden there was a group of people sitting round a burning torch on kitchen chairs. Adrian introduced me to a couple of them, whose names I didn't take in, and we sat down.

The night was still warm, the sky clear. Up through the trees you could see the big fat moon.

'Full moon,' said a Japanese woman. Small, with very dark eyes and a perfect round face, immaculately made up. Black was the dominant theme of her look, from her glossy black hair through her short black dress and down to her shiny black leather boots.

'Werewolf moon,' she said, her voice cultured, with no trace of a Japanese accent. 'Do you believe in were-wolves?'

'No,' I said. 'Do you?'

'No.' She laughed. She sounded like an upper-class product of an English boarding school, but with that old-fashioned, impossibly posh and precise manner of speaking that only foreigners managed these days.

'How about ghosts?' I said. 'The Japanese are strong on ghosts . . . You are Japanese?'

'I suppose so. I've lived so many places I don't know what I am any more. But I do know I don't believe in ghosts . . . So what does that make me?'

I shrugged.

162

'I think it's sad,' said a woman on the other side of me who'd been listening to our conversation. She was short and rounded in a red velvet dress and a self-consciously funny little embroidered hat with a tiny bell on the top. 'What was it Hamlet said?' she went on. '"There are more things in heaven and earth than are dreamt of in your philosophy, Horatio"? I think people should believe in ghosts.'

'Why?' I asked. 'You might as well believe in Father Christmas, the weather forecast, virgin birth and economic recovery.'

'Oh, but I do believe in those things,' she giggled. 'Utterly . . . and fairies at the bottom of the garden.'

'You've probably got a row of teddy bears on your bed, haven't you?' I asked, and she laughed again.

'Six teddies – Jasper, Benji and Fluff, Arnold, Bear-Bear and Louis. Plus Dolly, Horsey and Wongle. Wongle's a duck, or at least he used to be. He's just a bit of old tattered cloth now.'

'Do you believe in God?' the Japanese girl asked her.

'Of course I do. I think everyone does, really. I mean, it's just . . . It would be awful otherwise, wouldn't it? I mean, look at the moon, look at the stars . . .'

We looked, and as we did so a red veil passed across the moon. I don't know what it was – a cloud, pollution, reflected street lighting, but we all fell quiet, as if we'd been shown something important.

'Götterdämmerung,' I said.

'What's that?' said Tinkerbell.

'Wagner's opera. The last part of the ring cyle. The twilight of the gods. Brünnhilde lights a funeral pyre for her betrayed lover and the flames spread up to heaven. The final image is of a red glow in the sky as the fire destroys Valhalla.'

'The Germans nicked it all off the Vikings, of course,' said Adrian. 'It's all based on Norse myths, though Wagner changed them to suit his own thesis. The Norse myth about the destruction of Asgard, the Viking heaven,

163

is a lot more fun, to tell you the truth. The final battle, the clash of heaven and hell.'

'Hell is something of a specialist subject for Adrian,' I said.

'Ragna Rök,' said the Japanese girl.

'Yes,' said Adrian. 'The fatal destiny, the end of the gods. Ragna Rök, which through time became corrupted to Ragna Rökkr, the twilight of the gods, Götterdämmerung.'

'Go on,' I said. 'Let's have all the gory details.'

'The whole thing was inevitable,' said Adrian. 'The gods had sinned, broken contracts, lied and stolen. They knew how it would end. In a strange way the stories exist in the past and the future at the same time. It's hard to tell if it's a prophecy or a history, because it's all bound up with fate, they none of them had any choice in their actions.

'It begins when Loki, the Norse equivalent of Satan, the bad god, the evil one, is thrown out of Asgard for orchestrating the death of Baldur, the good one, their Christ. Well, he's had enough of it, so he joins forces with the enemies of the gods.

'In a forest in the east a giantess gives birth to a brood of wolves, the offspring of Fenrir, the great wolf. One of this monstrous brood chases the sun and each season it gets nearer and nearer, until one day it'll finally catch up and eat it and the sun will turn blood red and die.

'Winter will grip the world, senseless fighting will break out everywhere, like closing time in Middlesbrough, brother against brother, father against child, that sort of thing, and the world will slowly sink into the abyss of nothingness.

'From the west a ship will come, manned by a phantom crew, with the giant Hyr at the helm, surfing on the waves whipped up by the thrashing tail of the Midgard serpent.

'From the north another ship will come, its crew the inhabitants of the underworld, its captain Loki, with

Fenrir at his side, flames spurting from his eyes and nostrils, his upper jaw touching the heavens, his lower jaw scraping the earth and blood dripping from his fangs.

'From the south will come the fire giants, led by Surt, burning everything in their path, and when they reach the rainbow bridge which links the earth to heaven it will disintegrate and collapse.

'The gods will meet their enemies in front of Valhalla, on the field of Vigrid, and there an almighty battle will take place.

'And that's the end of the weather forecast for tomorrow. In summary, eternal winter, raging fires, storms and destruction. In the east, monster wolves. In the south, fire giants. In the east and north, ghost ships, serpents and more giants.

'And the sun will be eaten by a wolf . . .

'And to the woman who's rung in to say she's heard there's a hurricane coming – don't worry, there isn't.'

'So what happened to the gods?' I asked, taking a hit from a proffered joint.

'One by one they fell,' said Adrian. 'Their king, Odin, was first, swallowed whole by Fenrir. Then Thor killed the Midgard serpent but was so badly poisoned that he dropped. Heimdal and Loki similarly killed each other. Tyr faced up to Garm, the infernal hound from hell, and they too slaughtered each other. It was like *Reservoir Dogs*. Mutual destruction. The stars fell from the sky, Surt set the whole earth on fire and destroyed everything. Conflagration . . . The burning sky from the Götterdämmerung. But then the rivers and the seas rose and put out the fires, drowning everything in the process.'

'They're good, those old stories,' said stupid hat. 'It's funny what people used to believe in.'

'I thought you believed in all that stuff,' I said.

'Oh, no. I have a more modern set of beliefs. I suppose I'm a Christian, really, if that's not a drastically untrendy thing to say.'

165

'You don't think the Bible's full of somewhat far-fetched stories? Like, Noah's ark?'

'But its a nice thing to believe in.'

'Nice to believe in? To believe in lies. Tell me how it works. Tell me about the fucking flood, forty days and forty nights, and all the animals, he took in all the animals, two by two, did he? Old Noah? And what about the fucking fish? And the whales? And the otters and frogs and crabs and mussels . . . Did they drown? Did the fish drown? No. So how come they got such a good deal? Tell me *that*.'

'Well, it's a nice story and children like it. It's like Father Christmas and the tooth fairy, those are just fun things, aren't they? It's sort of nice to pretend that they exist. Though I do believe in ghosts, of course. I saw one once. I was staying in this house, and I didn't know at the time, although I found out afterwards, that it was haunted by the ghost of a young girl who . . .'

'Please stop,' I said. 'There is only one thing more tedious than listening to people's real-life ghost stories and that's listening to people's dreams.'

'Oh, but dreams are important . . .'

'God save me,' I said.

'You are an old cynic, aren't you? I mean, tell me, are you really sure that when you die, that's it? Don't you believe that there's got to be more? There's got to be something. Don't you believe in the soul? In the after-life? And, surely, if you believe in the afterlife you have to believe in ghosts, really, don't you? So you see – it's all explained. It's scientific. I mean, you have to believe that your soul lives on for ever, otherwise . . .'

'Please stop,' I said. 'Please. You're driving me crazy. I may not be responsible for my actions.'

'What?'

'I can't function.'

'What?'

'I can't function. I can't function. I can't function. That buzzing in my head. Maybe it's my soul trying to get out.

166

Eh? Trying to find somewhere nicer to spend eternity. Tell me about it. Tell me about the immortal fucking soul. Tell me about God and all his angels and archangels. Tell me about Jesus H. Christ. Tell me about the prophets and the kings, about Matthew, Mark, Luke and John. Tell me about Revelations and Genesis. Tell me about my immortal soul. I want to know. Tell me about heaven and hell and the afterlife. Tell me – if I die a drooling, brain-damaged and incontinent pensioner, is that who I get resurrected as? Do I spend an eternity wetting myself and laughing at jokes that nobody has told? Who am I? Who do I live for ever as? Because, let's face it, we change. We change every day. Every thing that happens to us changes us. I'm not the person I was when I was two. I've seen photographs. That boy is dead. The boy I was when I was five is dead, the man I was yesterday is dead. The foetus in the womb aborted. I've died a million times. Do we all go to heaven? Tell me, because I want to know.'

'Well, there's no need to get so worked up about it.'

'Why?' I laughed. 'For God's sake, woman, we're talking about what the fuck is going on. That's what we're talking about. Should I not get passionate about my immortal soul? You've got no fucking passion, with your watery New-Age-Anglican beliefs. Next you'll be telling me you don't really believe that God is a kindly old man with a white beard, but he's more of just this, like, cosmic force.'

'Do you have any better alternatives?'

'Yes, I fucking do. Look . . . What is this?'

'A cigarette.'

'More specifically?'

'Mmmmm . . .'

'It's a lit cigarette . . . And what is this?'

'An empty beer can.'

'Half empty . . . And what am I doing now?'

'You're putting the cigarette into the beer can . . . Is this some sort of magic trick?'

167

'No, it's the opposite. I am making the hidden visible. I am explaining the trick . . . Now, what's happened to the cigarette?'

'It's gone out, I should imagine.'

'Yes. Exactly.' I poured the beer out of the can and shook it. The wet fag slopped about inside. 'Listen to it, a dead fag rattling around in an empty can.'

'I don't get it,' she said. 'What's the point?'

'I don't fucking know,' I said. 'I just wanted to put my fag out.'

The Japanese girl laughed.

'You're interesting, you know,' said funny hat. 'I'd like to talk to you when you weren't drunk.'

'No, you wouldn't,' I said. 'I'm worse when I'm sober.'

Luckily my tormentor was distracted by someone else in the group who asked her a question and drew her into another conversation.

'I'll settle for you drunk,' said the Japanese girl. 'I'm Miko, by the way.'

We shook hands and I was just about to introduce myself when I saw a shaven head disappearing into the conservatory. A shaven head and a black leather jacket.

'Will you excuse me?' I said, getting up. 'But I've just seen someone I know.'

# SIXTEEN

I shouldn't have got out of my chair so quick, and I certainly shouldn't have tried to run on the crutches. I wasn't up to it, my system overloaded.

Trying to ignore the fact that my brain had started to spin inside my skull, I clattered through the conservatory, my vision flipping like a faulty television. I tried to keep an eye on that bald head and thought I saw it bobbing into the kitchen, so I blundered on, but then a mat slipped out from under one of my crutches and I was dumped on to the floor, cracking my forehead on the tiles . . .

I guess I blacked out for a moment, and came round sick and dizzy, not quite sure where I was, not fully conscious of what the hell I was up to.

Luckily nobody had seen my fall, so I didn't have to put up with any nursing. I hauled myself back up and tottered out of the conservatory, dimly aware that for some reason I had to get into the kitchen. Once there, the bright lights and strong, primary colours of the décor flattened everything. I was suddenly in a cartoon, hemmed in by crazy, Loony Tunes characters going yibber-yibber-yibber-yibberty-yibber, with bulging eyes, rubbery mouths and hands which turned into power tools . . .

There was crazy, speeded-up music, tinkling and beeping, and all the voices were supplied by Mel Blanc. I stood there, unable to go forwards or backwards, gasping to get breath into my jittery lungs. I looked from face to face; there was a guy who was speaking too fast, a woman

169

with a voice like a foghorn, and a middle-aged bloke in the corner who kept turning into a frog and going, 'What do you think of that, then?'

I closed my eyes but there were funny little coloured men chasing backwards and forwards across my eyelids, bashing each other with mallets.

I opened my eyes and saw that the bottles and cans on the table had come alive and were dancing around and singing like they were auditioning for an advert. Now the cheese and bread got in on the act. This was all I needed, tap-dancing food.

I had to get out of there.

I backed away, a chorus-line of fag-ends high-kicking towards me across the floor, and bumped into Terry.

'Take me away from here,' I muttered.

'Fockin' hell,' she said, laughing. 'Look what the cat's dragged in.'

'Please, Terry . . . I'm on my last legs.'

'You're on fockin' crutches, man.'

'I'm dying.'

'We're all dying, darling.'

'Some of us quicker than others . . .'

She at last took pity on me and helped me into the quiet room. It was dimly lit with discreet table lamps and full of bookcases and heavy old furniture. There was a separate CD system playing what sounded like Arvo Pärt and a few people with shifty faces like dogs lurking in the shadows muttering to one another.

I sank down on to a faded green Chesterfield and tried to uncloud my brain. Terry sat next to me, shaking her head and grinning.

'You been beaten up or something?' she said.

'Or something,' I replied. 'Have you got my keys?'

'Naw,' she said.

'Shit,' I said.

'I left them in the studio . . . I didn't know . . .'

'It's all right,' I said, letting out my breath in a long sigh. 'It's not your fault.'

'You didn't come here to find me, did you?'

'I'm afraid so.'

'Well, you're lucky you did.'

'Oh, yes. What luck. You haven't got the keys.'

'No, what I mean is, this isn't the party I was meant to be at. I've just been down the road, it was crap, except I copped off with this real slut and she was coming here, so . . . You should see her, long blonde hair and tattoos, tits to die for . . . In fact, I don't think I'll stay here long. If I play ma cards right I'll be going back to hers. I reckon I'm on for a shag.'

'Have you got your keys with you?'

'For the workshop? No.'

'Shit.'

'Well, I've got all the inside ones, the alarm and fire escape and that, but not the ones for the big outside doors. They're too heavy to lug about the place . . .'

'Oh, well, that's a start. I couldn't borrow them, could I?'

'Don't see why not,' she said and got out her keys. 'Can't see they'll be much use to you, though, without the outside ones.' She took the various keys off her keyring and handed them to me. 'Why do you need to get in there so badly, anyway? If you wait till tomorrow, I can let you in . . .'

'My house keys are on the keyring. I can't go home without them.'

'Bummer.' She put her keyring back in her pocket. 'Listen, I'd go home and get the other keys for you now, but . . . You gotta see her, man, she's fockin' gorgeous.'

'Terry . . .'

Sensing I was going to ask her a big favour, she got up. 'Hey, like, I hope you find somewhere to crash.'

'Terry . . . I'll drive. Take me back to yours . . .' I looked at her pleadingly, but she was resolute. 'Terry, please. I'll give you a pay rise, I'll . . .'

'Sorry.'

171

'Bring her with you. Afterwards I'll drive you wherever you want to go . . .'

She laughed. 'It's late. It's too late.'

'It's not too late,' I said, but she was going. 'Terry . . .'

She was gone.

I held my head in my hands and squeezed out a big painful tear from each eye. As I did so I became aware of someone standing in front of me.

'Aha! There you are . . .' It was the woman in the stupid hat. 'I was wondering where you'd got to.'

I tried to think of something witty to say, some devastatingly clever put-down that would get her off my back for good.

'Fuck off,' I said.

She shook her head and tutted. I hoisted myself up on to my crutches and tried to make my escape.

She followed me into the garden.

'I know you don't really mean it,' she said. 'Your bear with a sore head act . . .'

I stopped and turned on her. 'Please, please, fuck off, or I will rip your stupid little head off and kick it into the next garden.'

'You don't have to be so male. You don't have to resort to threats of violence, you know.'

'Stop being so fucking understanding. I don't want to be understood, I just want to be left alone.'

I carried on across the lawn towards where Adrian still sat with Miko and the others. I managed a surprisingly brisk pace on the crutches and stupid hat struggled to keep up with me.

'Who are you?' she said.

'Who am I?'

'I know you're one of Adrian's druggy friends, but who are you? I'm sure I recognise you from somewhere.'

'I am one of the walking wounded.'

'I can see that.'

I stopped again. 'I'm a walking wound, if you must know. An open wound. I am a headache, a bad dream that

172

doesn't mean anything but leaves you feeling anxious and distracted all day. I am the yellow sugarlump in the tin urinal, the traces of black blood in your spit, the blue of hypothermia and the green of mould. I'm a moonless night, a vegetarian restaurant. I'm the limericks of Edward Lear where the last line's the same as the first. I'm an irritation, a pain in the neck. I'm a Gilbert and Sullivan operetta, I'm a Norman Wisdom film. I am Jerry Lewis, Robin Williams, Basil Brush and a trad jazz band playing "Hello Dolly". I am drivel, the outpourings of a poetry club, Frank Sinatra duetting with Bono. I'm your cheek when you bite it, the roof of your mouth when you burn it, your toe when you stub it. I am that burning smell you get on Inter City trains. In short, madam, I am a cunt.'

I turned and crutched on. There was only one chair free and I got to it before stupid hat, who hovered on the fringes like a child at an adult party.

Adrian was holding forth on one of his favourite topics. 'You know what? Twice as many people in this country die from methadone as they do from heroin. Heroin's not so bad, but it's become demonised. It's only dangerous because it's uncontrolled. If aspirin was banned, thousands of people would die from it every year, from buying street aspirin, where you could never be sure of the dose and the purity . . .'

I stopped listening. I was at the end of my rope, exhausted, strung out, wrung dry. Miko passed me a bottle of whisky and I took a long pull.

'You're falling apart,' she said in her Roedean voice.

'I've fallen,' I replied.

'Is Henrietta giving you a hard time?'

'Henrietta?'

'In the hat.'

'I'm sure she's a saint,' I said.

'She likes to save people,' said Miko, taking the bottle back and drinking from it. 'If you're not careful, she'll make you one of her special projects.'

173

'I don't want to be saved.'

'Who does?'

I tuned back into Adrian; it wasn't difficult, his strong, confident voice was drowning out most other conversation. '. . . All drugs are natural. Of course they are natural, ultimately everything is. Where else can we get any ingredient from but nature? But we have our drugs in a form many times removed from the original plant extract . . .'

What was I going to do? What now? It was the middle of the fucking night and I was stranded here in this strange limbo, this purgatory. Each step closer to the finish, I was ten steps back; I find Terry's friends – no Terry. I find Terry – no key. Only the inside key. Useful, but no fucking use. One step closer, ten steps further away. A mockery. Taunting me. This was like some massive bloody test, some obscure trial.

'. . . Nobody knows any more where drugs come from, or even how they work. Take aspirin, for instance, how does aspirin work? We all know you take an aspirin and it cures a headache. Everyone uses it – it's just there, isn't it? In packets. But who knows how it works . . . ?'

'Look at the stars,' said Miko, and I looked up.

'What about them?' I said.

'I don't know. Sometimes they make me feel cold.' She reached out and held my hand. It didn't feel cold, it was warm and soft. It drenched my body with warmth. Just to hold someone, to be held, soothed all my rough edges, drained the battery acid from my system, dissolved the crust in my veins. And the warmth soaked into the bruised glob that was my brain. Calmness. Clarity. I could start to think again.

Don't give up. Make plans. You can beat this. All right, I was halfway there, but no nearer at all. Unless, of course, I could go in via the fire escape. First, though, I'd have to get past the devil dog.

'. . . Who knows that the bark of the willow tree contains an active ingredient called salicin which for

174

centuries was used to cure headaches, fevers and inflammations . . . ?'

I looked down from the stars and turned my eyes on Miko, her face tilted upwards to the heavens. Then she, too, looked down, and her eyes were on me. We said nothing, just stared dumbly at each other. I knew nothing about her, and she knew nothing about me, except that we were probably both on drugs of some sort, and it was late, and we'd shared a bottle. She smiled at me, then let go of my hand. I rubbed my sore eyes and looked past our little group down the garden where there was someone wandering about. A man by himself. He looked drunk, weaving about in an aimless manner.

'. . . Aspirin; acetylsalicylic acid. One of the most miraculous drugs in the world. It prevents the production of prostaglandins, which are part of the body's defence system, they're produced in body tissue when you're attacked by illness, or whatever . . . Get rid of them, you feel better. *Voilà*. So what about sleeping pills, then? How do they put you to sleep . . . ?'

Now, that was an idea, wasn't it? It worked in films, fill a lump of meat with pills, chuck it to the dog . . . No. That was too much like some James Bond movie. There had to be a simpler way. If only Terry could take me back to hers, I could get her keys and . . . But Terry wasn't going home tonight. She was going back to her blonde slut's place . . .

In that case, she wouldn't need the keys to her flat, would she? Therefore she could give them to me. Yes. I could go back to her flat, let myself in, pick up her workshop keys, then return all Terry's keys to her tomorrow.

Of course. Borrow Terry's flat keys. What a twat I'd been.

'Thank you,' I said to Miko.
'What for?'
'For bringing me back to life.'
I stood up.

175

'What's that bloke doing?' said Henrietta, and I glanced back down the lawn at the drunk.

Only it wasn't a drunk, it was Mister Kitchen, stumbling about, white as a ghost and with no shoes on.

If it hadn't been for the stimulants coursing through my system, I think my heart might have stopped.

My initial thought was that he was a hallucination, a Kitchen of the mind, proceeding from the heat-oppressed brain. But the others had obviously seen him as well, so he had to be real.

'I'll go and see if he's all right,' I said.

'Do you know him?'

'Don't think so. He looks a bit lost . . .'

I crutched across the grass towards him. When I got there he looked at me with dull, uncomprehending eyes. He was out of it. There was only one explanation: I hadn't killed the bastard. But how had he got out of the boot? I'd have to find the answer to that one later; the immediate problem was what to do with him. I looked down at his shirt, at the neat puncture hole with blood dried around it. I had to stop him from going up to the house.

Supporting myself on one crutch and leaving the other to dangle from my elbow, I put an arm round him.

'You all right, mate?' I asked.

He said nothing. Christ, maybe this was a real zombie. But then he mumbled something.

'You what?' I said.

'I've come about the car,' he said, his voice quiet and hoarse.

'This way,' I said, and led him back down the garden away from the flaming torches and into the darkness. Then we got in amongst the trees and I took him deeper still.

What was I going to do with him? Maybe I should just leave him here. But then sooner or later he'd get his faculties back and he'd remember. Remember what I'd done to him, and I'd be right back to square one, facing a messy and public court case.

176

I had to get him back in the car.

I began to skirt round the lawn towards the front of the house.

One of us was guiding the other to hell. I didn't know which of us it was, and I didn't much care.

'What sort of mileage has it got on it?' he asked.

'It's hardly used,' I said, pushing branches out of our way. 'It's just a town runabout.'

'Is it leather trim?'

'Sure is.'

'What about a sun roof?'

'Yep. Electric. Electric windows, electric aerial . . .'

'Can I take it for a test drive?'

We came to a small clearing in the trees. There was something being built there, an ugly concrete construction, hidden from the house by the trees. There were bricks and concrete slabs, some sacks under a tarpaulin and a few tools left lying around. A pickaxe, a spade, a wheelbarrow.

'Why have you brought me here?' said Kitchen.

'Shut up,' I said.

'What is this place?'

'Shut up, will you?'

He broke away from my embrace and looked at me with a wild expression. Then his look changed to one of understanding.

'You,' he said and launched himself at me.

'Not again,' I said.

# SEVENTEEN

'You ponce,' screamed Kitchen. 'I'm going to kill you, you fucking ponce.'

I tried to defend myself, but my bad ankle gave way and I tumbled over, falling awkwardly on a pile of bricks.

Kitchen jumped on me and got me by the throat.

'You fucking lunatic ponce. I'm going to kill you until you're . . .'

CLUNK. I got him in the side of the head with a brick and he rolled off me.

'*Au contraire*,' I said, getting to my knees. 'When it comes to killing I've got a head start. And I don't intend to stop now. Let me see,' I said, looking round for a better weapon. 'How shall I kill you? Let me count the ways . . .'

But before I could find anything, Kitchen came back at me with a brick in each hand. I managed to get up and tackle him before he could land a blow, however, and we skidded across the clearing and into a tree.

'I will burn you in my funeral pyre,' I said, pummelling him in the stomach. 'I'll stab you, I'll flay your flesh from your bones, I'll poison you, you git, I'll drown you, I'll gas you . . .'

He bocked me on the top of the head with one of the bricks and I was down again. I didn't stay down, though; ignoring the pain in my ankle, I forced myself up and butted him in the chin.

This time we went down together.

'I will tear your heart out and shove it up your arse,' I

yelled. 'I will choke you on your own skin, I will cut you with razors, I will crush you and smash you and bury you alive, I will hang you and personally jump on your legs . . .'

He got me with one of the bricks again and I clutched my nose. Then, shielding myself as best I could, I scuttled away on my back.

'I will eat you,' I said, lying on the concrete foundations of the building, nursing my ankle. 'I will drain the blood from your body, I will tear you apart with horses, I will electrocute you, I will infect you . . . I will give you AIDS, cancer, TB.'

Kitchen clambered on to a stack of big stone slabs and leapt at me. I rolled out of the way and he landed in a heap, winding himself. I had a moment's grace, but he'd loosened the slabs when he'd climbed on them and I saw, too late, that they were tipping over. I tried to get clear but wasn't quick enough . . . With a crunch, the pile came down on my bad foot.

I shrieked in agony and desperately tried to tug my leg out but it was trapped, crushed beneath the slabs. I grabbed a spade and was attempting to lever them off me when I looked round just in time to see Kitchen coming at me with a pickaxe. The sudden blast of fear was enough to give me the strength to pull my foot free and fling myself out of the way.

The pickaxe sparked as it cracked into the slabs.

Still clutching the spade and hopping crazily, I made for the trees. I felt Kitchen behind me and instinctively ducked and fell to the ground.

The pickaxe thunked into a tree and stuck there. Kitchen started to wrestle with it, jerking it up and down, grunting, his back to me.

I aimed the spade at his head and swung, but he moved and the edge of the blade got him in the neck, sinking in like a blunt executioner's sword and jamming.

He let go of the pickaxe and waved his hands about,

179

dancing and gibbering incoherently like a cheeky monkey.

I hung on for dear life as he pulled me about. Hung on and tried to stop him from breaking free of the woods and back out on to the lawn. Hung on and tried to bring down this mad ghoul with a spade embedded in its neck.

I thought he'd never stop. He jumped all round the place, crashing through the trees, colliding with things, flailing his arms and legs. I'll say one thing for the bastard, he had a lot of spunk, but slowly the fight went out of him and he sank to the floor and finally lay still.

I sat down next to him on a pile of dead leaves and rotting wood, put my good foot to his head and pulled the spade out. It took some doing, I can tell you. An eternity of pulling one way and the other until, at last, with a squeak, it came free and I threw it away.

There was no blood; it really had been like doing battle with one of the undead.

I sat there for a while and stared at him. This was the second time today I'd killed him.

'Now stay dead, you bastard,' I said.

I half envied him, lying there so peacefully without a care in the world, while my problems got worse and worse.

Things were getting *desperate*.

My white suit was even more ragged. My face more bruised. And my foot hurt like fuck. If it wasn't for Kitchen's requisitioned steel-toe-capped boot it would have been a lot worse, but I could still sense that it was badly broken. I couldn't move anything . . . Dammit, why mince words? Let's face it, I had a boot full of pulp. I didn't want to risk taking it off and having a look. I really didn't want to know. Besides, I might never get it back on again. It was probably all that was holding my foot together.

I pulled the laces as tight as they would go and retrieved the crutches. As I was getting up on to my good

180

leg I remembered that I was supposed to be finding Terry to get her keys off her. Quick as I could, which wasn't quick at all, I picked my way through the woods towards the house, my broken foot held out behind me.

I emerged from the trees at the side of the house, near to the small gate I'd come through earlier. I went round to the garden and found that it was empty. Adrian and the others had come in off the lawn, and the barbecue was unattended, the coals slowly cooling. I went into the house and found that the whole party was winding down. I desperately searched from room to room, getting even stranger looks than before, but I couldn't find her anywhere. In the end I went to the front door, only to see her and a blonde girl getting on to the monster purple Honda motorbike which had forced me off the road earlier. The bike girl was dressed all in leather armour and was just slipping a silver helmet over her long blonde locks.

I clattered down the drive like a trodden-on insect, calling Terry's name, but she didn't hear me, or chose not to, and I watched pitifully as they roared off into the night.

'Oh, you shit!' I yelled at Kitchen and myself and Terry and the world and everything; then I saw my car, with the boot wide open. I went over to investigate and found the sheet tangled in the lock. That explained how Kitchen had got out; the sheet must have prevented the lid from closing properly when I'd got the bottle of wine out earlier. I freed it, took it out and closed the boot. I couldn't risk being seen putting Kitchen in there again, he'd have to ride in the passenger seat.

When I got back to the woods Kitchen was luckily still lying where I'd left him. I couldn't carry him back to the car in my state, so it was wheelbarrow time again.

If you ever want to really test someone's strength and ingenuity, I recommend the following exercise: with the use of only one leg, get a dead man into a wheelbarrow and wheel him through thick woods in the dark.

181

It seemed like I was there for hours. First I had to get the barrow on its side, then I had to roll Kitchen into it, then, kneeling on the hard earth, I had to lift the whole thing up. Time after time it slipped halfway, or Kitchen rolled out, or I simply couldn't get it off the ground. And time after time I tried again, until at last it was done.

Then, on one leg, I picked up the handles and shoved the whole thing away from me and dropped it. Then I hopped forwards, lifted and pushed again. It took forever, and twice the barrow tipped up again, but I eventually reached the edge of the trees and the path. I left him hidden there for a moment and went to check that there was nobody around. Who should be coming out of the house but Henrietta of the stupid hat.

I tried to back away but she'd seen me.

'Aha,' she said, coming towards me, wagging a finger. 'I've just worked out who you are.'

'You have?'

'I knew I recognised you. You used to go out with Carrie, didn't you?'

I nodded. 'Guilty as charged,' I said.

'I thought so. You helped her deliver the baby, didn't you?'

'How do you know that? Have you seen her?'

'I was up at the Royal Free this evening.'

'You saw her? How is she? How's the baby?'

'They're all fine. Exhausted, in pain, but fine. I couldn't believe it, seeing him, couldn't believe that it had been inside her, growing there, and now alive, a new human being. It must have been fantastic for you, being there, seeing him come into the world. Being born, what an amazing thing.'

I grinned. 'So they're going to be all right?'

'Yes. God knows what would have happened if you hadn't gone round to see her.'

'Who knows? Maybe I shocked her into having it.'

'I think it was meant to be. You were supposed to be

there. It was atonement, redemption for all you'd done to her in the past.'

'If only it was that easy,' I said.

She came closer and looked into my eyes. 'In your case,' she said. 'I don't think it is.'

So saying, she turned on her heel and strode away across the parking area, down the drive and off down the road, the bell on her little hat tinkling with each step.

The coast was clear now, so I hurried back and as I rounded the end of the building I bumped into Miko.

'Bloody hell,' she said. 'You look even worse than you did before. What's going on with you?'

'I fell off my crutches.'

'You poor man.' She kissed me lightly on the lips and it was like something exploded inside my head. My every sense leaped into life; my mouth was electric with taste, my nose drunk with perfume, I could hear every noise in the house, all the music, all the voices, I could understand what everyone said, like the wax had popped out of my ears. My skin was glowing and tingling, every cut and bruise alive, the smashed bones and jelly in my foot singing, but it was a good pain, it was life running through me.

'Who are you?' I asked.

'What does it matter?' she said and kissed me again.

I tried to suck her mouth out of her head, gorging myself on her tongue like a lizard eating a snake, and she sucked back. Our mouths became one big bucket of eels, a clash of teeth and tongues and hot breath. I put a hand to her small breast and felt the nipple hard through the black material of her dress. Then I slipped my hand down and pulled up the hem and felt for the warmth beneath her knickers.

She, too, was fumbling at my clothing, her hand unladylike, yanking at my flies. In a moment my prick was out and her knickers were pulled to one side.

Still standing on one leg, propped on my crutches,

183

pressing her back against the wall, I slid up into her and she grunted.

She had her eyes open wide, a serious look in them like a wild mixture of fascination, anger, fear, pain and joy, but really none of these. It was sex. Life.

I couldn't last in this position for long, and soon we slipped to the ground in an untidy tangle, still joined at the crutch.

She pulled away from me, grabbed me by the shirt and dragged me into the trees. I kept up as best I could on damaged limbs.

In the mottled darkness of the trees she tugged off her knickers and lay on her back, her skin white in the moonlight, her pubic hair jet black, her eyes glinting. She pulled me down on top of her and I pushed her knees up over my shoulders, opening her, pinning her small body down on the warm leaf mould.

I could see the wheelbarrow, just feet away, with Kitchen's legs dangling over the side, and as I slipped back inside her I prayed that she wouldn't see him.

I lost track of how long we rutted in those woods. Every time I felt myself flagging I looked at Kitchen and set to with renewed vigour. It nearly killed me.

She twisted and threw herself about and gripped my arms with iron talons, she yelped and sucked in her breath through gritted teeth, but didn't come. Neither did I. I tried, I stared at the barrow, closed my eyes and imagined it was Gaia beneath me, but it was no good, I was too cranked. We both used every means known to try to trigger the other, fingers, teeth, tongues . . . but it wasn't to be. In the end, exhausted, spent, we flopped down side by side and lit up, watching the smoke drift off up through the branches towards the stars.

After a while Miko got up and pulled her knickers back on. She straightened her hair and brushed herself down and in a few moments she was immaculate again.

'I'd better get back,' she said, then knelt and kissed me

184

on the mouth. 'Goodbye, good luck and sweet dreams,' she said.

I said nothing, just listened as she went away, snapping twigs and rustling fallen leaves.

I was left with a semi-hard dick and an ache. There was a pent-up orgasm within me, I felt like a Spanish fly victim; the more I scratched, the more I itched, and was now too drained to do anything.

Drained, but alive.

Unlike Kitchen.

I crawled over to him and bit one of his legs.

I hated that man.

Nothing else happened to me on the way to the car, thank God. I got the wheelbarrow to the passenger door, tipped Kitchen in and was just doing up his seat belt when someone put their hand on my shoulder.

I guess I must have jumped a few feet.

'It's okay.' It was Adrian.

'Jesus, don't do that,' I said.

Adrian looked at Kitchen. 'He looks in a worse state than you,' he said.

'Adrian,' I said, 'I'm in big trouble.'

'Is he dead?'

'No . . . Yes. At least I fucking hope he is. What am I going to do?'

'Exactly what I told you earlier. Get rid of him. Lose him so that no one will ever find him.'

'That's what I've been trying to do all day. I've been trying to get him to the furnace at work.'

'That's a good idea.'

'Adrian . . .' I held his arm. 'You're taking this very well.'

'It's not my business to sit in judgement. I'm neutral, I don't have any kind of moral position.'

'But . . .'

'We've all of us had to do some terrible things in our time.'

I looked at him.

185

'I shot a man in Reno,' he said, 'just to watch him die.'
He smiled.

'Johnny Cash,' I said.

'Yes. Only it wasn't Reno, it was Germany, and it was a knife, not a gun, and there was a reason for it, though I couldn't tell you what it was now. I was a junkie at the time, just getting into the life. And since then, well, you only see the nice side of what I do. But it's a business, a bad business, and business is business, if you know what I mean.'

'Have you got any downers? Sleeping pills?'

'On me?'

'Yes.'

'I've got a car full of the stuff. I've got librium, mogadon, barbitone, phenobarbitone, diazepam, temazepam . . . What do you want it for?'

'I need something to knock out a dog.'

'I won't ask why.'

Adrian went over to one of the other cars, a dark-blue Volvo estate with a 'Child on Board' sticker in the back window – he'd told me once that the police never stop Volvos – as I hobbled round to my side of the Saab and got in. I was ripping a thin strip off the sheet when Adrian returned with a handful of pills.

'These might do the trick,' he said. 'Diazepam. Should put a dog to sleep, but you'll need a handful.'

'Thanks,' I said, putting them in my pocket. 'And while you're here, could you possibly strap my foot to the clutch with this, please?' I handed him the strip of sheet.

He did as I asked, then gave me another packet of pills.

'Here,' he said. 'These are for you. Just some DF118s, they should help kill your pain. You could do with some morphine really, but that's not advisable with the amount of other shit in your system.'

'Thanks, Adrian,' I said. 'I won't forget this.'

'Neither will I. I'm sure one day you'll be able to do

something for me. I'd drive you myself, but if we were stopped . . .'

'You've done more than enough.'

'I'm going to get caught one day,' he said. 'But not tonight.'

'You're immortal, Adrian.'

'It's all front. Wear a decent suit and tie and people think you've got everything sussed. But I know it won't last for ever, I've got no illusions. Sooner or later I'm going to get caught, or killed, or just beaten senseless. It's inevitable in my line of work. But I save. I put away ninety per cent of what I earn for a rainy day. Put it away where it can't be found. So, when they lock me up, I'll know it'll be time to call it a day, then I'll sit things out till I'm released and can claim what's mine.'

'And if you get killed?'

'Let's just hope I get caught before I get killed, eh?'

'Talking of getting caught,' I said. 'I'd better go.'

'Take care. And remember, nothing lasts for ever. Happiness is an illusion, enjoy things while you can. And when your number's up, pray that you can accept it with good grace . . . I got that out of a cracker last Christmas.'

I closed the door, started the engine, eased my shattered foot down on the clutch, screamed and pulled away.

# EIGHTEEN

I don't know if Adrian's pills helped at all – I don't know how bad the pain in my leg would have been without them – all I know is that the drive from Highgate to St John's Wood, with my shattered foot strapped to the clutch, was the most extreme form of agony imaginable. I drove along blubbering, shaking and moaning. I couldn't even listen to any music, it hurt my ears too much. There was only one consolation: the pain kept me alert – let's face it, it kept me awake.

I drove slowly and stayed in second as far as possible, as changing gear was, obviously, the most painful process. I couldn't drive too slowly, however, or I knew I'd be stopped. Crawling along at five miles an hour late at night is an unmistakable drunk's tactic. Plus, there were the inevitable lights and junctions at which I had to stop and start again, so I used my foot more than I could bear and by the time I'd made my way round Parliament Hill, down through Belsize Park and into St John's Wood, I was a mess; a raw, jangling, aching, radioactive monster. My body felt like it was constructed entirely out of damaged nerves; all that was keeping it together was the pain.

It was a relief to get home, and the relief gave me fresh strength. No time for self-pity, get on with it. I parked the car outside my front door and untied my foot from the clutch pedal, then, leaving Kitchen where he was, I went inside to get everything I needed for an assault on the workshop.

Getting up the stairs on my crutches used up all my

new-found energy, but I did it. Nothing was going to stop me now. I rested for a while on a chair by the door, torrential sweat pouring down me, my throat dry, my eyes sore, my heart leaping and stuttering like a rodeo bull. Then I forced myself up and crutched into the bathroom post-haste. Once there I filled the sink with cold water and put my face into it. I held it as long as I could, then pulled out, emptied the sink and refilled it with hot water. I used a flannel to bathe my wounds and after a while I looked almost presentable. I drank a glass of water from the tap and felt the soothing coldness creep down inside me. I brushed my hair back off my face and studied myself in the mirror. Not bad. This was the face of a man with a future. This was the face of a man who would succeed.

This was the face of a man who needed drugs.

I mixed up a nice sulphate/cocaine mix; I didn't know if I had any reserves left to tap, but if there was anything left to burn up I intended to burn it.

I snorted the lines as best I could – a feeble suck up the hooter. As much fell out again as went in and I was suddenly gripped by a terrible itching of the snout. The last thing I wanted to do now was sneeze, it could shake my whole body apart, so I massaged my nose and squeezed the bridge and rubbed my eyes, but it just got worse and worse. In the end I decided I had to risk it; if I lost my payload of drugs I could always refill, and anything was better than this agonising suspense. I relaxed and waited for it to hit.

And waited.

And waited.

And it wouldn't come. I couldn't sneeze, my system had forgotten how. The eruption just lingered there, infuriating me, a Spanish fly of the nose.

'Come on, come on, sneeze, you bastard!'

I glared at my red and twitching nose in the mirror, but it was obvious nothing was going to happen, so in the end I left the bathroom and got on with my preparations.

First, the dog.

I had the knockout pills from Adrian; all I needed now was a big juicy steak to hide them in. So I went to the cupboard but the cupboard was bare. Or, more specifically, I went to the fridge and it was empty. No steak, that is. Just beer, and milk, some Belgian chocolates and a Marks and Spencer egg sandwich, still in its wrapping.

Never mind. Dogs ate sandwiches, didn't they? To my knowledge dogs ate anything. These particular sandwiches were about a week past their sell-by date but, as I say, dogs aren't fussy. I opened the packet and recoiled from the stink. Breathing through my mouth, I peeled back the top layer of bread and pressed the pills into the rotten egg, then I re-sandwiched, wrapped them in clingfilm and put them in a shoulder bag.

That was the devil dog sorted out; now for the fire escape door.

Terry had given me the keys to the padlock, but I'd still need to break the window to get at it. I kept a tool bag under the sink and from it I selected a crowbar, a screwdriver set and a large hammer. I thought it best to be prepared for anything. No point in going off half cocked. My adventures today had taught me that.

I put the tools in the holdall with the spiked sandwich and I was set. All I needed to do now was get out of my ruined suit and into some fresh clothes – only my itching nose was driving me crazy.

I had to do something about it.

I propelled myself back into the bathroom and pulled off some sheets of toilet paper. Then I blew my nose . . . and the insides of it came out in my hankie. In a flood of blood and mucus the septum slid through my left nostril, followed by some fatty lumps of membrane and cartilage. I looked at the greyish mess of gristle and bits of human tissue in the toilet paper and a wave of nausea came over me. I was suddenly chilled to the core. I dumped the mess in the bog and threw up after it.

190

So that was my nose gone. What was next? Leaking blood, I crawled out of the bathroom back into the sitting room, and it was at that point that I most seriously considered giving up.

I thought, sod it, I would just lie there on the floor and wait for morning, wait for them to come and take me away, lock me up in the deepest dungeon, never to see the light of day again.

Oh, let them lock me up for forty lifetimes, nothing could be worse than this. I curled up and whimpered for a while . . . but what was I doing? Shit, you know, you can buy yourself a new nose, a nice silver one that'll never let you down, you can mend that shattered foot, heal those cuts and bruises, get yourself a whole new range of suits, in every style and colour.

You can finish this thing, you can dispose of Kitchen.

I felt my cock; it was warm and semi-hard, storing that pent-up orgasm that it couldn't deliver with Miko. I squeezed it and rubbed it, and it was then that I noticed that the red light on the ansaphone was winking. Jesus, I could do with some company, even if it was just old, dead voices on a machine. I yanked the unit off the table by the cord and pulled it towards me across the floor.

I pressed the play button. There were the usual two or three bleeps indicating that people had rung and not left a message, and then a familiar voice came on. It was Crispin, my right-hand man. As I've said, he was out in Japan where he was negotiating with a trendy, and fearsomely expensive, store in Tokyo who wanted to stock a range of my designs. He sounded drunk.

'. . . Listen, hey, crack open some bubbly, mate. Shit, look, I know it must be the middle of the sodding night over there, but I had to tell you. I've been in round-the-clock meetings for bloody hours now. When these guys meet they bloody meet. But listen, listen, not only do they want to take all the original stuff, they want to increase the order and, in their words, "enlarge their relationship with you". You know what this means?

191

You've cracked it, old son. Nippon is opening up to you
. . . Listen, I'll ring off now, but call me soonest, yeah?'

Oh, holy mother of God, I was truly on the verge of
the big time . . .

In the midst of darkness there is light.

In the midst of hardship there is . . .

Be-eep.

'. . . Hello? This is your father.'

Most people get tongue-tied and self-conscious on an
ansaphone, leaving vaguely coherent messages, but not
my father . . . 'Well, I hope you're proud of yourself.
Thank you for a lovely evening. Your cousin Jill has just
come back in a terribly distraught state. Come back alone
in a taxi, I might add, even though you promised us you
would look after her. Thank you very much indeed, I'm
glad to know you're as reliable as ever. She informs me
that the two of you had some sort of argument, and then
you picked a fight with a total stranger, at which point
she wisely decided to leave you to it. Splendid, at least
your behaviour is consistent.

'I'm only ringing because your mother, God bless her,
is worried about you. For some reason she actually cares
whether you're all right or not. Old habits die hard, I
suppose. So, if you could do us the courtesy of calling
back when you get in, no matter how late, I should be
most grateful. You can rot in hell for all I care, but I
don't like to see your mother upset, so for her sake, get
in touch. Good night.'

Be-eep . . .

In the midst of lightness there is dark . . .

Be-eep . . .

'Hello, it's me again. It's two o'clock and your mother
has very kindly just woken me in order to inform me
that you haven't rung back yet. She is talking about
telephoning the police. I have no idea what hours you
normally keep, but if you are there, could you please
ring so that I can get a good night's sleep? Thank you.'

Be-eep . . .

192

I punched in their number, and when, after four or five rings, I heard my mother's voice on the little speaker, I picked up the receiver and said hello.

'Hello?' Mother sounded sheepish and querulous.

'Mother,' I said, 'it's me.' My own voice was cracked and hoarse.

'Oh, you're home . . .'

'Yes, I'm home. So you can stop worrying.'

'Jill said you got into a fight with some tourists.'

'It was just an argument. Nothing happened. I'm all right.'

'You sound awful.'

'I'm tired . . . I'm very tired.'

'I was going to call the police.'

'For God's sake, Mother, you don't have to call the police. You have no idea what I get up to any other night of the year, so why tonight you feel you have to . . .'

'But Jilly said you were acting very strangely . . .'

'I was just a bit drunk. It's my birthday . . .'

'I know, darling, and I was worried about you in the car. I thought you might have an accident or, I don't know what. I was going to ring the hospitals, but your father . . .'

'Go back to sleep, Mother, and forget all about me.'

'I can't. I worry, darling. I don't know if you're looking after yourself. Since you broke up with Carrie you haven't had a girlfriend . . . I don't know, you looked so peaky.'

'Peaky?' I laughed and coughed, which hurt me all over, so I stopped coughing and groaned instead.

Then I stopped groaning.

I stopped everything. Everything stopped, and as I sank into a state of dizzy oblivion, Mother babbled on and I lost the thread. When I eventually tuned back in she was asking me if I got enough exercise . . .

'Only there was a programme on Radio Four the other day about men's health, the importance of exercise. Most men go through life assuming they're indestructible, but they're not, you know, women outlive them by . . .'

'Mum, it's four o'clock in the morning. I'm tired, you're tired. There's blood pouring out of my nose, I just want to . . .'

'What do you mean, there's blood pouring out of your nose?'

'I've got a nosebleed.'

'You *were* in a fight, then?'

'I walked into a door.'

'Have you been in a fight?'

'Yes. Yes, I've been in a fight, but I'm all right, I . . . AAARGH!' This yell was caused by the fact that I'd foolishly tried to stand, and slipped, putting my weight on to my bad foot.

'What's the matter? What's the matter?'

'I'm all right.'

'What's the matter?'

'Fucking leave me alone, for fuck's sake . . .' I lay on my back and held my calf, trying to choke the pain out of my foot.

'What's the matter? You sound terrible. I'm worried.'

'Mum, please,' I sobbed. 'Just leave me alone. I can look after myself.' My throat was so dehydrated now that I could hardly get my words out, I could feel my strength floating away from me.

'It's the weather forecast,' I whispered. 'It's all their fault. If they hadn't got it so wrong, none of this would have happened.'

'What? What did you say? What's happened?'

'It's those lying bastards, the weather people . . .'

'Who are the weather people?'

'They try to control the elements, but they only control us . . .'

'Who controls you? I can't hear you properly. Are you concussed? What's the matter? What are you talking about?'

'The forecast.'

194

'The weather forecast?'

'Yes.'

'They say the fine weather's going to last. It's nice for us, but the farmers must be suffering terribly . . .'

'Fuck the farmers.'

'What?'

I croaked something back, but sleep was taking me. Mum was babbling again now, talking about hospitals and casualty and emergencies, I wanted to stop her.

'I've had enough, Mum . . . I've really had enough . . .' I don't know if she heard this last bit, I don't know if I even said anything or just imagined that I had, I heard it in my head. I heard a lot of things, my own voice, church bells, heavy guitar chords, Adrian talking about aspirin, my mother saying 'Hello?' over and over again.

I was too weak to hold the phone and it dropped to the floor with a clonk. I rolled over and tried to pick it up but I couldn't see it, the room was spinning and flipping, flashing on and off like a strobe . . . The cacophony in my head grew louder and louder, mother's squeak coming down the line drowned out by a tidal wave of noise, everything that had ever been said to me, every record I'd ever heard, every car engine, every jet, every barking dog . . . Louder and louder . . .

Then silence . . .

I was an only child, I grew up in High Wycombe and when I was ten we moved to Notting Hill. It was funky in those days, dirt-cheap slum housing up for grabs. My father, I don't know if he knew he was on to a good thing. He boasts about it now, about how the house he picked up for peanuts is now worth over a million. I don't know . . .

So I suppose I'm a west Londoner, a classic white Notting Hill boy. Except I don't have the accent, the fake, black, street, my-old-man's-a-dustman twang of the middle-class whities. I was sent away to boarding school in Wiltshire and sponged up the Queen's English, RP tones of my peers. I guess I could have gone either

195

way; I spent enough time in west London, I spent enough time hanging out with jive-talking wannabe niggers, but, as you know, I have an ornery streak. I just like to get up people's noses, and not do the done thing, and so my life has been fucked.

I had trouble with my accent from the start.

We had a lovely school uniform; red blazer with gold trim, grey shorts well into teenagerdom, little grey caps on our innocent little heads and, when older, straw boaters. I suppose in my own small way I knew what it was like to wear the hated uniform and badges of a minority. But, let's face it, everyone in Britain is a member of a minority, what is the majority? The majority is everyone else. Live in the wrong area, go into the wrong pub, cut up the wrong driver and we're all fucked. We're all minorities. Aristo, prole, black, Jew, leftie, city-boy, homeless, blind, northern, southern, scouse, cockney, man, woman, vegetarian, scientist – we're all outnumbered by the rest, we're all given a hard time and made to feel unwelcome. We all know where we call home, and where we'd rather not go. I've had 'GET OUT YUPPIE SCUM' painted on my front door, my car keyed countless times, I've been spat at in the street, beaten up, chased and insulted from an early age.

Oh, yes, I hear you bleat with your pained and pitiful liberal tones, but you can't possibly compare your suffering to that of genuine persecuted minorities. What about slavery? You have no knowledge of the suffering of the blacks . . .

The thing is, though, that the history of slavery has been the history of the world. I remember in school being told about some Roman emperor checking out his newest bunch of slaves and commenting that these are not Angles, they are angels. And that was us, the English, white men, slaves. All right, it was a long time ago, but, then, Britain abolished the slave trade in 1807, and that was a long time ago as well. Whites

196

have enslaved whites, blacks have enslaved blacks. It was black slavers who sold us the slaves in Africa.

But what about real persecution? What about genocide? The middle classes have never had to face mass organised slaughter. But they have – in France in 1789, the Terror, in Russia in 1917, the Red Revolution, and what about the Cultural Revolution in China under Mao Tse Tung? What about Cambodia under the Khmer Rouge? Christ, in Cambodia, if your hands weren't calloused from work, it was good night sweetheart, which was why the country was suddenly overrun with middle-class types claiming to be taxi drivers. In all those places, under all those regimes, the middle classes were systematically wiped out. And they are my brothers, all of them, just as much as the Jews of the world are brothers, and the blacks, and the working classes, and the aristocracy – quite literally, in their case.

And so, as yet again the town boys slammed me into a wall, stole my books, smashed my boater, kicked me with their big boots and belted me in the guts, I cursed my parents for not being working class, but I guess, like everyone else, it eventually made me stronger, more proud of what I was. I mean, at one time I thought I could never forgive my parents for giving me a decent upbringing. But I got over it.

And now I wear expensive suits, I talk loudly in restaurants, I'm beastly to prole shop assistants, I arrogantly hail taxis, I'm rude and domineering at dinner parties, I condescend to the ignorant, I insult beggars, I go skiing . . . just as the black guy speaks in heavy Jamaican patois and wears gangsta threads, the Jew wears his homburg and ringlets and heavy black coat and reads Hebrew in the synagogues, the road protester wears his tribal rags and lives in trees, and . . . shit, where was I?

What was I talking about?

My childhood.

My mum and dad.

I remember as a child I was often feverish. I can

vividly recall sweaty hallucinations and visions more clearly than anything else that happened to me. Many times my room would become filled with people, sepia-skinned people wearing very little, people crowding on all the surfaces, at the end of my bed, on my toy box, on the chest of drawers, on the wardrobe, on the windowsill, chattering, fidgeting, like shipwreck survivors, clinging to wreckage. A more superstitious mind than my own might have thought them ghosts, or phantoms; demons, even, but for some reason I thought they were fishermen. Probably Portuguese. I certainly didn't speak their language and had no idea what they might all be talking about.

Why fishermen? It must have been a story I'd heard, or a television programme I'd only half understood, but fishermen they were and as such they didn't frighten me. Other visions did, visions of nothingness, an enveloping blackness that flowed about the floor, separating and joining like mercury, growing, obliterating everything until it threatened to blot out the whole room and me with it, and then I'd bolt, scramble away from the void, away from the room which had become a vacuum . . . But I could never go to my parents, as I wanted to, because there was a light on the landing between my bedroom and theirs, and in my feverish state I believed that there was a line drawn on the underside of the bulb, a line past which I could not go. So my parents' room was forbidden to me.

Some nights I would sit huddled on the landing for hours, looking at the light, wanting to pass but being unable, too frightened to go back to my room where the Big Nothing waited for me.

I could never tell my mother about the line in the morning because I knew that it was foolish; when the fever had passed I knew there was no line. During the day I would sometimes get a chair and stand on it and study the bulb and, of course, there was no line. But in the depths of the night, when the fever had a hold of me, and my pyjamas were crusty and reeking with sweat, and oblivion was eating away at my room, it was there.

The line I must not pass.

So I never told my mother, and she never knew. Still doesn't.

Since then I've often tried to regain that heightened fever state, to be out of control, to see and feel things I couldn't normally feel, to bring back the Portuguese fishermen, and I worked my way through the usual teenage catalogue of mind abuse – Benylin, acid, alcohol, solvents, amyl nitrate, you name it, I've defiled my holy temple with it, but somehow I never could get back there with either the fishermen or the void. These days I look after myself, I hardly take any drugs at all, certainly not any of the mind-benders, just enough sweeteners to keep me going, but I still look back fondly on my more adventurous youth, fondly recall some of those hallucinations and wonder if . . .

RRRRRRRRRRRRRRRRRRRRRRRRRR . . .

What was that noise?

Jesus, what's going on?

Demarcation.

I was on the landing, cowering beneath the bulb, ten years old again. A mewling, puking wretch. No, I wasn't. Don't be a twat. The twat in the hat comes back.

RRRRRRRRRRRRRRRRRRRRRRRRRR . . .

What the fuck was going on?

I saw the phone handset lying abandoned, static spilling quietly out of it. Come on along and let the good times roll. I was on the floor, damp and lost. There was a foul taste in my mouth, a mixture of blood and vomit.

And there was something else . . .

Oh, yes. That's right, I wasn't breathing.

199

# NINETEEN

RRRRRRRRRRRRRRRRRRRRRRRRRRR . . .

Shit. I was dying. I don't pretend to know much about the complicated workings of the human body, but I do know that if you stop breathing that's it, your time's up. Panic gripped me. My throat was blocked, bulging and throbbing like a shotgun in a Bugs Bunny cartoon after someone plugs the end and pulls the trigger. I pounded my chest with my fists. My lungs wanted to explode, they wanted to burst out of my body, scuttle across the floor, throw the windows open and suck in some fresh air. My feet were dancing a crazy Fred Astaire tap dance on the boards. My head swelled up like a balloon . . . Reality spun away from me again and the room fell apart into its constituent atoms . . .

Come on – do it!

Live.

I coughed, and a lump of congealed blood and vomit shot out of my throat and splatted into the side of the sofa. Oxygen whistled back into me. The consequent scalding pain in my tubes was just one more agony to add to the list. Thanks very much.

There was a small patch of dried sick crusting on the floor, and there was more of it down my front.

RRRRRRRRRRRRRRRRRRRRRRRRRRR . . .

I'd also pissed myself. There was a dark, cold, wet patch on my trousers. I got up shakily, a puppet on a crutch, put the phone back on its cradle and brushed the pieces of food from my shirt front. Christ, if I hadn't woken up I'd have probably died there, in a festering swamp of my own bodily fluids. I tried to remember a time when I'd had some dignity, but it seemed somewhere far off and unreachable.

Well, it was time I got my shit together, as it were.

Dammit, how long had I been passed out? I looked at my watch – four thirty. The sky was starting to brighten, there were some birds nearby cheeping in an irritating manner.

I crawled into the bathroom, pulled myself up at the sink and started to wash myself.

RRRRRRRRRRRRRRRRRRRRRRRRRRR . . .

I splashed cold water in my face and turned on the shower. I was just about to undress when I realised that the incessant ringing sound wasn't in my head, it was the doorbell.

I went to the living room window to try and see who it was. If it was the police I wouldn't answer, even though they would have found Mister Kitchen in my car by now.

It wasn't the police, though, was it? It was my darling parents.

Fuck, I'd have to deal with them. Who knows what manner of mischief they'd get up to if left to their own devices?

I went downstairs and opened the door.

'Oh my God,' wailed Mother. 'Look at you.'

'I'm all right.'

'Are you aware that there's somebody asleep in your car?' said my father.

'Yes,' I said. 'Now, can I assure you I'm fine?'

'Who is he?'

'Go home to bed. What are you doing here?'

'I thought something terrible had happened to you,' said Mum.

'We've been ringing your doorbell for quarter of an hour,' said Dad.

'I was asleep,' I said. 'I just fell asleep on the phone. I'm sorry. I've had a long day . . .'

'You smell,' said my father.

'We're taking you to hospital,' said Mother. 'You might be concussed. You might be . . .'

'You're not taking me anywhere,' I said. 'You're going home to bed, and I'm going back to bed.'

'Your mother thinks you may be in trouble,' said Dad.

I smiled. 'I need to sleep. That's all.'

'There's something going on.'

'Please,' I said. 'Please . . .' I went down on my knees, my hands clasped in prayer. 'Please go away.'

'Get up,' said my father. 'You're drunk.'

'I beg you,' I said. 'Leave me in peace.'

'Oh, this is ridiculous,' said my father and he walked away over to the Saab.

Mother helped me to my feet. 'I'm not going to leave you,' she said. 'I couldn't live with myself if I went home and something happened to you . . . Have you been sick?'

'I look worse than I am.'

'But you're on crutches, and your face is all bruised, and . . .'

'Who is this?' said Dad, peering into the car.

'No one,' I said. 'A friend.'

'Is he all right?'

'For fuck's sake!' I yelled. 'I'm all right. He's all right. Everything's all right. I have never felt better.'

The strain of shouting must have loosened something in my nose, because a fresh torrent of blood burst forth and washed down my face. I put my sleeve up to staunch it. Dad looked at me with renewed disgust.

'Never better,' I said.

'There's something going on here,' he said. 'I don't mind about you, but if you are in trouble and it gets out, it could affect me. I won't hesitate to co-operate with the police, you know. I write respected books of advice; how would it look if . . .'

'Right,' I said. 'What do you want me to do? Hmm?'

'Let us take you to Casualty,' said Mum.

'Okay,' I said. 'You wait here. I'll get some things just in case they want to keep me in.'

202

Mum smiled with relief. 'I'm glad you're being sensible,' she said.

I went back inside, clumsily puffed up the stairs, and fetched the shoulder bag with the tools and doctored sandwiches in it, then I got my biggest and sharpest Sabatier knife from the kitchen drawer and dropped that in as well.

I went back to my parents.

'Let's get this show on the road,' I said and opened the boot. 'I'll just put my bag in here . . . Good God!'

'What is it?'

'Come and look at this.'

They dutifully came and looked.

'Look at what?' said my father.

'Look at the boot space.'

'If this is another one of your childish jokes . . .'

'You could fit two people in here,' I said.

'Yes, very amusing . . .'

I brought the knife up. 'Get in,' I said.

'What?'

'Get in the boot.'

'What on earth are you talking about?'

'GET IN THE FUCKING BOOT!'

I think I must have scared them.

'Maybe we should get in,' said Mum.

'I'm not getting in there . . .'

I put the knife to his throat. 'Get in, please, Dad. There's something I have to do, and I can't have you interfering. I didn't want it to be like this, but I'm at my wits' end. So just get in the boot and this will all be a lot easier for all of us.'

Dad stared at me for a long time, then slowly climbed into the boot. He suddenly looked very old, as if all the life had gone out of him.

'Darling . . .' said Mum.

'Look, I'm sorry,' I said. 'I can't explain right now, but believe you me, it's for the best if I shut you up in my boot.'

'"Up"? Why "up"?' said Dad, helping Mum in.

'What?'

'You don't need to say "up". What's "up" about it? You simply have to *shut* us in the boot, not shut us *up*.'

'Shut up.'

'All your life you've disappointed me,' he said.

'I know,' I said and slammed the lid.

'What's the matter with him?' I heard my mother say.

'He's gone crazy, if you ask me,' said Dad, and I wrenched the boot open.

'I am not crazy,' I said. 'I'm just having a bad day.'

I slammed the lid again and got in the car.

I got a joint out of the glove box and lit it, then I drew the smoke into my lungs with a cooling mix of air, held it for as long as I could and let it go.

And it was like I was already dead. Like I was a ghost and could travel through walls and hear things that were being said elsewhere. As the smoke went out of me, I lifted. Talk about out-of-body experiences. And I heard them nattering away, my parents, squeaking like mice in my boot.

Birth, nappies, nursery school, primary school, big school, measles, chickenpox, mumps, nursing me in their arms, taking my temperature, holding my hand, buying me my first pair of shoes, so tiny, drying my tears when I fell over, burying my hamster when it died.

All that, all that for this.

> Squeak, squeak, squeak.
> Good O levels, good A levels . . .
> Squeak, squeak, squeak.
> All that for this.
> 'That's enough,' I said. 'That's enough.'

I started the engine and pulled away. Gliding slowly down the empty road.

It had become dark, big clouds had come up from nowhere and were scrumming together in the sky, killing the rosy dawn. As I turned the corner I put my lights on, and there was another car coming straight for me. We both swerved and I was aware of a face lit by my headlights, wide-eyed and startled.

And there had been a spark of recognition as well.

It was Kitchen's brother. I was sure of it. I put my good foot down and looked in my rearview mirror.

He'd stopped his car and was turning round.

I was sure of it.

I barrelled through a red light and drove away from there as fast as I could. I bombed down to Maida Vale, then back up St John's Wood Road, past Lord's cricket ground and on to Prince Albert Road. I did two high-speed circuits of the park before I was sure the brother wasn't on my tail, then I headed down Portland Place into the West End.

I don't know if the various drugs I'd taken were finally kicking in, or if my pain circuits had simply overloaded and given up the ghost, but I was suffused with a sort of warm numbness, like I didn't have a body any more. I was the car, I'd melted into it, and I was the road. I'd been plugged into the very city itself . . . I was the streetlights, the buildings, the billboards. I was London . . . Christ, if I wasn't careful I'd multiply like one of those children's addresses – Mister Lucky, Parminter Road, St John's Wood, London, England, Europe, the World, the Galaxy, the Solar System, the Universe . . . Everything.

I had to rein myself in; if I got that big I'd be stretched so thin I might as well not exist at all.

I settled for being the car.

BROOM. BROOM.

And now I came to think about it, maybe it hadn't been Kitchen's brother. I don't know. I wasn't sure of anything any more.

'I mustn't lose it now,' I said to Kitchen. 'We've had some larks, eh? You and I, today. Haven't we? Eh? Oh, what larks! Now, how about one last tour of London before you go in the pot?'

Kitchen said nothing, so I assumed he didn't object.

'Look at the place,' I said. 'The size of it. It's an illusion, isn't it? It has to be. London is impossible. It's a dream . . . There isn't any way that an idea like London could work. Nearly seven million people living in one place. A huge city, six hundred square miles of it. You couldn't sit down and invent London from scratch, you'd go crazy with the logistics of the thing. The miles and miles of sewers, of underground cables, the tube, the roads, the trains, the buses. The people, each dependent on the other. All those people, crammed together, the whole system working like a machine, it boggles the mind . . . All the galleries and institutions, the orchestras and shops and theatres, the clubs and bars and restaurants – thousands upon thousands of restaurants. What is this place? It's a whole world, and it's taken hundreds of years to create, since the Romans founded it at the narrowest point in the Thames forty years after the birth of Christ – about the time he was being crucified. Londinium. What a thing it's become since then, sacked by Boadicea, ruled by people speaking a score of different languages, a wall built around it, growing bigger and bigger, spreading out from the old city, down the Strand to Westminster, bigger and bigger, spilling over the walls, small villages and suburbs getting swallowed by it as it spread like a fungus, finally a touch of planning introduced in the seventeenth and eighteenth centuries, as the squares were built and the big public buildings went up. It's been bombed and burned and developed and redeveloped, smart houses have become slums, then smart houses again, tower blocks have gone up and come down . . .

'Docklands, the City, the Nat West Tower, the East End, Limehouse and Whitechapel, Wapping . . . You forget, sometimes, don't you? Living here. You forget what a place London is, you forget what an extraordinary thing it is to live here, how these landmarks are known throughout the world, Trafalgar Square, Buckingham Palace, the Houses of Parliament, the Albert Hall, St

Paul's, the Tower of London, Tower Bridge, Piccadilly Circus, and there's history here, there's Noël Coward and Sherlock Holmes, Jack the Ripper, Dick Whittington and Paul Raymond, Charles the First beheaded at the Guildhall, there's Oscar Wilde and Gladstone, Pitt the Elder, Pitt the Younger, Watt Tyler, Charles Dickens, the Ally Pally, the BBC, Samuel Pepys, the Great Plague, the Sex Pistols, Dan Leno, apples and pears, pearly kings, fuck, listen to me. Knees-up, knees-up, knees-up.

'It's all here, Mister Kitchen, all on your tour, all the statues and blue plaques, the gold-paved streets, the football clubs, Tottenham, Arsenal, Millwall, Fulham, Chelsea, Crystal Palace, QPR, West Ham . . . Knees-up-knees-up-knees-up. Look, here's Admiralty Arch, Charing Cross Station, there's Nelson on his column . . . impossible, isn't it? But it's all here, the West End, Oxford Street, Regent's Street, High Street Kensington, Knightsbridge, Chelsea . . . The parks, Hyde Park, St James's Park, Regent's Park, Hampstead Heath, you could live a lifetime and never see all of it, never visit all the museums, all the art galleries, all the shops . . . the churches and temples . . .

'The Muslims and Jews and Hindus and Buddhists and atheists and agnostics, and pagans, the gospel singers, the evangelists, the scientologists, the Russians, the Spanish, the Chinese, the Indians, the Pakistanis, the Irish, the Greeks, the Turks, the West Indians, the Africans, the police, the hospitals, cranes and diggers, the births and deaths and tragedies. Sleeping now, but not sleeping, never asleep, lights burning through the night, cars crawling round its roads, music playing, people working, phones ringing.

'And us. Sat in my car at the centre of it all, this huge great device rotating around us . . .

'What if you could make it all just stop? Fall silent and dark, all movement cease? It would be like stopping the world from turning, stopping the planets from rotating, the stars creeping across the sky. It would be like stopping time.

207

'Shepherd's Bush, Chiswick, Richmond, Kingston, Clapham, Brixton, Deptford, Greenwich, Woolwich, New Cross, Hackney, Islington, Camden, Highgate . . .

'What if the jaws of the wolf scraped the heavens and the earth? Closed around the place, its teeth dripping blood, the Blitz, see it all go up, St Paul's silhouetted against the flames, the wails of sirens, the shouts of seven million people, hands on car horns, exhaust fumes rising like smoke to the sky.

'Black sky.

'Soho, Mayfair, Southwark. The Embankment. Going west now. South of the river? No problem, guv. I'll go anywhere, me. A city split by a river, the narrowest point but not narrow enough. Knees-up, knees-up, knees-up . . .'

It was nearing the end now. We were hurtling towards Battersea and the furnace. Kitchen wasn't saying much, so I put the radio on . . .

'Well, it's a warm, clear night, and it looks as if this settled weather is here to stay.'

'You are all wrong!' I yelled, pushing in a tape and looking up at the black sky. 'You all think you know what you are talking about, but you are headless chickens. You are phantoms, no sooner born than you drift away on the wind. Confetti.'

'They call me Mister Lucky, bad luck can't do me no wrong . . .'

There was a warning light on the dashboard. I looked at the petrol gauge. Empty.

Empty.

Well, we'd just have to get there on my rage, on the fuel within me, juiced on pain. My will would keep us going.

'Go. Go. Go.'

Foot down. Invulnerable. Hoiotoyo!

'Here we go, Kitchen. This is it, pal. The first, the last and everything. Emptiness rushing to embrace oblivion!'

And as the last of my petrol ran out I freewheeled to a halt outside the workshop.

# TWENTY

I got out of the car. There were muffled shouts and bangs coming from the boot but I ignored them. I took my shoulder bag and went over to the workshop, where I fished the sandwiches out. I lobbed them over the wall into the devil dog's pen and waited . . .

There was a horrible stillness; the air was solid, not a piece of rubbish stirred on the ground. It was like it had happened – the world had stopped turning; it was trying to move, events were trying to transpire, but the engine had got jammed and it was overheating. Time was about to burn itself out. It was quiet; the dense, constipated air was blocking out all sound. I felt as I had done when I was choking, that moment when I thought I couldn't last a second longer, trapped and isolated within my body, a far-off whining in my ears, pressure behind my eyes, just wanting to burst . . .

There was a splat, then another. Big, heavy drops of rain, swollen and sick with water, hit all around me, water-filled condoms thrown from the roof by an irritating child. Spat, spat, spat. One struck me in the face, warm and stinging. A few more spats followed, then there was a blinding flash, the whole sky lit up, the buildings around were flattened by the white light, standing out as if they were part of a huge fake film set.

Then, twenty seconds later, there came a roar of thunder.

Don't you find it infuriating in films, you know, horror films, when the thunder and lightning come at the same time? That only happens when the storm is right on top of you, and then only for one or two strikes before it moves on. In the real world the two are always separate, and somehow that always seems more frightening. The disorientating flash, and then the long, uncertain wait for the bang, like everything's out of joint, out of synch. And when the bang comes, it comes in darkness. Cracking, breaking, with that deep, deep bass sound underpinning it.

It was a deafening explosion, the first crash of thunder, coming as it did in that awful silence, and it shook everything loose. The world began to turn again.

The volume was turned up.

The skies opened and rain came down in a thick, unrelenting torrent, hissing and slapping on the ground. And it brought down with it the smog, all the filth that had risen on the hot air, cloying and acrid, a foul, dry, poisoned stench.

Within seconds I was soaked, stumbling around like a man underwater. I fought my way back to the car and took shelter, watching the slow progress of the minute hand on the dashboard clock.

I wanted it over.

The rain showed no sign of relenting, and when I'd waited as long as I could without going crazy, I ventured back out into the storm and headed for the wall. Once there I threw the crutches over and started to climb, trying to take hold of the rain-slick bricks. Clawing, breaking my nails, trying to find toeholds with my one good foot. At last I got both hands to the top and pulled myself up, gasping and grunting, fighting for air, the water streaming down my face, filling my mouth and nose, blinding my eyes.

I lay along the top of the wall and peered into the yard. The spotlight on the side of the building lit everything a harsh, vile yellow – the grey walls, the iron fire escape, the falling rain, the concrete floor covered in festering piles of dog shit. There were the crutches, four foot apart and ten foot from the base of the wall.

210

Of the sandwiches and the devil dog himself there was no sign. I prayed to God that he had eaten them, that he was curled up asleep, sheltering from the rain, that he wouldn't notice me, that he'd rather stay dry than chase a sorry soul like myself.

I prayed to God. Because I knew for sure now that there was one. The universe could only be so fucked up if there was somebody in charge who thought they knew what they were doing, some big, useless, fat bureaucrat with a patent system. All the things that should work but don't were proof there was some fuck-up tinkering with it all. Childbirth, electric razors, superglue, the United Nations, those cheap sets of screwdrivers you buy that seem to be made out of tin and which bend when you try to use them and the heads wear down before you've got one screw in. Thank you, God. And thank you for book clubs, private pension schemes, aromatherapy, democracy and free love.

And thank you most of all for this fucking guard dog, which, for all I knew, was sitting waiting for me.

But my mind was made up.

I quickly let myself down the wall before I had time to talk myself out of it. I had to drop the last few feet, and, attempting to land on one leg, I slipped on the wet concrete and instinctively put my other leg down to brace myself. It buckled, shooting pains right up my spine and into the base of my skull.

I sat there in a pool of water and wept with the pain. That was when I heard, above the sound of the pounding rain, a growl.

There was no time to try and get to the crutches; I scrambled to my feet and set off across the yard. It was about twenty feet to the fire escape but, hopping, slipping and hobbling, I made desperately slow progress. Behind me I heard the dog, its claws scuttling on the concrete, its growl growing to a roar.

If it wasn't for my broken foot, I might have made it. Who knows? But at the last moment, inches from the ladder, I made another mistake. I looked round. I had to. My back was tingling, tense, waiting for the dog to leap. I had to know how near it was. I had to see it coming. And I did. Just as I turned there was a flash of lightning. I saw this huge black shape, big as a cow, flying towards me, its black eyes glinting, its teeth wide and bright. In my terror I slipped in some dog shit and fell, just as the dog slammed into me with the force of a car. Back I went, back and down. I was flattened. My head whipped back and cracked against the ground. I puked and blacked out at the same time.

I was only out for an instant, and when I came to the thunder was rumbling in heaven and the dog was flinging me about on the wet floor. It had me by my right shoulder and was worrying me like a rat. I guess I screamed – though there was so much adrenalin and so many chemicals coursing through me I was rapidly going beyond pain – and the noise distracted the dog. It let go my shoulder. I thought I was clear, but before I could get up, it turned its great head on its massive shoulders and sank its jaws into my face.

I stopped breathing altogether now, I thought my heart had packed in, but I was still alive.

The dog's mouth was clamped over me like a mask, one set of teeth buried in either cheek. I was looking straight down its pink throat. I froze, and the dog, too, fell still. It just stood there, holding me in its mouth. It seemed calm and patient, like a dog with a stick waiting for its master to take it from him. There was no anger in it, no attack. It was cool and in control.

It panted, its foul breath hot in my face, its tongue rhythmically bobbing, licking me, covering my bleeding face with drool. I could feel its teeth scraping the bone. I began to shake. I knew I was on the verge of passing out again, and this time I might not wake. I feebly put my hands up to try and prise the jaws apart, and the dog growled a warning, tightening its grip. I stopped. It was pointless anyway; I might as well have tried to

212

open the jaws of a stone lion. It was utterly solid and immovable.

It gave another quiet growl. I could hear the sound coming from deep within him.

I couldn't let it end like this, in the jaws of some dumb animal.

Ignoring its growls, I put my hands up again and felt around its face until I located both eyes. Then I gathered all my strength and plunged my thumbs in as deep as they would go. The dog snarled and yelped and twisted its head, snapping its jaws, and I was flung free.

I hadn't damaged the dog, but it had been enough to make him let me go. I scrambled for the ladder, slithering along the ground through the dog shit, all the while expecting to feel its hot teeth at my neck, but I made it.

I got to the bottom step and hauled myself up the ladder.

I looked back. The dog hadn't followed, it was playing with something, something fleshy and flapping. I put my hand up to where my nose should have been and realised the dog had torn it off. It was chewing it now, tossing it from side to side, clacking its jaws in great sloppy snaps.

I scrambled up the fire escape, clattering all the way to the top, trying not to think about the ghastly sight of the dog calmly eating my face.

At the top of the ladder was the door, and a flash of lightning suddenly showed me my reflection in the window. I gagged and stepped back. My top lip and most of my nose were gone. A wave of faintness and nausea washed over me but I fought it.

Don't think about it. Get rid of Kitchen.

I didn't seem to be bleeding as much as I might have expected, but I was still losing a lot of blood. I removed my holdall then took off my tattered and filthy linen jacket, finally I ripped off my already torn shirt and wrapped it around my face. The action reminded me of the dog's attack on my shoulder, and I looked at it. There was a big flap of loose flesh, but not too much blood. Luckily I could still use my arm, though I could feel it stiffening.

I had to keep moving. I took the hammer from the shoulder bag and smashed the window.

That set off the alarm system. A long, monotonous ring trailed up into the hissing night air. I had to shut it down before it set lights a-twinkling in the local police station.

Move it. Move it.

I got Terry's keys out and found the one I needed, then I stuck my hands through the broken window and fumbled for the padlock. Come on. I located the padlock and jiggled the key into it. In a moment it snapped open and I unthreaded the chain from the bar on the door.

Come on. Move it.

I pulled the bar towards me and the door popped open.

I was in.

Keep moving.

The first thing I had to do now was switch off the alarm at the foot of the stairs.

So down I went, stumbling and unsteady. Halfway there I slipped and fell, rolled down half a flight, bouncing my head off the concrete steps.

I crawled the rest of the way.

Once at the bottom I somehow got back on to my feet and opened the alarm box with Terry's key.

1–2–8–0.

I punched the numbers in in sequence.

Merciful silence.

Had I been quick enough, though? For all I knew the police could even now be racing round here with sirens blaring and lights flashing.

I had to not think about that.

I leant against the wall, dripping water and blood on to the stone floor. That fucking dog, I hope my face poisoned him.

I looked back up the stairs.

Don't think about it.

I took them one step at a time. Clutching the banisters, hauling myself up.

One step at a time.

Up.

Up.

Up, until I was at the top again.

Yes. I could do it. Faceless, legless, battered, I could still do it. Nothing could stop me now.

I unlocked the workshop door and went in.

The furnace was going full power, rumbling and clanking, sending a red glow around the high walls.

There was a flash of lightning and I saw Pluto picked out in white light, his big eyes alive. Judgement day. Oh, pathetic fallacy. That all this great show was somehow for me. This final mistake of the weathermen.

I turned on the lights and there were my keys, hanging on a nail by the door. I grabbed them and staggered over to the hoist. I wound the door up and switched on the motor. Acting quickly, at home, in my world. A skilled professional.

I punched the down button. Slowly the steel rope spooled out and the hook was lowered towards the car park. When it was down I kept it going until its whole length was unwound, then I hit the stop button and prepared myself for the next step.

The big double doors, you see, could only be opened from the outside. I'd realised that when I was at the foot of the stairs.

There was only one thing for it. I put on a pair of heavy working gloves, leaned out to grab the cable then swung out into the rain-lashed night. I wrapped the few working parts of my body round the cable and sort of slithered. But it was slick from the pounding rain and my gloves began to slip, so that I descended in a series of jerks. The last few feet I came down in virtual freefall, but I somehow managed to land on my good leg and hop across the forecourt to my car. I don't know what reserves of energy I was working off, I was a robot, a headless fucking chicken.

215

I opened the passenger door. Kitchen's eyes were open; he was chalk white, drained of all blood. Like a wax model. Not real. The slash below his jaw was wide open but curiously ungory. I took the end of the cable, wound it around his neck and hooked it on to itself, then I undid his seat belt.

I hopped over to the double doors and unlocked them then, step by painful step, I crawled back up the three flights of stairs to the workshop.

There was a broom propped against the wall and I used it as a makeshift crutch to get me back over to the winch. Once there I started the engine and watched as Kitchen was slowly dragged by his neck from the car, across the tarmac, then up into the air, like a corpse on a gibbet.

'I told you,' I said. 'Told you I would hang you. I would destroy you. Wave goodbye to London, it's a lovely view from up here.'

At last he got to the top and swung there. I tried to push the iron platform out to lower him on to, but it was a forlorn effort; I couldn't shift it one millimetre. So I tried to hook him with the broom. On the third try I got him and I pulled him over to the opening and somehow got my arms around him.

Then something happened.

His body jackknifed.

Holy shit. Sweet Jesus. Was it possible the bugger was still alive, and fighting me to the end? He sure was one resilient bastard. He'd been stabbed, beaten and whacked with a spade. He'd been suffocated, bitten, shot in the arse and hung and still he was going right on living.

Or was it just some muscular spasm?

I didn't have time to find out, because, as his body twisted, I was thrown off balance, my bad leg gave way and I fell out of the hatch. Luckily I had a hold of him and the two of us were left hanging there fifty feet above the ground.

Hanging by Kitchen's neck.

216

The cable was pulled very tight now, cutting into the spade wound.

I tried to swing us back, kicking in the air, but I only succeeded in losing my grip and sliding down his body. Lower and lower I slipped, scrabbling at his rain-slick clothing, until I was dangling from his stockinged feet.

I wondered how long his neck would hold out before the cable pulled his head off. I remembered Carrie's baby, the doctor tugging the forceps with all his might.

We could be here for hours, and any moment now the police could turn up and find me dangling in this all-too-compromising position. I yelled and forced myself into one final desperate attempt to climb his body, exploding with my last bit of strength, like a weightlifter pushing up an impossible weight . . .

And I was there, hauling myself up his trousers, his jacket, and finally taking hold of the cable at his throat.

I knew where my strength was coming from now. It was my ego. More powerful than blood. The same ego that had kept Kitchen going when he should have been dead.

All I had to do now was get up on to the winch arm and then over to the building.

I reached up and Kitchen jolted again; his body jerked and turned and I slipped.

Right back down to his feet.

If he'd been wearing boots I could probably have got a hold.

But he wasn't wearing boots, was he?

I was wearing them.

Fuck.

All I had hold of were his socks, and slowly, slowly, they slipped from his feet.

I fell with the rain.

My life attempted to flash before my eyes but, my memory being what it is, the result was very patchy. Mostly Portuguese fishermen and Miko's pale body in the moonlight. If it had been a film I would have asked for my money back.

The next thing I knew, I hit the deck, feet first. My body crunched, concertinaed. I felt myself squash like a cartoon character, and I crumpled to the ground.

Far off, growing nearer, I heard the sound of police sirens, and closer, I could hear my parents in the boot, shouting and banging.

My good leg was shattered now, and I guess my spine must have gone somewhere, because I couldn't move a muscle. I was totally painless. Like a child in a soft, warm bed.

The dog had done something to the nerves in my face and I couldn't close my eyes, so I lay there looking up into the black sky, the rain falling down and the white shape of Kitchen, swinging on his gibbet. There was a creak and I saw him slip a little. I realised that if his head came off and he were to drop he would come down like a thunderbolt and smash me into oblivion. After all I'd been through I had no desire to be killed by a corpse. I had to get out of there, away from the drop zone. There was a tiny tingling of life still left in me and I urged every working part of me to move, to shuffle me across the wet ground on my back.

Like a snake that had been run over by a car I slithered and shuffled, millimetre by millimetre, rain-stung eyes fixed on the white thing above me. If anyone had been watching they probably wouldn't have been able to detect any movement at all, but I was moving, pulling myself along by the hairs on my back, by my twitching skin . . .

What a day. What a brilliant day. And to end it all here, now, being pissed on by rain which hadn't even been forecast. Crawling, waiting, not able to close my eyes and blot out the punishment that hangs above me, wriggling, sliming, moving but not moving, alive but not alive, adrift in a sea of sound – the barks of the devil dog, the wails of the police sirens, a crack of thunder, my parents, the squeak of the winch, the relentless pounding rain, for ever and ever, unchanging, for all eternity, till hell freezes over, et cetera, et cetera, et bloody cetera . . .

**AMEN**